TWIST A ROPE OF SAND

# TWIST A ROPE OF SAND

*More Adventures of Anya and Corax*

K.M. del Mara

ISBN 978-1-7348488-2-3 Twist a Rope of Sand paperback
ISBN 978-1-7348488-3-0 Twist a Rope of Sand ebook

Library of Congress Control Number 2021924165

Published by K.M. del Mara
kmdelmara@hotmail.com
www.kmdelmara.com

Cover design by the author.
Photo of "Corax" by Marc Garstein
Photo of "Anya" by Petra Fischer Art & Photography
Cover photos reworked by the author.

Other books by K.M. del Mara

·

From 'The Silent Grove':

Whitebeam

Willow Oak

Passage Oak

·

Beautiful as the Sky

·

Vagabond Wind, The Adventures of Anya and Corax

·

# DEDICATION

I proffer, to all the By-Gones that were ever clasped to bosom,

not a dedication, but a farewell.

Easier far to twist a rope of sand
than to stop Time's arrow or change the past.

You are about to discover that some of the characters in this book have chosen to be children. Three children and one dog, actually, which is to say five children. The reason for this can be traced to Madelaine L'Engle and her thoughts about writing a difficult book. Don't write it for adults, she said. Write it for children. She may not have been referring to the immature brain's capacity, but more to a precious quality in the mind of a child. Because who but a child might see possibilities in twisting a rope of sand? Who but children dream of sailing off into the "dingle starry" on a grand adventure? And no adventure is complete without a dog alongside, as every child knows. A grown person could decide to tag along too. Come to think of it, whyever not?

# TWIST A ROPE OF SAND

There has always been a Trickster.
Since the Time of Beginnings, the Old Ones regarded
him as a symbol uniting opposites:
Transformer and Destroyer, Joker and Truth-Teller.
He is contradiction and paradox,
because everything in our world is balanced by its opposite.
We may complain that nothing ever changes,
but if that Trickster puts his nose over your doorsill,
your life can turn in the space of one pawprint.

And herein, as the saying goes, lies a tale.

2

PARADOX
Circa 1050 C.E.
Near Frijoles Canyon, New Mexico

She rides the hot thermals with barely a flap of her wings. High she soars, impenetrably black against the sky. That is how Raven is the first to see what is coming, one day while she circles lazily over the sweltering Parajito Plateau.

Out there, far away across the mesa. Something strange.

But her interest is lost a moment later when she spies her enemy. Coyote! The enemy she so loves to hate. That old trickster himself, creeping along the rim of the canyon, slinking among the boulders, probably stalking a marmot or a pica.

Haha, Senor Coyote! No pica for you today, Raven croaks to herself.

Coyote, glimpsing the shadow of Raven hovering above him, crouches low, ready to lunge at her. *Aaugh!* Raven screams and dives. She swoops past him, nearly clipping his ear and hoping to alert any prey to Coyote's presence. Coyote rears up, snapping his ferocious jaws but catching only the odor of Raven's dirty feet. She, gloating and inattentive, nearly collides with a branch of a pinon tree.

As often happens for Coyote, though, the encounter works in his favor. Raven's attack alerts him to another danger. He notices something, but what *is* that out there? Anxiety sharpens his perception. Vague, indistinct forms, rippling in the shimmering heat of the plateau, the oddest band of creatures he has ever seen. He sits up and watches them, yipping small panicked cries, ears alert, nose scenting. What are those strange animals? There are many of them, definitely coming his way. Alarmed, Coyote turns, disappears over the rim of the canyon, and threads his way down the cliff.

He and his extended family have made homes in this canyon for time out of mind. What would happen if those strange creatures discover this beautiful place? Would they want to stay? He fears that, in a blink of his yellow eyes, his life could be upended, his home dislocated, his children endangered, the prey he hunts no longer in their customary haunts. Everything would change.


Ah, Senor Coyote is right to be afraid, even he, with his breed's superior ability to adapt. His old habits, old comforts may have to be left behind, and it may happen that he is allowed only a sliver of time in which to move on. Things can change just that quickly, and in no time at all, he will sense the shadow that stands again at his shoulder – the dark angel of fear.

The dark angel, though, is no stranger to Coyote. He knows he must banish him. Because then and only then may the archangels enter. Only then can Coyote discover what is waiting for him, and Time can spin loose from the eddy that snagged it and flow on to its secret destination.


Meanwhile, far out on the dusty plateau, those strange creatures, the People, are dragging their feet. Wandering, homeless, with no set destination. Some dark angel stalks them, surely. Why they have been displaced from their former land, no one today can recall. Perhaps they were driven out by enemies, or drought; perhaps they are nomads searching for new territory. But in any case, the last of their water is gone. There is not a drop to be had. They have found no place on this scorched plateau that would shelter them from the hot furnace of summer sun, from the icy blasts of winter, from greedy enemy tribes.

Some of the People begin to complain, and complaints start arguments. We have made a mistake, say a few. We reminded you many times, say others, of sacred places in the distant mountains that ring this plateau. We should have gone there, because it will take a miracle to find sustenance in this flat dry place where only scrub juniper and sagebrush grow.

It would indeed take a miracle, and as miracles go, the one that appears just now might not seem auspicious. He is, in fact, terribly deadly, but when they spot him, the People know that finally there is hope for them. If he, creature of dust and rocks, can thrive here, they will be able to, as well. Crawling on his belly, so well camouflaged they almost don't see him until he is right at their feet, his rattle is what warns them.

A snake, even coiled and ready to strike, is to them a blessing. His presence means that water, most precious of all the earth's gifts, must be close by. Water, more valuable than gold. Respectfully, with heartfelt thanks, they give him a wide berth and pick up the pace. Water, somewhere near. At this point, in this sere landscape, they would rejoice to find any little trickle.

Then, abruptly, the plateau ends. They hadn't even detected the long fissure of a canyon that now blocks their way, so narrow it is. They stand at the edge and stare at the rocky cliff wall opposite. Granted, there are good-sized trees clinging there, box elder, pine, and pinon, but no waterfall. When they look down, however, peering cautiously over the cliff edge and deep down to the canyon floor, they almost weep with relief. They never expected paradise.

The canyon walls are steep. It means a difficult descent. It takes hours to pick their way through the treacherous rocks. The men hurry ahead and women, children, old people, and a few bony animals follow slowly, carrying everything they own in this world. When they finally reach the bottom they find, not a narrow stony stream bed, but a broad green and hospitable shore. Not a trickle of water, but a river, flowing from out of the western mountains even in this dry time.

The river canyon was to them a gift from the gods. They stayed for many generations. The People cut caves to make homes, literally carving them out of the soft pink *tufa* of the cliff walls. Game was abundant. They formed clay into pottery, and found pleasure in painting it beautifully. They learned to plant corn, beans, and squash, and their children's children inhabited this place and worshiped its gods for three hundred years by our count.

Then life turned for them, too. This time, they moved down to the Rio Grande River, where their descendants live to this day. Again, no one knows why they had to go, apparently in great haste. Was it fear of enemies? Plague, or drought? Their men did not even take time to gather all their weapons. Some, they hid. Others they just dropped. Women left tightly woven baskets and their precious pots, too heavy to carry. A child forgot one little shoe, a grandmother discarded an image of her fertility goddess. They left these things behind, and the years buried them.

Almost every trace of the People, buried by Time.

They were gone. No drums, manifesting the heartbeat of Mother Earth, sounded in that canyon for another six hundred years. The deeply worn foot trails blurred a little more with passing seasons. The hand-and-toe trails, leading straight up sheer faces of rock, eroded and became impassable. Forsaken shrines lay untended, and the wind wailed lonely through the hollow canyon.

Empty.

The canyon, riven into the volcanic *tufa* more than a million years ago, once again seemed empty.

But in truth the gods of the place had never left. They weren't entirely forgotten. Occasionally a passing hunter would honor them with a turquoise shard or a piece of shell from some far shore, laying it beside the boulders that had long ago been arranged in a keyhole shape. A few of the Old Ones sometimes came back to pray next to the two stone lions that guarded the entrance to Shipapolima, their Underworld.

But mostly the gods now kept their vigils alone. Wisps, phantasmas, they waited in their sacred places. Perhaps one day a traveler might come through and recognize them, commune with them; some traveler who would know without seeing, who could feel without knowing. For him or for her, the unchanging gods of ancient earth were waiting.

Come to us, be quiet, feel.

INDIFFERENT PILGRIMS
A village in upstate New York


Thursday, a week before Thanksgiving, 1933


It's a fact, and well-known, for who hasn't found it to be true? Just when everything is going well, life decides to teach you something. It's almost always painful. And it always, always comes at you backwards. First life administers the test. Then it teaches the lesson. Unkind, it must be acknowledged, and not even reliably effective.

On this particular evening, in a big house at Five Elm Street, a young red dog was taking a nap in the study. His nap was going very well, as almost all his naps did. His girl, nine years old, was quietly doing her homework at a small table. She didn't find her studies too difficult. The holidays were coming, and she and the dog were going to spend them on a trip out west with her dad. She was happy, the dog was happy. Everything was going very well.

Now, people have claimed that dogs are clever at recognizing signs of coming calamities. So we have here a sleeping dog. Though there is a saying about sleeping dogs, this isn't about that.

It is about the best way, if you are a dog asleep, to stay in touch with your person. Resting your chin on her foot is good. As long as you don't drool, she doesn't mind.

But the human foot is a busy little appendage. There are likely to be disturbances because, from a dog's-eye view, a person's foot is almost continually sending signals. Toes extended toes curled; foot jiggling foot wagging; heel bouncing toe tapping. The foot is almost as expressive as a dog's tail, though maybe not as adorably cute. Therefore, that claim that dogs are deeply intuitive, that they can sense moods, even illness? It really just comes down to paying attention to the feet.

So when Anya Netherby slammed her pencil down on the table, her dog Corax received a split second warning from a stomp of her forefoot. It caught him sharply on the chin. He gave his head a good shake to get his lips phlumphed back into place. He blinked. He was then obliged to jump up immediately, to see what needed to be done. The reason for his girl's gesture need not be explored. That was beyond his scope. But perhaps the sequel could be modified.

Corax's best effort at modification was to lay his chin on Anya's knee and weep gently. This usually brought sympathy. Tonight, no. It didn't help.

PANIC.

"Oh Dad, no!" Anya slapped her schoolbook shut. "That's just – no! You can't let him come with us!"

Jack Netherby spread his hands. "I just couldn't refuse, Anya. Sometimes things are required of us and, like it or not, we have to rise to the occasion."

"Noo! Not him!I don't want him to come! He's horrible!"

"Well, it's all arranged. I just got off the phone with Aunt Helen. He's arriving tomorrow."

"Da-ad! No! Please! You don't know him! Please?"

Corax pressed his chin against Anya's leg, squealing softly.

His tail swept once, twice, then seized up with angst.

"Don't worry. We'll work it out. This way you'll have someone to do things with while I'm working."

"Not Robert! He never ever wanted us to do stuff together. He thinks I'm stupid. And besides, Dad, he's just plain mean. He is!"

"It'll be different out west. There are lots of things to do there."

"But he hates me! You don't understand! He'll ruin the whole trip."

"Anya, you might try to have a little compassion. He's had a tough time this fall."

"I don't care!" She leaned her chin on one fist and pounded the table with the other. "I don't care! I don't care!"

Robert! The cousin she despised. He'd gotten her into so much trouble last summer. Never mind that all that trouble had brought a world of good into her life. At the moment, that hardly mattered to Anya. Robert was still Robert. Robert was a jerk.

Jack Netherby pulled a chair close to his daughter's. He put his hand on her back. "I do understand why you're angry. But it was hard for me to say no to Aunt Helen. She took care of you for all those years, don't forget."

"She did not. Mrs. Wright took care of me. And Betty and Neil. They took care of me. Aunt Helen didn't care two pins about me."

"Hey." Jack, trying to be patient, tugged the arm she was leaning on. "Listen. I know how much of that was my fault. I feel bad about it. You know I do. But we're trying to be a family now. And Robert and Aunt Helen are family."

"They never felt like family to me, Dad." Anya pulled away from her father and stood. "I'm going to walk the dog."

Corax bounced to his feet.

WALK? DOG?

Jack reached for her hand again. "Now wait, Anya. What if I

told you –?"

She pulled away. No sense talking about "what if". Everything had been decided. Her holiday was ruined. "Robert is horrible, Dad. He just loves making me miserable." She yanked open the closet door, found her coat and a scarf. "Come on, Corax." She clipped on his leash and banged out the door.

Stomping down the sidewalk, hands in her pockets, she pulled the dog onto Main Street, heading toward Betty and Neil's house. No one would be home there. They had already left for their Thanksgiving holiday. Betty, who cooked for Anya and her dad, had left a dinner for them to warm up tomorrow night. Anya felt sick just thinking about sitting down at a table beside her disgusting cousin Robert. Mrs. Wright, their housekeeper, had left on her holiday today too. Nobody to remind her that she was making a fuss over nothing. Nobody to assure her it would all work out.

It won't work out, she told herself stubbornly. It won't. Somehow she had been tricked out of the best Thanksgiving of her entire life. Now her holiday was hopelessly ruined.

She waited by a picket fence while Corax read the roll call of passing dogs. Windows glowed in houses along the street. People were making happy preparations for the Thanksgiving holiday next week, and here she was, out in the cold with no desire to go home. She turned the dog around and headed uptown. She crossed the green iron bridge and stopped to peer at the canal below. It had been emptied for the winter. Now its bare banks were an eyesore. Streetlamp reflections polywogged all night on a shallow trickle of water that had been trapped there for the winter, going nowhere. Like me, thought Anya. Trapped, still to this day, by Robert, the big bully I can't get away from.

While Anya and the dog were out for their walk, Jackson Netherby sat hunched by the fire, his elbows on his knees. He had messed up, messed up with his daughter again, and he didn't know how to put things right. He carried a load of guilt where Anya was concerned, guilt about how he had handled things in the past. He realized now he had been selfish and weak. Admit it, he told himself. You've been a terrible father. But the past was a locked chest. It would not allow him to go back and do anything over.

When Anya was four years old, they had lost her mother to an accident. Unable to imagine being without his wife, much less imagine himself as a sole parent, Jack had entrusted his little girl to her grandparents and disappeared for almost five years into the back country of New Mexico. Five years is a long time in a child's life. It went by in a flash for him. When he and Anya were finally united a few months ago, he had sworn to himself that he would do what he could to make up for those missing years.

Now he had ruined the holiday they had both been looking forward to, and after all his efforts, he had almost surely ruined her trust in him.

Time. It was supposed to heal all wounds. It sure took a long while doing so.


Anya stayed out walking for so long that even Corax was tired by the time they returned to climb the steps to the front door.

"Here you are," her father said. "I was about ready to send out the troops."

Anya hung her coat in the closet without speaking.

"Did you finish your homework?"

"Just about." She would be missing several days of school. The teacher had sent home an assignment so she wouldn't fall behind the class.

"Come in here. Let's sit by the fire for a minute."

"Nah. I'll just go to bed." She was being horrible to her Dad. She knew that, and it didn't make her feel one bit better.

"No, come sit with me."

Groaning, Anya flopped into a chair and stared at the fire. The dog longed for his second evening nap, but he couldn't bear to leave her side when she seemed so upset. Sneakily, he tried to edge his way into her chair.

"I wasn't going to tell you this til tomorrow," Anya's father began, "but I have a surprise for you. Two surprises, really."

Silence.

Jack tried again. "I've been planning them for weeks. You'll be happy, you'll see."

Impossible. Anya frowned mightily and didn't take her eyes from the fire.

"Or, I don't know." Jack threw up his hands. "Maybe you're not interested."

She shook her head and pushed Corax off her chair. He walked in a circle, once, twice.

ANXIOUS. ANXIOUS.

"Okay. I'll call and cancel her then."

Anya pulled her shoulders up to her ears and snatched a look at her father. "Who?" she growled softly.

"Oh, never mind. You're not interested. I'll call and tell her not to come." Jack half-rose from his chair. "It was only Hattie."

"Hattie?"

Corax sat abruptly, looking from one to the other. He wrenched his mouth wide into a nervous gaping dog-yawn and started to pant.

TENSION. THE TENSION.

Anya sat up too. "Dad!" she shrieked. "Hattie Fish?"

"Of course Hattie Fish. I arranged it all with her mother. Hattie was going to come on the noon train tomorrow. She *was* going to come to New Mexico with us. But I guess you don't want her now."

"Dad! Stop fooling around! Really? Hattie?"

"The very girl."

“But what about Thanksgiving? Won't her mom – you know – since her father just died and all? Won't her mom be sad without her?”

“Hattie's brother's family will be there. I guess Mrs. Fish thought maybe a little trip would help cheer Hattie up. She's been pretty glum, her mom said.”

“She has. I know. Her last letter was so sad. But what if she can't afford train tickets?”

“I mailed her tickets to her.”

“You are the best.”

“Well, I try.”

“You are!” Anya threw her arms around her father's neck. Corax bounded over to butt in. “Wait til you meet her, Dad. She's amazing!”

“So about Robert --”

“Yeah yeah. I won't have to pay any attention to him if Hattie is there.”

“I would hope you could spare him a little kindness.”

“Robert does not deserve kindness.”

“We all deserve kindness, Anya.”

“What's the other surprise?”

“I think I'll make you wait for that one.”

“It can't be better than Hattie!”

HAHA! HAHA! Corax bounced hither thither, craving a share in the affection.

Finally he got the big hug. Because if anyone gets the overflow of kindness, it's always the pets.

Isn't that the truth?

Friday

The train slowed as it approached Rochester, New York, and Hattie Fish, almost twelve years old, let out a long sigh. The idea of spending days in a New Mexico desert held about the same appeal for her as lying on a hill of fire ants. Desert? Empty and dry? Blowing sand? If she was going to be depressed and bored, which she was, why bother to go clear across the country to a place like that? But her mother had insisted she accept the invitation for a holiday with her young friend.

So here she was, feeling somehow tricked into all this. Normally she would have liked spending time with Anya. Her friend was two years younger than she, and they had shared some exciting adventures this past summer. They had written to each other faithfully all fall. But the prospect of pretending to enjoy herself for the next ten days? No, she absolutely did not feel like it, no matter who she was with.

It was no reflection on Anya. Ever since Hattie's father died in September, she couldn't seem to take an interest in anything. She wished she could find something to be glad about, but she could not. Even thinking about it made her tired. The only thing she felt was regret. A dense mass of regret was clamped like a hot iron fist to her insides.

The truth was, she didn't care for anything in the whole world anymore. She just didn't care. The only thing she wanted was to have things go back to the way they were. She wanted that in the worst way. Sure, she and her dad had rarely agreed on anything lately. She thought he was old-fashioned. He thought she was trying to be too much like white girls. She had argued, contradicting him. He had turned on her. Angry, so angry. Unspeakably angry with her.

She didn't want Anya to ask her about any of that. She didn't want to try to explain why she felt so low. Besides, how could a nine-year old girl understand what Hattie was going through? Granted, Anya had lost her own mother, but she had been only a small child at the time. Anya didn't know what it was like to have your dad standing next to you one minute, more angry with you than you had ever seen him, and be gone, gone forever, the next.

Hattie looked out the train window and sighed. Oh, no. Already? They were pulling into the station already. She wished the train would just keep going on and never stop. There was Anya, scanning the faces in the train windows. That must be Anya's father, next to her. Hmm, a good-looking man. Hattie stood up, feeling like she carried a fifty pound weight on her shoulders. She sighed again. Here we go.

When she stepped onto the platform, she saw Anya's face light up. The next thing she knew, Anya had barreled into her and thrown her arms around her. Surprised, Hattie patted her friend's shoulder.

"I was so sorry to hear about your dad." Anya pressed her face into Hattie's shoulder.

To her own amazement, Hattie found herself suddenly clinging to Anya, almost sobbing. She finally let go, dug out a handkerchief, and looked at her friend. She tried to smile but her face seemed to have forgotten how. "I'm sorry, Anya. I thought I was all done crying."

"It's hard, I know." Anya shook her head and took Hattie's arm. "Come and meet my dad."

Jack was surprised, after hearing so much about the amazing Hattie Fish, at the woebegone look of this drooping girl, her long face, the frenzy in her eyes. He offered a handshake and held Hattie's hand for a minute. "All my sympathy for your loss, Hattie.

We're so pleased you've come." When he put his arm around her shoulders, Hattie felt her lips trembling again.

"Let me carry your suitcase. I hope you brought some hiking clothes."

She nodded, a little relieved. Hattie owned one dress and she was wearing it. It wasn't even a dressy-type dress, just a simple cotton frock, homemade. Maybe, on this trip, she wouldn't need to get dressed up too often after all. That had worried her. She felt marginally less anxious. Jack led them to the car and opened the door.

"You girls sit in the back. I'll put the suitcase in the trunk. You all right, Hattie?" Hattie was staring.

"What year is this?"

Jack laughed. "The car? 1929. You like it?"

"It's amazing. I've never seen that color."

"Burgundy, I guess they call it."

"Six cylinders?"

Jack was delighted. "Why – no, eight."

"Eight? This is beautiful! And is that ...?" Hattie pointed to the dashboard.

"The tachometer. It's tells ...."

"No, not the tach. That one."

"That's the engine thermometer. And this is for your cigar." He pulled it out. "May I offer you a light?" Jack was pleased that he had gotten a little smile out of her.

"What horsepower?"

"One-fourteen. You want to drive?'

"I – I could. I drive around the airport where I work. I'd love to, but I'd better not."

"I'll let you drive it up the driveway when we get home. Get in. I have to take you girls home, and while you're settling in, I'll come back downtown for Anya's cousin."

"Cousin?" Hattie looked at Anya who only scowled and turned

away. "Not that boy cousin you told me about?" Hattie asked Anya as they climbed into the back seat.

Anya nodded grimly. "Robert."

Hattie settled back and rubbed her hands appreciatively over the seats. "You didn't tell me your father drives a Studebaker."

"Only you would get excited about that." Anya was so glad to hear Hattie laugh a little.


Much earlier that same morning, as soon as he saw his train slide into the Montreal station, Robert Netherby stood, picked up his suitcase, and without a word of good-bye to his mother, boarded the train. He didn't look back when she called to him. He knew that would be a punishment to her. He wished he could be glad she was miserable but it only made him feel worse. Who did he think he was punishing?

His seat was at the window. He could see his mother on the platform, a hankie to her face. Stupid Harvey, her new husband, had his arm around her. Gag. It made Robert ill. He snapped his head around, and he didn't look back or wave when the train finally pulled out. They didn't care about him anyway, and he didn't care about them.

Seemingly overnight, life had become a rocky road for Robert Netherby. For thirteen years, he and his mother had lived with his doting grandparents. Thirteen years of his Grandmother Netherby constantly insisting that second place was no place for her grandson. His needs must always come first. His achievements must be unparalleled. Robert must be Number One in everything. And in her mind, he was. In her mind, he was the only person in the world who could do no wrong.

Thirteen years of living on a pedestal. Then, seemingly out of nowhere, his mother had taken it into her head to marry. They moved to Montreal with her new husband and she packed Robert off to a school in Quebec, a boys' school where he knew no one. His French was terrible. He made no friends. Within a few months he had made enemies though, and by the middle of November, he had been expelled for trying to beat up one of the students. It wasn't bad enough that he lost the fight, but expelled too? Humiliating. Not fair. Not fair at all.

And all of that turned out to be a problem for his mother. She and stupid Harvey had planned a little trip for themselves in November. To Europe. Antwerp, she said. To go to a sale of gemstones for her new business. She hadn't planned on taking Robert. Thanksgiving was not celebrated in November in Quebec, so she thought he'd still be at school. Now what were they to do?

He could still go with them, couldn't he? No, sorry darling, it was too late to get a ticket.

Robert, left behind? Robert, his mother's darling, no longer Number One? He was obviously nobody's darling any more. Nobody's. Just – just don't think about that. Forget it.

His mother couldn't leave him home alone in Montreal. No, he'd have to take the train to Rochester, New York. Stay in the house that used to be his. Mother had telephoned his uncle and, she claimed, Uncle Jack had said he looked forward to Robert's visit. Oh sure. Sure he did.

This would be wonderful for you, his mother had said. Uncle Jack was planning a trip to New Mexico and thought Robert would love seeing the southwest. Oh absolutely. He really would. New Mexico? Nothing but ugly dry desert? Oh, he'd just love it. And he'd get to spend time with his charming cousin Anya. Three years younger. How wonderful. The little rat-cousin who loved him. Yeah right. Spend time with that goody-goody? He'd rather eat pigeon droppings.

Robert gnawed on his knuckle. He felt a prick of shame when he thought of his cousin, but he stifled that in a hurry. He had learned it was useless to try to deal with shame. Anger – it was always his best defense. Anger was his default trait. These days, he woke up angry and he went to bed angry.

So here he was, somehow tricked into this whole escapade. Caged for ten days with the world's dumbest cousin. He wished this train would travel on forever so he wouldn't have to get off.

He went from the train station in Toronto to the ferry. Standing in the cold wind on the bow of the ferry made him feel marginally better. But all too soon, they arrived in Rochester.

Now the hard part. He spotted a man in a long overcoat who he thought might be his uncle. Robert had been six or seven years old when he had last seen Uncle Jack, so he couldn't be sure. There weren't many people waiting on the platform, though. Anya was definitely not among them. Thank goodness. Robert stepped off the ferry, hesitant.

"Robert?"

"Yeah. Hi." So that was his uncle. They shook hands and Jack pulled him close, an arm around his shoulders, clapping him on the back. All this good-buddy stuff. It could just about make you barf.

"The car is over here. Let me take one of those bags."

Robert slumped along after Uncle Jack. Ah. Okay. A Studebaker.

"Hey, nice wheels."

"Thanks." Jack slid Robert's suitcases into the trunk. "So how was your mother when you left?"

"Okay, I guess. Married." A pang, thinking of Mother. Forget her! Robert turned to look out the window as they drove. He had lived on the outskirts of this city for his whole life. It was strange to be returning. It wasn't long before they were passing Neil and Betty's house and turning into Elm Street. His old address, really his grandparents' place, up until this past fall, when they had all moved out.

Robert had no father, so he and his mother had always lived

with his grandparents. And his dumb cousin had lived with them too. Now she and Uncle Jack still lived there, while Robert had been forced to move to Canada. Stupid little Anya, living in his old house – with her father, because she had a father now. She had everything now, it seemed. The tables had turned. That was enough to make anyone want to smash something.

At the thought of seeing Anya again, Robert felt sick to his stomach. If he found out that she had moved into his old bedroom, he would turn around and walk out. Honestly, he would. They pulled into the garage.

"Come on in. I've got this bag. Grab the other." Jack turned back. "Robert? Would you mind grabbing the other bag?"

Robert turned back to retrieve his bag, and shuffled through the big front door. He had not anticipated being hit with an embarrassing wave of nostalgia. He had forgotten how nice it was here. What a hideous turn of events, he smoldered. Why couldn't things have just stayed the same, the way they used to be?

What was this now? A red dog came trotting into the hall. His rat-cousin even owned a dog now?

"This is Anya's dog Corax."

Grateful for the dog's welcome, if no one else's, Robert knelt and ruffled his fur.

"I think the girls are in the study." His uncle steered him through the door. Anya looked up, glowering through squinty eyes. He felt his neck grow hot, remembering how he had last seen her. In this very room, cowering under their grandmother's wrath, blamed for something he knew perfectly well that she had not done. Though he had never confessed that.

There was someone else in the study. A girl? With that chopped-up haircut, he had to look twice.

"This is Hattie. She'll be coming with us," Jack said. "This is Anya's cousin Robert."

"Hello," Hattie said without smiling.

She doesn't look exactly pleased to meet me, was the way Robert interpreted her look, though he stole only a glance. She could have been pretty if she weren't so crabby-looking. Dark-skinned, very short black hair. He wondered if Anya had told Hattie about the trick he had played last summer. At Anya's expense. Just a stupid little trick. He had never meant it to go as far as it had. Really, he hadn't.

Jack tried to cover the awkward moment. "I'm going to warm up the dinner that Betty left. We'll eat in about half an hour. Then I think we should go to bed early tonight. We have a long train ride ahead of us."

"Sure, Dr. Netherby," said Hattie.

"Robert, you can sleep in your old room tonight. We've changed things around upstairs, but we haven't had time to do anything to your room. It's pretty much the way you left it. You can go get washed up now, if you like."

Robert escaped, relieved, up the stairs.


When Uncle Jack called him for dinner, Robert found the girls setting the table. Jack came in with a casserole.

"Macaroni and cheese," he announced.

"How nice," said Hattie, just to be polite. Her stomach said a definite 'no thank you'.

They sat down and Jack, trying to fill the silence, took over the conversation. "Well, tomorrow night at this time, we'll be in Chicago." He looked up and smiled. Anya and Robert were both overly-intent on spearing macaroni. Hattie was pushing her food around her plate. "Then on Sunday morning we change trains and by Monday afternoon we'll be in New Mexico."

"Is it all just sand dunes there, Dr. Netherby?" asked Hattie.

"Sand dunes? No. No dunes where we're going. I hope you'll like it. I think it's very beautiful."

"Are we staying in Santa Fe?"

"No, we're not actually going to Santa Fe. We'll be near there, at a place called Bandelier. We were able to get rooms at my favorite lodge, luckily. It's quite rustic, but very comfortable."

Rustic. Again, Hattie was relieved that it might not be too dressy. Nobody else seemed willing to talk, so to make conversation, she asked, "Is there stuff to do there?"

"Oh, I doubt you'll be bored. Mrs. Frey, the owner, has a son who'll show you around. Do you kids like to hike? Robert?"

Robert shrugged and kept his nose in his plate. "Dunno."

"Have you done much hiking?" his uncle asked.

"Well – not with girls." He had never been on a hike in his life.

Hattie bristled. "Hey!"

"You'd better be careful what you say," laughed Jack. "These aren't ordinary girls. For one thing, I hear Hattie's pretty good with a lacrosse stick."

"Well, my father and all my ancestors were players."

"She's so good, Dad, she plays on the boys' team. 'Course," teased Anya, "she's very bossy. The girls are probably glad to be rid of her."

Hattie's father, in his youth, had been a champion player. In the tradition of their people, he had given baby Hattie a lacrosse stick as soon as she could walk, and again as was the custom, his own stick now rested beside him in his coffin. Hattie's people took their game seriously.

"Anyway," Jack continued, "you kids will be free to do what you want because I'll be busy with the photographer."

"For your book?" Hattie asked.

Jack nodded and smiled enigmatically.

"What is your book about?"

"It's about the Native Americans who used to live at Bandelier."

Hattie sat up straighter. "Natives? They are not there

anymore?"

"They deserted the place early in the fourteenth century, a mass exodus, apparently."

Hattie, a member of the Onondaga Nation, was curious. "What tribe were they?"

"Historians have been calling them the Anasazi, but that word is actually not in their language. So now we, or at least I, refer to them as the Old Ones. The Pueblo people down on the Rio Grande River claim to be their descendants."

"Why do you want to write about them?"

"I'm glad you asked, Hattie. I'm trying to show how the landscape of Bandelier changed these people. I'm proposing that a small band of nomads wandered into a certain canyon and realized it could be a safe haven. When you see this place, you'll know what I mean. They gave up wandering and began to grow food and medicinal plants. A better diet helped their population grow and they stayed for three hundred years. And then, very suddenly and mysteriously, they disappeared."

"I don't get it," Robert interrupted.

"What don't you get?" asked Jack.

"Why should you care what happened way back then? It's over. Done."

"That's a very good point, Robert. But if you imagine that every yesterday holds the seed of today, then the past fits into the present like a jigsaw puzzle. Do you see what I mean?"

"Yeah, okay," snorted Robert. "Well, I still say the past doesn't mean a thing to us. Not to me, anyway."

Hattie folded her hands in her lap. White people, she brooded. They have no respect for their ancestors.

Anya frowned at her cousin. He was upsetting Hattie.

Robert was oblivious to either girl. "You're wasting your time, if you ask me, Uncle Jack."

"Maybe you'll change your mind when you get to New

Mexico."

Robert rolled his eyes, shook his head, and went back to his noodles.

"What was it, Dr. Netherby, that got you interested in archaeology?" Hattie asked.

"Oh ...." Jack folded his napkin. "I guess you could say the Old Ones kind of saved me."

"You mean, learning about them made you —?"

"My old job was boring. I — Anya and I, we — had lost her mother. I couldn't pull myself together. The Old Ones brought me back to life. Made me rethink some things."

Hattie stared at her plate.

Anya watched her father as he spoke. She had wondered and wondered. What had been so fascinating to him back then, that he couldn't come home to her for so many years?

"So you were saying," Hattie continued, "there is a lodge in Bandelier?"

"Yes. Years ago, someone built the lodge we'll be visiting, hoping he could protect the ancient site from vandals and looters."

"What were they stealing?" Anya rejoined the conversation. Robert pretended to ignore everyone.

"They stole any antique things they could dig up and sell to collectors. Europeans are fascinated by Native American objects and will pay practically anything for them. So there has been extensive damage to an important historical site. Then, maybe fifteen or twenty years ago, Mrs. Frey bought that lodge. Well, she bought the rights to live there, anyway, from the government."

"Are there still vandals?"

"Not nearly as many as there were. Word has gotten out that Evelyn Frey has a rifle, and, believe me, that lady knows how to shoot. I've watched her. So she and her son try to keep out trespassers, cattle herders, loggers. She's an amazing lady. She also rents cottages to visitors. That's where we'll be staying, and she was kind enough to say we could bring Anya's dog this time, which isn't normally allowed."

Anya rose from her chair. "Dad, can I get the dessert?" Betty, their big-hearted cook, had left a carrot cake. Anya was a bit miffed that she had baked Robert's favorite. But who could complain about carrot cake?

"Thanks, honey." Jack put a hand on her arm. "Hey, can you make me a cup of tea, too?" She nodded. He pulled her back. "No, maybe I'll have coffee."

"Okay."

"Unless there is ice cream. Do we have any? If we do, I'll have chocolate." He put his hand out again. "Or maybe just a glass of water, no, make it tea, after all. Or – I don't think we have any juice, do we?"

"Dad," Anya giggled. "You're being silly."

"I know. Cake is just fine."

Robert, his face a dark cloud, watched Anya and her father fooling around. He could not remember ever hearing Anya laugh. Seriously, never. It wasn't fair, the stupid little twit. A year ago, she had essentially been an orphan, her mother long dead, her father away for years. Even her own grandmother ignored her as much as possible. Now she had her father back and they owned the house he used to live in. And what did he, Robert, have? He tossed his fork onto his plate with a loud clatter.

"We three will do the dishes, Dr. Netherby," Hattie offered.

"Uh, no no! Not me," protested Robert.

Anya frowned and Hattie stared at him. "Fine. I'll help you clear, Anya," she said.

"You didn't finish," Anya said, looking at Hattie's plate.

"I ate as much as I could."

"Hardly any, Hattie."

They went to bed shortly after dinner. By Saturday night, the train had taken them almost halfway across the country to the city of Chicago.

Sunday


Very early the morning after that, they stood in the dimness of Chicago's Union Station, numb with sleepiness. From here, their train would be stopping in several cities and then traveling on to California. They were taking the handsome Santa Fe Chief, its gleaming silver locomotive trimmed in red and yellow. Blazing across its prow was the star logo of the Atchison, Topeka, and Santa Fe Railroad. Robert walked toward it, enthralled, and Hattie followed. He turned abruptly and frowned at her.

She stopped short. "What?" she demanded.

"Are you following me?"

"It's not you I'm looking at. It's the machinery, dumbo."

"Machinery? What kind of girl are you?"

Hattie froze. "A normal girl! And what kind of pinhead are you?"

Robert pulled back as if stung. "Listen to you!"

"Oh, leave me alone!" She brushed by him and bent to peer at the underside of the engine.

Robert rolled his eyes and kept his distance.

The engineer, about to board, noticed their interest in his engine. He stopped to speak to them. While Anya watched from a distance, Hattie and Robert listened to him with their mouths open, fascinated with his explanations of the arrangement of the wheels, the top speeds, and the affection that develops between engineers and their favorite steam locomotives.

"The most human machine ever invented, this is," Anya heard the engineer declare. "Each locomotive has its own quirks and every engineer has a favorite that he knows as well as a person.

Maybe better. This one here is my baby."

That sounded pretty weird. Anya didn't join them. Instead she squatted next to her very distraught dog. Corax was panting nervously, peering into the crowd, watching for porters in uniform. He seemed to sense that he was going to be forced into a cage like the day before, and loaded again into the baggage car. Anya tried to reassure and comfort him, knowing what he could not, that there were still two long days ahead before he could finally be free again.

Robert drifted away from his family. He took a stick of gum from his pocket, wadded the wrapper and absently flicked it to the ground. He was wandering nonchalantly along the platform when he heard his name mentioned.

"Netherby!" That was strange. Robert stopped. His name, muttered with evident disgust by a tall, stoop-shouldered stranger with salt-and-pepper hair that was definitely in need of a trim. And a shampoo. Sticking out from under a very large cowboy hat, his greasy locks curled over his silk ascot.

Crazy outfit, thought Robert. An ascot and a cowboy shirt?

The man continued speaking, but not in English. "What is Netherby doing here? Speak French, in case he comes over."

Robert had been trying to learn French at school for the past few months. He was able to understand most of what they were saying. It turns out they were not talking about him after all. The tall man seemed to know Uncle Jack.

"Ahh. He's rather handsome, isn't he? Who is he?" Robert heard the man's short, bespectacled companion ask, tilting his head back and blowing a cloud of cigarette smoke into the air. His voice was light and very high, and his speech sounded to Robert's ear like perfect French.

The tall man answered. "He's a real (unintelligible phrase), just what we need on this trip."

"Some kind of detective or something?"

"No no, an archaeologist. A nobody in the profession. He's been living out west but somehow just landed a (swear word?) job at (unintelligible) Cornell University. I figure he must know somebody, to get a job like that."

"Are those girls with him?"

"I don't know."

"One is an Indian."

"Yeah. I noticed. Huh. What's he doing with a (another unintelligible word), I wonder?"

"Is she a guide?"

"Maybe. Yes, I bet she is. Netherby is very (something?) with the natives. Practically lived with them, so I'm told. Just a publicity stunt, if you ask me. He knew it would look good on his resumé."

"So this person, this Netherby will be a problem, you think?" asked his companion.

"Oh he will! You're (A swear word. That was definitely a swear word.) he will!"

"What you should do is (?) up to him. Find out what he knows." The short man dropped his cigarette butt to the floor and ground it out with his shoe. "I would relish the opportunity, if you don't want to."

"(?) his brain a little, you mean."

"Why not?"

"Quick. Turn around. He's looking this way."

Robert had the distinct impression that man did not like Uncle Jack. A minute later, he watched Jack recognize the tall man and step forward to speak to him. Oh well, none of his business. Robert jingled the change in his pocket and went to the concession stand to see if they sold chocolate milk.


Meanwhile, while they waited to board, Anya and Corax watched people striding across the station platform, most of them blank-faced, preoccupied, hurry-hurrying, buying magazines at the newsstand, searching pockets for tickets, stuffing last-minute items into bags. She noticed an older man in a somewhat ridiculous cowboy hat who was looking their way and speaking out of the corner of his mouth to a short plump man beside him. The tall one was staring. Anya followed his gaze. He was looking intently at her father. She didn't think too much about it until her father noticed the same man. Just as Jack's eyes were raised to him, Anya saw the man turn away and lean over to speak to the bespectacled man beside him.

Her father took a couple of steps toward those men. "Doctor Ravilious?"

The man looked back over his shoulder. "Yes. Hello."

"You probably don't remember me. Jack Netherby." Jack stuck out his hand.

Cackling, the man pumped Jack's hand. His smile was a tight stretch of liverish lips over stained teeth. "Of course I remember you, Doctor Netherby," he chirped.

The man knew her father. Why hadn't he greeted Jack when he first saw him? Strange.

"So you're headed out west too," said Jack.

"Y-yesyes. Yes. And, uh, how nice to see you again."

"How far are you going?" Jack asked him.

"I – my assistant and I are staying near Santa Fe."

Jack looked at the portly assistant and hesitated, waiting to be introduced. Apparently that wasn't going to happen. "Jack Netherby," he said, offering his hand.

"Honoré Ouisel," the short man squeaked, switching a fresh cigarette to his left hand, and barely touching Jack's hand with his fingers.

Ravilious squinched his face in what passed for a smile. "Oh yes. Sorry, I should have introduced .... Honoré is here from Paris. He, uh, yes, um ... hmm." Ravilious hesitated.

"Very nice to meet you." Jack looked from one to the other and shifted his feet awkwardly. "Well." He smiled. "Maybe we'll have a chance to chat. We're headed for Bandelier."

"Ah. Bandelier. That's just wonderful. Doing some collecting?"

"No, I'm not a collector. I don't like to disturb the sites any more than I have to."

Ravilious looked perplexed. "You aren't looking for artifacts?"

"Yes, I am. But I try to leave things as I find them."

"Oh, come on! That's a load of crap. The people that left that stuff behind are dead. Nobody cares about any of it anymore, obviously, or they'd have dug it up themselves."

"They care. They just don't care to sell it. So it's partly out of respect that I don't disturb the sites, and partly in the interest of scholarship. Also, as you know, it's against the law to remove artifacts."

Ah. Ravilious rubbed his palms together. Well, good. This jerk will leave all the loot for me. Aloud he said, "Uh huh. Well, I'm hoping to get to Bandelier myself. We should talk. Yes. Let's do chat sometime." Now that he thought about it, Ravilious couldn't believe his good luck. Jack Netherby might turn out to be his best find all week.

Abruptly, Dr. Ravilious waved a signal to a couple of porters. He strode away, calling to direct them to his large pile of trunks and bags. The assistant, ignored, ground another cigarette underfoot and wandered after his boss. Jack watched them both disappear into the crowd.

Anya and Corax went to Jack's side. "Who are those men?"

"The tall one is an archaeologist. He's done a lot of work in the southwest."

"Like you?"

"Yes, but he's much better known than I am. He's built himself a big reputation. He's pretty famous actually. He's published a lot."

"Uh huh," sniffed Anya.

Jack looked at his watch. "We should be boarding soon. Excited?"

Anya nodded.

"Isn't the Santa Fe Chief a handsome train?"

She smiled. "Yeah, sure, I guess."

The shining silver train was being oiled and steam-cleaned. Fresh linens were being loaded, bags of mail, and case after case of food. An important-looking man in uniform, jingling an impressive collection of large brass keys, hurried down the tracks to check the signals. Porters were stowing baggage. Corax began to tremble when two men in uniform came toward them. It took great effort from both of those porters to push one red dog into his cage. Corax refused to move, pouted, made his back into a hump shape – he tried with everything he possessed to root himself to the platform.

"It'd be easier to move a baby elephant," said one porter, when they finally got him in and latched his cage door.

"You'll keep him where we can get at him?" Jack asked them. "My daughter is going to want to walk him at some of the stops."

"No problem, sir. We'll see that he's comfortable. Just come forward to the baggage car."

Anya watched her dog being carried away. He barked frantically only once and then cried piteously all the way to the baggage car. Anya dropped her head, feeling like she had committed some criminal act.

"Bo-oard!" bellowed the conductor. It was finally time. They were led through the Pullman cars to their berths, one compartment for Jack and Robert, one for Hattie and Anya.

As the four of them went down the narrow passage to their compartments, Hattie was last in line. Dr. Ravilious, the man who was acquainted with Jack, happened to step out of compartment number nine, right in front of her. His companion followed.

"Oh. I beg your pardon," Hattie said, and tried to slide past them.

Ravilious took a large breath. His bulk, his over-sized cowboy hat, and the heavy briefcase he carried took up most of the narrow space. He glared down at Hattie.

She straightened and pulled her overnight case in close. She had been brought up to respect adults. Of course you don't ever want to be rude, Mama had always told her. Be polite, *but* .... That "but", highlighted by her mama's sternly arched eyebrow, communicated an entire code of behavior. Hattie Fish had not been brought up to be a meek flower of a girl.

"Excuse me, sir," she said in a clear voice, "may I get past?" She tried to force herself to stop staring at the man's incongruous silk ascot. Its raw salmon color, clashing with his red plaid shirt, almost made her feel bilious.

Ravilious crowded her against the wall. This might be his only opportunity. He thrust his unshaven jaw forward, speaking confidentially. "Listen, I uh ..." He decided he'd better mention his lofty title, just to clarify his status. "I'm Doctor Ravilious. And you uh, I – I assume you know the area around Bandelier pretty well?"

She shook her head.

"Okay, look. I'll come straight to the point. Just – just tell me. How much is Netherby paying you?"

"Pardon me?"

"Whatever – whatever it is, I'll double it."

"I don't understand." What in the world did he want?

He dropped the smile. "Don't play dumb with me, sister."

"I have no –"

"You wouldn't be here unless Netherby hired you as a guide. My money's just as good as his. So how much?"

"Mister, I don't know what you want. But whatever it is, I doubt you could pay me enough." She tried to slip past him, frowning when he gripped her arm. She shook him off.

"My my. Aren't you the uppity little Indian."

Hattie straightened her shoulders. "Yes. Yes, I am an uppity Indian. And I'd like to get past."

He pointed a finger in her face. "You're a cheeky little rodent as well. Geezis." Ravilious turned to his companion. "Didn't I tell you, Ouisel? You can't deal with these people. Come on. This one's a waste of time." He turned away, letting his briefcase bang against her leg.

Hattie watched them go. It certainly wasn't the first time she had been treated this way. But the women of the Onondaga Nation were not brought up to be submissive. At home, they had important roles in their democracy. By ancient law, men deferred to women in certain situations. It was, for example, the clan mothers, not the men, who nominated their chiefs.

Hattie had been groomed to take her place among such women. Still, her first encounter with Dr. Ravilious left a sour impression. It upset her more than she liked to admit. "I see you, sir," she whispered to his disappearing back. "I see you."

Distressed, she hurried along the passage. Thank goodness! There was Anya, sticking her head out of their compartment.

"Hattie! Here you are. I wondered what became of you."

"Here I am." Something about those men ... they had made her feel horrible. Hattie tried to brush the whole incident away and speak normally. "What a – what a nice little room. Is it just for us?"

"Dad and Robert have a room of their own. He said the porter will make these seats into beds later."

"I thought we'd have to sleep sitting up."

"Nope. There's a bathroom down at the end, too."

"The strangest thing just happened, Anya."

Hattie wanted to tell Anya about meeting Ravilious and Ouisel but just at that moment, Jack knocked at their compartment door. "Will this work out okay for you girls?"

"It's very nice, Dr. Netherby. Thank you for inviting me." Hattie had to admit that, if nothing else, this trip was giving her something new to occupy her mind. Maybe Mama was right to insist that she come.

"Our pleasure, Hattie," Jack said. "Why don't you three kids look around a bit? They usually have games and snacks in the club car. We can meet in the dining car for lunch." He looked round at Robert, who hung back with a sullen expression. "Come on. I'll show you all where the observation car is."

They entered, found seats, and plastered their faces to the windows. Then, with a loud puff-belch, they heard a rush of steam escape from the cylinders in the engine. Anya had never ridden a train until this weekend. She grinned excitedly at Hattie.

The Santa Fe Chief was about to get underway. A blower lifted the smoke. They heard the beat of the air pumps. The engineer dropped the reverse lever and blew his whistle.

Shoo. Shoo shooshoo, and the Santa Fe Chief was pulling them out of the dark Chicago station and into the dawn, into the railyard packed with a hundred train cars and snarls of train tracks. They picked up speed. They passed miles of warehouses and factories, and on to neighborhoods where tilting houses crowded close to the tracks. Bells clanged, and little boys larking about in their Sunday-school clothes ran to the crossing to wave their caps at the engineer, and dance for joy when he tooted his whistle and waved a hand to them.

The Chief sped faster. The houses thinned and brown fields, sliding by at breath-taking speed, stretched for miles. They rolled south through Illinois, over brown rivers, the scenery a grey-brown blur, flatter than the fields at home, but otherwise not that different from what they were used to seeing. The train cars swayed to the music of the clacking wheels.

A porter came in and asked for their attention. "Hello, folks.

My name is Frank Rawlings," he said politely. "My job is to make sure you have a pleasant trip. I am at your service and here to help with anything, so please ask. I'd like it if you'd call me Frank, but if you forget, just call me Porter." He pointed to his cap. The word was embroidered there. "I ask you please though, ladies and gentlemen, do not call me Boy. Do not call me George."

Everyone in the car stared at him, silent. Anya looked questioningly at her father. He nodded slightly and raised a finger, signaling her to wait.

Frank the porter continued. "Now. You can rest assured that the Atchison, Topeka, and Santa Fe Railroad will to get you to California, if you're going that far, in practically no time at all. So just sit back and relax. Thank you, ladies and gentlemen. I sure do hope you enjoy your trip on our beautiful Santa Fe Chief. " He touched his cap and bent to speak to a passenger beside him.

"He's talking," explained Jack softly, "about people, rude people, who pretend to forget his name, just to be insulting. They call him George, after George Pullman, who designed these train cars. Or they call him Boy, even more insulting."

"I hate that," said Hattie fiercely. "I hate it."

"Pfft," Robert sneered. "What's the big deal?"

"It's rude, Robert. Why be rude? There's no sense in it." As soon as the words were out of her mouth, Hattie was reminded of how rude she had been to Robert earlier that morning. Flustered, she stood up to look at the map that hung near the door.

Anya was glad that Hattie had put Robert in his place. She wished he would just go away and leave them alone. He and she had not spoken a word to each other for the entire trip.

But Hattie always surprised her. She beckoned to them. Robert ignored her, turning to look out the window.

Jack got up. "I love maps. Let's have a look." He prodded Robert out of his seat. "Here's our route." Jack pointed. "And we're getting off here, in Lamy, New Mexico."

"This trip would have been a lot better if we were going over the Rockies."

"Well, next time, Robert."

"Let's go to the club car," Hattie suggested, "and see if they have jigsaw puzzles. The three of us can work on one together."

Anya wondered why Hattie was insisting they hang out with Robert. She refused. "That's all right. I have to visit Corax." She wanted nothing to do with her cousin.

"Sure," Hattie said. "Come back when you're done. Come on Robert, let's see what we can find." She paused, biting her lip and watching Anya walk away. "Robert!" She waved him back. "Hey. I'm sorry I turned on you this morning. It's just – I had so many arguments with my dad about girls and – you know, machines and stuff, I – I kinda lost it ... y'know?" She shrugged. "Wanna see if we can find a puzzle to work on?" Robert hesitated, then trudged after her.

Anya asked Frank the porter for directions to the baggage car. She swayed toward the front of the train and opened the door. What was that old guy with the dumb cowboy hat doing in here among the trunks and suitcases?

Ravilious and his short companion looked up from where they leaned above a very small desk. A big sheet of paper was spread open before them. Anya could see it was a map, though he had snatched up the edge to hide it from her. As if she were remotely interested. She ignored him and smiled at Corax, who squealed excitedly in his cage.

"Hey! You! No kids in here," Ravilious growled.

Anya halted. "Pardon?"

"No kids allowed in here. Beat it."

Was this an order, almost a threat? An angry feeling, too powerful to ignore, drew a scowl across her face.

She crouched down beside Corax, who wept softly.

GET ME OUT OF HERE, WOULD YOU PLEASE?

Doctor – what was his name? Doctor Somebody's cowboy boots clomped toward her. He leaned over her. "You don't understand English, kid? Leave the animal and get out of here."

Corax growled low in his throat. He didn't like the tone and he hated the boots – nothing to do with their style, just a deep personal prejudice against boots in general.

Anya wondered what Hattie would have said to this man. She always had a store of snappy sayings. Go take a long walk off a short pier. Move out, Brussel sprout.

Anya took a breath and steeled her nerve. "I need to see my dog," she finally blurted. Her insides did a flip followed by a flop.

And then a piece of luck came to her aid. Luck came in wearing a porter's uniform, complete with cap.

Anya looked at Frank the porter and cowered. Would he, too, tell her to beat it?

Frank glanced at Doctor Ravilious, who stood almost menacingly over the girl. He noted the expressionless eyes of Monsieur Ouisel. He looked at Anya, scared, kneeling beside her dog's cage. He sensed he had interrupted something ugly. This situation called for diplomacy and his Frank-the-gracious-porter persona.

"Good morning, folks," he said with bountiful cheer. "We got a lotta people in this here car this morning. I just stepped in to see the conductor, but if I can be of any assistance ...?"

The baggage car was the conductor's domain. He kept his lists and charts and timetables here. Generously, he had allowed Frank the porter to claim two inches of real estate on his little desk, just behind the box labeled 'Documents'. Back behind that box was where Frank the porter liked to store his two rolls of Lifesaver candies (one roll of butterscotch, one lime, for preference). Ravilious had spread his map out on that desk.

Ravilious glared at Frank. He puffed air through his lips. He fumbled with his map, a spiteful piece of paper if ever there was one. It refused to fold. He thrust it at Monsieur Ouisel and began to gather his briefcase, pencils, ruler. Muttering angrily, as he put his stuff away, he snitched a roll of Frank's Lifesavers. "I just needed a place to – I couldn't – somewhere private – away –, " he sputtered. A business card fluttered to the floor, unnoticed.

"If you have paperwork, sir, our club car has lots of room. Why don't you go there? Better light, nice comfy chairs, and tables where you can spread out your maps." Frank sounded like a radio advertisement.

"Yeah yeah." Ravilious drew back when Frank touched his sleeve as he passed. "What?"

"Excuse me. You picked up a roll of my Lifesavers by accident."

"Oh. Yours? Sorry. Yes, accident." Ravilious stomped out, the square toe of his cowboy boot thumping Anya's knee on the way. Monsieur Ouisel waddled slowly after him, without a word.

Anya, kneeling beside Corax's cage, worked the latch while he nosed her fingers.

The porter waited until the door closed behind the men, then looked at Anya and tilted his head. "Care for a Lifesaver? Lime."

"Thank you."

"Everything okay with you, little lady?"

She nodded. She let Corax out and he revolved in glad circles in front of her.

Frank crouched beside them. "What's your pup's name?" He stroked Corax's chest and won the dog's instant devotion.

"Corax."

"Cute name."

"Is it okay if I let him walk around a little?"

"Sure, sure! Long as he don't go tearing through the entire train."

"He hates the cage."

"Course he do. Anybody would, right? Next stop, you can give him a short walk on the platform. But it'll have to be short. We just pick up the mail and a passenger or two and we're away again. But the lunch stop, you get more time. Gotta keep to the schedule, you know. The Santa Fe Chief ain't never late!"

"Thank you, Mr. Frank." Anya palmed the business card she had seen Doctor Somebody drop, and stuck it in her pocket.

When Anya returned to the club car, she saw Hattie and Robert leaning over a table, working on a puzzle. Her father was in the corner, books and notebooks open. And sharing his table, his back to Anya, was the nasty Doctor Somebody and his plump assistant. Mr. Ouisel noticed her first. He shoved his glasses up the bridge of his oily nub of a nose and cleared his throat. Ravilious looked back at her.

Anya wouldn't normally interrupt when her father was meeting with someone, but she was curious to see what Doctor Nasty would now have to say to her. She went over to stand beside her father's chair and looked at the two men across the table. Her eyes flicked away from Ouisel's, then back again. His face was creepily immobile, unless he really was a corpse, which she thought he greatly resembled. Cold stupid eyes, like the sharks she had seen in pictures.

"Let me introduce my daughter Anya," Jack said. "This is Doctor Ravilious and Mr. Ouisel. These gentlemen are getting off the train at Lamy too."

"How do you do?" Anya said, her eyes back on the doctor's face. If he was surprised to see that she was Jack's daughter, or if he was embarrassed because he had behaved rudely to her, he never showed it.

"Very nice to meet you, Anya." Ravilious was a bit aloof. Mr.

Ouisel was only present in body. But he watched. He watched everyone.

Jack said, "I'll have to excuse myself, gentlemen. The kids are probably hungry for lunch."

"Let's have a drink together before dinner," said Ravilious, all heartiness again.

Jack smiled and gathered the papers he'd been working on. "Maybe. I'll have to see how the afternoon unfolds."

"I want to hear all about your plans for this trip," Ravilious said. "It sounds very exciting."

Walking away, Anya whispered, "I don't like those men."

Her father only replied, "Why don't you get the other two and meet me in the dining car?"

After lunch, Hattie and Anya worked on the jigsaw puzzle for a while, but when Robert joined them, Anya left to find her book.

"What's her problem?" Robert growled, pretending to be insulted.

"She went to get her book."

"I don't know what her gripe is," Robert claimed, watching her go. "I haven't done a thing to her."

"Really, Robert?"

"Well – ." He shrugged. "Whaddya want from me? A confession?"

"No. Nobody wants to make a fuss. So maybe you can take off that warrior mask of yours."

He looked at Hattie blankly. She never said what he expected her to say. "Has Anya been complaining about me?"

Hattie ignored the question. "Do you want to help me with this puzzle for a while?"

"No thanks," he said. "Maybe I'll wander around for a bit."

He walked aimlessly through the cars until he came to the

baggage car. The conductor was in there, working at his stand-up desk. Corax saw Robert and immediately tried to rise, barely possible in the small cage. He barked, and Robert knelt beside the cage. It wasn't locked, so he let the dog out. Corax pounced a few happy hops around Robert's feet. Robert leaned down to accept the invitation to play and they tussled on the floor.

"Don't forget to latch his cage before you leave," said the conductor on his way out. He turned back. "You handed in your dinner order, right son?"

"Yessir. Roast beef!"

"It'll be real good eating!" the conductor declared, and left.


Anya yawned. She had fallen asleep in her seat. Her book was on the floor. She felt the train slowing and noticed the porter moving through the car.

"Where are we, Mr. Frank?"

"We're just coming into Kansas City, little lady. But if you want to give that pup of yours a nice walk, wait til the dinner stop. Topeka, Kansas. It's only another half hour from now. You'll have lots of time to walk him then."

"Thank you."

Anya got up and headed to the baggage car. Poor Corax! He'd be so lonely. He had been by himself all afternoon. She went in and closed the door to the baggage car carefully so Corax wouldn't be tempted to make a dash for the exit. She turned around.

Her dog was gone.

His cage door was open and he had disappeared.

This was impossible! Where could he be? Resentment flooded her mind with the worst possible scenarios. She ran back through the train. Her father was alone at a table in the club car, his papers spread out in front of him once more. His fingers drummed thoughtfully on the table.

"Dad! Dad! You've got to help me! Corax is missing!"

"What?"

"His cage is open. He's gone! And I know who took him, too!"

"Who? Who would take him?"

"Robert!" she hissed softly.

"Don't be silly."

"Seriously, Dad. He does stuff like that."

Jack began stuffing his notes in his briefcase. "Don't worry. He can't have gone far."

"He threw him off the train! I bet he did!"

"Now why would he do that?"

"To be mean. He's a big huge meany."

"Hold on. I can't leave my notes here. Let me take them to my cabin."

"Hurry, Dad." On the other hand, why hurry? Her dog was probably lying dead, ten miles back down the tracks. Anya, with a little whimper, stumbled after her father.

Jack opened the door to his cabin. It had already been made into sleeping bunks for the night. Stretched out there, his back to the door and sound asleep, was Robert.

"Ha! Look," said Jack. Corax's head was ensconced on Robert's pillow. Robert's arm was slack across the dog's back. Hearing the door open, Corax popped his head up. He leapt over Robert and into Anya's arms. His feet, pushing unconcerned against Robert's body, woke him up.

"Oof!" Robert sat up, groggy. "Oh. Guess I – oh. Hi." He swung his feet to the floor. "Guess I fell asleep."

"What were you doing?" Anya demanded. "How dare you take my dog!"

"Sorrreee! I went to visit him. He seemed so lonely that I just –" Robert stopped. "It's not like I hurt him or anything."

"That was kind of you, Robert," Jack said, knuckling the dog's head. "You're a lucky one, Corax, to have so many friends."

Anya seethed. She did not want her dog to have Robert for a friend.

"We'd better put him back in his cage, though, before we get caught."

"Mr. Frank said I could walk him in Topeka, Dad. It'll be dinnertime."

As before, it took all three of them to block Corax from escaping and push him into the cage. But Anya stayed beside him until they got to Topeka. She sat on the floor, trying to puzzle things out.

Imagine Robert, of all people, realizing the dog would be lonely.


Corax did get a chance for a good long trot along the tracks in Topeka. On their way back, Anya stopped at the window of the telegraph office, curious to watch the operator using his machine. Anya pressed close to the window. He was busy at the moment, taking a piece of paper from someone standing at his desk. That someone was Dr. Ravilious. He caught sight of Anya peering in the window and frowned angrily. She backed up quickly and hurried away to the train.

Then, for poor Corax, it was back in the cage once more while Anya had her dinner.

She found the table set with beautiful linens, china, and crystal. The food was delicious, cooked and served by the famous Harvey company, who took pride in providing immaculate service to the railroad. She was really getting to like train travel! Doctor Ravilious had sent a half-bottle of champagne to their table for Jack. Jack turned and bowed to him in thanks.

"He's a creep, that man," muttered Anya.

"Oh, he's probably not a bad person," her dad said.

"I don't like him."

"You don't want to give him the benefit of the doubt?"

"I don't like him either," said Hattie. "Dr. Raving Idiot, I call him."

Robert was tempted to give his opinion, but when he hesitated, Anya interrupted.

"Hey, Dad. Look at this." Anya fished in her pocket for the business card she had seen Ravilious drop to the floor of the baggage car. She told her father where she found it.

"George G. Lowe," read Jack, speaking softly. "Don't tell me Ravilious is consorting with this character."

"Who is that?"

"Lowe? He's a rich guy who calls himself an art dealer. A swindler, more like it. He specializes in Native American antiques."

"What?" asked Hattie, her head snapping up. "Antiques from where?"

"Anywhere in the west. People dig up ancient Native artifacts and sell them to this Mr. Lowe. He resells them and makes big profits. He has a pretty bad reputation among archaeologists."

"Are the artifacts valuable?" asked Anya.

"How can they be valuable?"growled Robert. "It's just a bunch of old junk nobody wants anymore."

Anya glared at him.

"Well actually, Robert," said Jack, "imagine yourself coming upon an object that was lovingly crafted six hundred years ago. And say you discovered it on your own, in the place where someone left it all that time ago. I feel sure you'd sense an enormous energy there."

Robert shrugged.

"I wish these ancient things could be left in place," Jack continued, "and certainly the native peoples wish that, too. But instead, stolen artifacts end up gathering dust on somebody's bookshelf. And not always properly cared for. This Mr. Lowe isn't fussy about where he gets the stuff, either. He doesn't think twice about selling stolen goods."

"What do you mean? He steals from tribal lands?" asked Hattie.

"Sure, and from private property, from national parks, from anywhere. People dig where they are not supposed to, like around ancient settlements. And graves are practically treasure troves to them."

"Graves? That should be against the law! It is! Isn't it, Dr. Netherby?" Hattie's voice rose. "They have no right! Why is it illegal to dig up white peoples' graves, but nobody cares about our graves?"

Jack put his finger to his lips. "I know. You're absolutely right, Hattie. And it is against the law."

"Dr. Netherby, I was wondering." Hattie hesitated. "I don't mean to be critical, but what about your work? Do you dig up graves to find stuff to put in your book?"

"My main focus is not objects. We'll mostly be photographing abandoned settlements, some that are almost unknown. And if I find an artifact, great. If I have to touch it to get a photo, I put it right back where I found it. But mostly I'm trying to learn about the way people lived, whether one settlement traded with another, stuff like that. I'm more interested in ancient societies than in artifacts. This will be a good time of year to be working out there. No tourists, no pot hunters. Just me and the photographer."

"I didn't mean to accuse you, Dr. Netherby. It just gets me so upset."

Robert was thinking about Ravilious too, about the angry conversation he had overheard that morning. Should he warn Uncle Jack that Ravilious had insulted him? The conversation had been in French. Maybe he had misunderstood. But, pfft! Never mind. What difference would it make? Those two men weren't talking about him. They were talking about Uncle Jack.

It is weird though, thought Robert, the way he found himself liking his uncle. He was kind of a cool guy. Of course, that probably wouldn't last. Something would happen. Something always happened. Jack would get mad at him and start to ignore him, and end up hating him.

Yeah, it was stupid to get upset about insults to Uncle Jack. Why should he care what that Ravilious guy said?

They had all finished their dinners and rose to leave. Filing out past the table where Ravilious and Ouisel sat, Ravilious stopped Jack with a suggestion. "We missed our drink together. It would be nice to share our resources on this trip, Doctor," he said to Jack. "I have a map you might be interested in, and I'm sure you and your Indian squaw – your – your guide here," he gestured to Hattie, "could show me some places of interest. Let's share notes this evening, shall we?"

Hattie stared at Ravilious. Had he called her a squaw? An Indian? She wasn't from India. Slowly she turned, outraged, to lock eyes with Anya.

Anya shook her head slightly. You could never be sure what Hattie would do when provoked.

Jack felt the insult to Hattie, too. He ended the conversation, politely but quickly, and wished Ravilious and Ouisel a good night.

Ravilious twisted in his seat. "We'll talk tomorrow, okay, Doctor?" he called.

While he was turned, Hattie's hand shot out. She snatched a cigarette butt from the pile in the ashtray and dropped it into Ravilious's fresh cup of coffee. She looked up. Ouisel was puffing a cigarette, watching her through a cloud of smoke. Had he noticed? She stared back, defying him to reprimand her. But Ouisel said nothing. Hattie lifted her chin and walked away with her companions.

Indian squaw indeed.

Anya, huddling close behind her, put her head down and

pushed Hattie through the door.

Robert was the last to pass Ravilious's table. He felt a touch on his sleeve.

"I'm in compartment nine," said Ravilious quietly, lifting his coffee cup to his lips. "In case you need a friend." He smiled at Robert and slurped.

As Robert walked away, he heard violent coughing.

"Geez, Ouisel! What are you trying to do? Choke me to death?"


Robert was puzzled. In case he needed a friend? What was that supposed to mean? A while later, he tapped on the door of compartment nine.

Ravilious pulled him inside. "Sorry I can't offer you a chair," he said, sitting down. Ouisel, in the other seat, was immovable.

"What's your name, kid?" asked Ravilious.

"Robert."

"You're Netherby's son?"

Robert shook his head. "Nephew."

"Care for a little wine?"

Robert hesitated. It wouldn't be his first glass. "Sure."

Ravilious poured. "Just a little. I don't want you falling on your face."

Robert sipped.

"Enjoying your trip?"

Robert shrugged and took a bigger slug of wine. "It's okay."

"Not very good company for you, is it? A little girl and an Indian."

"Eh, it's okay."

Ravilious sipped his own wine for a minute, thinking. "So. Richard."

"It's Robert."

"Robert. I bet you could help me out with something. I bet you're the man I need."

"Help you?"

Ravilious nodded and smiled.

Robert twitched his shoulders. "Doing what?"

"Your uncle promised to show me his maps. Maybe you can bring me a couple. He keeps forgetting."

"Why don't you just remind him?"

Ravilious smiled. "I hate to bother him. But I can trade information with him. Or with you, if you like. I can show you an old Spanish map I have. It shows where those famous gold bars are buried."

"What gold bars?"

"You haven't heard that old story about missing gold bars? Stolen fifty years ago from a bank in Utah, and buried somewhere near Santa Fe. I can show you where."

"Huh."

"You bring me your uncle's map and I'll show you mine."

Robert thought for a minute. "What, you mean steal one of his maps?"

"Noo! Nonono. I don't mean steal it. Borrow it. I just want to look at it."

"I – I don't know. I don't think I could."

"You're too chicken?"

"No!" Robert frowned and rolled his eyes.

"Then why are you acting like a chicken?" said Ravilious, wrenching a smile across his face.

"Me? A chicken? You must be kidding."

"Well?"

"Uncle Jack's stuff is all in his briefcase. I probably wouldn't get a chance –"

"Have you seen any maps?"

"Yeah. Sure I did. I saw one."

"Marked with sites?"

"Dunno. Some kind of marks."

"I just need some place names."

Robert bit his lip and emptied his glass. "I dunno."

"All right kid, look. If you don't have the guts, ...."

"Hey! I – I might be able to get a look at one of them." He banged his wineglass down and wiped his mouth with his hand.

"Nah. You're not up to the task, kid, I can tell. What did I tell you, Honoré? You can't send a boy to do a man's job."

Ouisel squinted and sucked hard on his cigarette.

"I could do it." Robert shoved his hands in his pockets. "I could. But I don't know if I want to." He hesitated. He leaned back against the door, feeling a little airy-headed. "What would I get?"

"Get? Get? What're you talking about?"

"What'll you give me?"

"I told you. I said I'll show you my map."

"How do I know your map's any good? If it's good, why aren't you digging for the gold yourself?"

"Hey! You think I'm lying?"

Robert bit his lip. "How about – I won't bring my uncle's map, but I could bring you some names of places he has marked. But you gotta give me something good in return."

Ravilious sat back in his chair, belched softly and smiled. "Whadya want?"

"How about that?" Robert pointed to a mechanical pencil sticking out of Ravilious's pocket. A small gem sparkled on the clip. "That gold pencil."

"This?" Ravilious pulled it out. "This was a gift. An award. It's ten carat gold, fer crissake. 'Sgot a diamond on it."

Robert shrugged. "So?"

"Nope. No dice, kid."

"Sorry, then. I can't help you." A little relieved actually, Robert turned the latch on the door.

"Okay, wait a minute. Here, kid. Take it. Yesyes, go ahead. I want you to have it. But you better bring me some information. And I mean good information," Ravilious smiled evilly, "or I'll have to take the pencil back somehow. Whatever that takes."

Again Robert hesitated. He shrugged. "Okay, then." He took the pencil and slipped it into his shirt pocket, stepped out of the compartment into the hall, and nearly tripped over his cousin Anya and her friend. The girls stopped, surprised. Hattie looked at the number on the door. She looked at Robert.

"What's up?" she asked.

"Wrong room," said Robert. "Made a mistake." He hurried on to the next car.

Hattie held Anya back for a minute. She gestured toward compartment nine. "Dr. Raving Idiot's room," she whispered.

"You sure?" asked Anya.

"Positive."

"That's weird."


Later that evening, Robert sat down at the table where his uncle was referring to a map he had spread out in front of him. Robert leaned his elbows on the table, chewing his thumbnail. His eyes searched the map.

"How's it going, Robert?"

"Okay. Okay I guess. Is this a map of where we're going?"

"It is."

"This place here. Stone Lions. That sounds interesting."

"It is. Very."

"So, uh, you going there? Digging or something?"

Looking up, Jack immediately noticed the clip of a gold mechanical pencil gleaming in Robert's pocket. "No digging this time," he said. "I want to hike into some of the canyons. Get my photographer to record some of the sites I've found, some of the rock paintings." He looked at Robert carefully. "Nice pencil."

"Yeah, I uh, my mother gave it to me or Grandma or, I don't know who – "

"AIA?"

"Huh?"

"The clip is engraved. AIA. The Archaeological Institute of America awards sets of those pencils to distinguished members. Doctor Ravilious has one. Have you noticed?"

Robert felt his face flame. "Oh yeah. The old guy's pencil. I forgot I had it. He lent it to me. Before. Mine broke and I – I forgot to give this one back."

"You'd better get it back to him right away."

"Yep," Robert stood up, a little dizzy. Whew, the wine. He bumped hard against the table and tripped over his own feet. "I should do that right now." He slammed through the door to the next car and stood for a minute to collect himself.

He could hear his mother's voice in his head. "Robert! Think! Use your head. You've got to learn to think before you do something."

A minute later he knocked on Ravilious's door.

"Robert, my friend."

Robert thrust the pencil at him."Here. Keep it."

"No no. We have a deal."

"I don't want your pencil. I don't want your deal," he blurted. He pulled the door closed before Ravilious could answer.

Robert banged his hand against his forehead. Wow, you handled that like an imbecile. You call that thinking before speaking? He hurried back down the passageway. He had to get into bed, pretend to be asleep before Uncle Jack came in. He didn't want to have to look him in the eye.

Why did stuff like this always happen to him? He hated Ravilious for making him seem like a fool. He hated him.

CLACK CLACK.

THAT NOISE CAN REALLY GET TO YOU.

CLACKETY CLACK.

SO COLD. NO ROOM TO MOVE. OUCH, THE HARDEST BED IN THE WORLD.

CLACK CLACK.CLACKETY CLACK.

NO ONE COMING TO TAKE ME OUT. HOURS AND HOURS. MY GIRL, THE BOY. NO ONE. WHERE ARE THEY?


Doorknob noises. Up comes his head.

OH PLEASE. His heart leaps. PLEASE PLEASE. He holds his breath. HOPE.

The door opens.

Crash. Back into the pit of depression.

IT'S ONLY THAT MAN.

Definitely not his girl. No way, not with legs like that. Calves the size of pork roasts and boots made of thick leather, thick as marrow bones. He had once been kicked by boots like that, so he knows. He knows how awful they are. The man passes his cage as always. No friendly word, nothing, and he hears the scrape of a chair or a stool. Papers rustling.

His heart actually hurts.

It is broken broken broken. Never to know gladness again.


Doorknob noises again.

WHY EVEN BOTHER TO LOOK UP?

No one would ever come for him ever again he'd been forgotten for all time forsaken for the rest of his life.

Alone. Abandoned again.

That nice man came to his cage.

"Hey, little fella. You sure look unhappy."

EH, SO WHAT ELSE IS NEW? Abandoned, just like before. IT'S HAPPENING ALL OVER AGAIN.

Grief, loneliness, he knows them. Oh yes. He is well acquainted with them.

SIGH. Loneliness crushes the life out of a dog.

"Come on, cheer up, fella. It won't be long now. A train ride ain't the end of the world. Wanna Life Saver? Here, take it. Come on, take it. No? Oookay then."

The nice man rose.

"This is one unhappy dog." The man popped the Life Saver into his own mouth. "How we doin' for time, Bucky? Have to be in Santa Fe by three seventeen tomorrow, on the dot. Got a dollar on it, me and Chuck, so don't let me down."

YAK YAK YAK.

SO COLD.

His elbows hurt. He tried to roll onto his side.

SO STIFF, NO ROOM TO STRETCH OUT.

His ribs hurt his heart has been wrung dry.

CLACK CLACK. CLACKETY CLACK.

BITTER BITTER COLD.

TRICKSTER'S COUNTRY

Monday


They woke up the next morning on the high plains of Colorado. The dry prairie grass lay brown and dead, dotted everywhere with clumps of silver-green sagebrush. Buildings were low, hunkered down into the landscape. Whereas, in the east, people liked building on top of knolls, out here they sheltered beneath them. A few sparse trees were sometimes planted around houses and buildings for protection from wind, but homeowners seemed to make no effort at landscaping or gardening. Hard times had taken a terrible toll on farmers out here. Many homesteads were surrounded with upended wagons, broken wheels, the skeletons of bent windmills, here a beat-up Model T Ford, and there a sway-backed horse or a matted droopy-headed goat. The kids saw no paved roads; only dusty two-tracks running alongside the rails or out into empty nowhere; the occasional horse and wagon, hardly ever a car.

"Look at the telegraph poles," said Anya. "They're so short."

"Where do they get their water?" asked Hattie. "No lakes or streams."

"There's a farm pond." commented Robert. "But pretty small."

"Out here the ranchers get into actual battles over water rights," Jack told them.

"There's no real dirt. Just sand everywhere. Or yellow dust. How can they grow things?"

"Lots of rocks, not many tall trees."

"Most crops don't do well," said Jack. "They raise cattle and sheep, mainly."

"Yeah, look. Lots of cows. Wow! Look at them all."

They made a brief stop in Trinidad, Colorado. As they pulled out of the station, the sky behind them was heavy with black stormclouds. Jack said he hoped they could get over the Raton Pass before the storm caught them. They weren't far from Lamy now. The train tracks held to the flat plain and the white peaks of the Rockies rimmed the horizon. Buildings became even more sparse and the fenced ranches went on forever. Fences and telegraph poles, that was about all there was to see.

When they began the zigzag climb up to the Raton Pass a sleety snow blew down and stuck to everything. The train slowed to a crawl, twisting its laborious way up to the pass. At places where the tracks crossed roads, they practically came to a standstill and the engineer blew long hoots on his whistle. They could feel the wind beating against the sides of the cars as they inched up the steep grade, and the snow flew thick and fast.

"We're going to get stuck up here," worried Anya.

"This is the steepest active grade in the whole country," Jack told them, "so they've got to take it slow. The tracks can get icy. Maybe after the tunnel ...."

"There's a tunnel?"

"We should be coming to it soon, and that will take us into New Mexico."

Once through the tunnel and heading down the other side of the pass, they picked up speed. The sun came out again. The snowstorm had not followed them over the mountain. When the train stopped at Raton, the pale blue sky was wisped with white clouds. There were a dozen people in dusty work clothes waiting to board, not even wearing coats, probably going to Santa Fe. The station, with its row of arches along the porch, looked small, nothing at all like the train station in Chicago. Anya and the dog ambled along the platform. There were a couple of shops across the way, no buildings above two stories tall.

"One last time into your cage," Anya told Corax. He was accepting his fate meekly now, defeated prisoner, outcast. She wished he could understand that soon he'd be free.


They watched eagerly for the station at Lamy.

Finally, there it was. Buff-colored stucco with a reddish-brown roof, it was the tiniest station they had seen. Its name was painted in giant letters on the side of the building. The porters helped everyone jump down to the platform.

They carried their coats. It was so much warmer here. All they needed to wear were light sweaters. The breeze was soft and the dry air was filled with a spicy fragrance. Hattie and Anya drank in smells like a healing draft. Robert stood blinking in the sun, like someone who had just awakened.

Corax, released from his cage, was ecstatic at seeing all his people together in the beautiful outdoors. He circled each person, begging to be petted, then ran back and nosed Frank the porter's knee.

Frank bent to scratch the dog's chest. "Oh, you like me now? See, I told you you'd be free eventually. Okay, little guy. Gotta go."

Frank waved to them. The train slid away down the tracks, wended its way across a wide plain of silver sagebrush, and disappeared into yellow hills. With immense satisfaction, Corax watched it and its abominable dog-prison depart.

So this was New Mexico, almost a different world. Off to the west were distant blue mountains, some topped with a dust of snow already. Overhead the blue dome of the sky was ribbed with thin clouds. Colors, roses and blues and golds and silver greens and dark piney greens; the fragrance of sagebrush; warm sun and soft dry breeze. None of this was the desert they expected. They sat down to wait near their luggage.

"That's not our hotel over there?" asked Robert. "El Ortiz?"

"No," said Jack, scanning the parking lot. "Somebody should be here soon, I hope, to pick us up."

"Well, how much longer before we get where we're going?"

"Be patient. It will take as long as it takes, Robert." Jack rose. "Let's carry our bags around to the back of the station."

They were lugging suitcases around the building when a black limousine came roaring up. The driver honked impatiently and then got out.

"Snyder!" he yelled. "Over here!"

"George!" Dr. Ravilious and Mr. Ouisel hurried past them without a glance, gesturing to a weary porter who plodded along pushing a cart piled high with cases.

"Dr. Raving Idiot sure needs a lot of luggage," said Hattie quietly to Anya.

"Yeah," whispered Anya. "All those silk ascots." They wondered how the men were going to pack that mountain of gear into the limosine.

Ravilious shook hands with the man from the limo. "Good to see you, George! Where's your driver?"

"He's here, but he drives so slow he makes me crazy. Open the trunk, Smith," George ordered his chauffeur. "And this is?" George held out a hand to Ouisel.

Introductions were brief. "Honoré Ouisel, this is George Lowe, the dealer I told you about. Ouisel wants to take some pieces back for his French clients."

George Lowe stiffened. "I trust he won't be in competition with me?"

"He and I have an agreement, George. You'll get first pick and a cut of everything. There will be no problem."

"Good. You realize I can't let valuable pieces slip through my fingers without compensation."

Ouisel had nothing to say to that.

"My telegram! Did you get my telegram, George?"

"Yep."

"You got all the stuff we need?"

"I got it."

"The tent and – ?"

"I got it, Snyder! Stop worrying! We'll pick it all up at the rental company. Let's go. You, Smith," Lowe told his driver, "you sit in the back. Give him your case, Snyder. He can hold it on his lap. Give him that other one, too. Pile it all in there."

The black limousine spun off, fishtailing in the dust and nearly colliding with a square brown station hack just pulling in. George Lowe blasted his horn, shouted something rude out the window, and sped away.


The station hack parked and the driver got out.

"Dr. Netherby!"

"Dick! Here you are!"

The girls watched a young blonde man coming toward them. Hattie's eyes widened. She gulped involuntarily for air. New Mexico was already beginning to look a little better. Robert sat back on his heels, hands in his pockets, squinting narrowly at the young man.

Jack greeted him with warmth. "It's good to see you, Dick. You're well? Your mom is well?"

"Both of us fit as fiddles, Dr. Netherby."

"All our bags are here, but let me introduce you to everyone. This is my daughter, Anya. This is Dick Frey, kids. He and his mother run the ranch we'll be staying at."

Dick laughed. "My mom's the boss, just so you know. Nice to meet you, Anya."

"And this is our friend Hattie." Dick's blue eyes felt warm as sunbeams to her.

"How do." He unhooked his hand from his belt and made a little one-fingered salute.

Hattie Fish, indefatigable lacrosse champion and aviation repair apprentice, was weak-kneed and strangle-throated. "Grzlg," she answered.

Anya wondered if that was Onondagan for "hello". No. Whatever it was, it was not Onondagan.

"This is my nephew, Robert."

"Hey, Robert." Smiling, Dick held out a hand and waited until Robert deigned to shake it.

"Oh yes, and our dog Corax."

"Hi there, little fella!" Dick knelt.

Corax hid behind Anya and put his tail between his legs, afraid. Boots again! He peeked around Anya's knees. Wait. Sweet-talk, he was hearing sweet-talk. Shy, wary, Corax humped closer to the stranger.

OH, AH, ALL RIGHT. Not only a sweet-talker. A good manly fur-scratcher, too.

"You'll have to pardon his enthusiasm, Dick. He's been in a cage for three days," said Jack.

"Okay. Let's get those bags loaded." Dick pointed to the dusty wood-paneled Ford.

"Will we all fit?" asked Anya. Hattie had temporarily lost the power of speech. Robert refused, on principle, to speak. How do you talk to a guy who was this good-looking without sounding like a jackass?

"This car has plenty of room. We've taken six, eight people before," said Dick. "Let me take that bag for you, Anya."

"Grab your suitcases, everyone," said Jack. "Robert, give us a hand. Come on. We still have a ways to go."

"You're right, Dr. Netherby. We should get moving. It gets dark early now, and that trail is treacherous at the best of times. Does your dog mind car rides?"

"He loves them," Anya said.

Corax leapt into the back and refused to give up his window seat. He vowed never, never to be confined again. Nothing would feel so good to him now as a nice wind bath. Ah, what a wonderful day he was having!

Dick slid behind the wheel and drove out to the road. When he swerved onto a one-lane track half an hour later, he blew the horn a few times.

"Letting Michael know we're coming. Wake him up," he laughed to Jack. A dust cloud billowed angrily behind them and chased the car across a flat plain covered patchily with greensilver brush.

The wide plateau wore a startlingly rich palette of colors, endless in variety and changing by the minute; the softest yellows and lavenders, the silveriest olives, blushes of apricot and almond. The cornflower blue of the Jemez Mountains in the far distance was a perfect complement to the soft pink of the plains, and as the sun lowered in the west, the whole mesa was washed in every shade of deep rose and lilac. Everywhere around them, a painted world of wonder, richly tinted in colors more varied than any of them had ever imagined.

When the car lurched to a stop next to a pair of barns, a little bevy of mules raised their heads and regarded the newcomers with bored expressions. Corax barked and leapt out immediately to investigate these strange creatures.

The mules showed only a slight interest in the dog and even less interest in the people. It was the end of their day. They had been hoping their work was finished.

Wearily, they evaluated their one requirement for a tolerable human being. Since humans were cargo, you would think these mules would be glad that these weren't large heavy people. But most days, gladness was not part of their emotional spectrum, or not for these particular mules, anyway. They had been mired in moping when the car pulled up. They went back to moping.

Dick got out of the car. "Michael?" he called. Hattie sat forward on her seat, surprised to see another person who looked like herself. He was a native man in his mid-twenties, with striking good looks. He wore a light, loose shirt, and his black hair was tied behind his head. He came out of a shed and began to help Dick take their suitcases out of the car.

Dick gestured toward him. "Michael Redbird, everybody."

Michael nodded. "Welcome," he said. "You have come from a long way. And still, we have further to go."

Anya jumped out of the car and looked around. "Further? Where's the hotel?"

"Down there." Jack pointed.

Craning their necks, they walked cautiously to a rim of land and peered over the edge. A deep scar of a canyon had split the earth in a gash so narrow and abrupt they hadn't even noticed it was there. Far below, soldered into the canyon bottom, was a silver ribbon of river, Rio de los Frijoles.

"Down there?"

"How do we get there?"

"It's sure a long way down."

"Don't worry. It's less than a two-hour trip by mule," Dick told them.

"Two hours?" "By mule?" "What do you mean, by mule?"

"We could walk, but it will be dark in a while. We're much safer trusting the mules on the trail," Dick said. "They can make this trip blindfolded. Go with Michael, everybody. He'll get you saddled up."

"Saddled?"

"What about the car?"

"The car stays up here."

"But --"

"We can't drive down," Jack told them.

"There's never yet been a car in that canyon," said Dick.

"No car?"

"No road. Everybody goes down by mule. But your bags, our groceries, lumber, everything but people can take the cable car."

"Why not us?" demanded Robert.

"No people, except for staff, allowed in the cable car. Sorry."

"Come on! You must be kidding," complained Robert.

"I'm not. We keep it free in case of emergency."

"It's not strong enough to hold us?" asked Hattie.

"It is. But we still have the no-people rule. Besides, we want you to enjoy the full ranch experience."

"That cable car is strong," Michael Redbird said. "Don't worry about that. It was strong enough to move his mother's piano."

Dick gestured them forward. "Even my mother's piano. The cable car was built about ten years ago. But when I was a baby, she had to take me down there by mule. Me and the seventy-five fruit trees and the five hundred baby chicks that came with us."

"So, you mean we –?" asked Hattie.

"We ride." Dick dazzled her with another smile. "Let me help you up."

This guy, those blue eyes, Hattie raptured, then immediately sobered. Her late father. No, he would definitely not like to hear what was going through her head right now. She tried to stifle a hiccup.

"You've never ridden?" Dick asked her. "Hey, Clive! Easy!" Clive the mule wanted to start immediately for the rim of the canyon.

"Stop, you – you animal! Help! How do you make a horse stop?" squealed Hattie, clutching his mane.

Dick laughed and held Clive's bridle. "Mule. Clive's a mule."

"I have to ride this thing down that trail? It's straight down!"

"The Pueblo people used it for hundreds of years."

"He's going! He's leaving!" Hattie beat the sides of the mule with her feet, which signaled to Clive to go faster. "Make him wait! Clive! Stop!" Again Dick caught him.

"I've got him. Easy, easy."

"Please! I'll walk. I don't like this animal! He's too dangerous! Aaah!" Hattie had never felt so awkward. Hiccup! She could hear Anya snickering behind her back.

"Hattie!" Jack laughed. "You said you've flown an airplane, for pete's sake. This is only a mule."

"He's going to spill me over the edge!"

"You've flown a plane?" Dick asked her.

"Only for a couple of minutes." Instead of going to school, a residential school despised by all her people, Hattie had a job assisting her uncle. He was an airplane mechanic. Flying with him was a piece of cake compared to riding this animal. Airplanes had mechanical controls, but mules had minds. Minds of their own, it appeared, over which Hattie had no control.

"Don't worry, Hattie. The trail is steep but Clive here has made this trip hundreds of times. He's just a little ornery today, is all."

"Ooh, I get the ornery mule. Great."

Dick touched her hand. "Maybe if you didn't pull on his mane …."

"Yeah, okay. Okay." Good grief, what was wrong with her today?

"Has anybody ever slipped off the edge?" asked Robert.

"I was afraid you'd ask that. Tell you the truth, years ago, a mule loaded with lumber died in a bad fall. But now we send all the heavy stuff down by cable car. We're not going to lose anyone tonight, I promise you."

Michael Redbird started the motor on the cable car and watched it descend, taking the luggage down six hundred feet to the bottom of the canyon. Dick soon had the riders lined up and ready to set off. Corax, wary of edging past the surly mules, took up the rear, stopping only every five steps to sniff excitedly.

The sun was warm on their backs as their mules slouched to the edge of the mesa. When they began twisting down the narrow trail, the shadows deepened, though it was just four o'clock in the afternoon. The temperature dropped and they buttoned coats and pulled gloves from pockets.

The trail was steep. It became alarmingly narrow in many places where it hugged the edge of the precipice. More than once, a long drop straight down appeared practically under their feet. If one mule loosened a stone at the edge and had to scramble to keep from slipping, as happened several times, the riders clutched their hearts in panic. Stones clattered down the slope. Their mounts puffed, back-stepped, and waited with seeming indifference until the threatened one regained his footing.

At first the riders marveled at how unflappable the animals were. But several long, loud, and shockingly malodorous eruptions soon betrayed a stunning lack of mulish intestinal fortitude. Rather unnerving, to realize your mule was terrified. Not to mention the singularly unpleasant sensory experience it created for those behind him.

The light in the valley dimmed. They plodded slowly down the narrow path, halting, back-stepping, cautious; the riders leaning back in their saddles against the steepness, more and more uncertain about whether there would ever be an end to this trail. Above them, the looming cliffs narrowed the visible heavens to a river of sky tinged with saffron light, then bluebell, deep periwinkle, gentian. A star appeared. And still they wound down, down the wall of steep bouldered terrain.

At long last, far below, a twinkle of lights. Never had human habitation looked so welcome!

And finally they were on flat ground. The river raced alongside them. The mules began to trot faster, knowing their stable was near. Their gait was rough and the riders bounced painfully on their saddles, but the little band of people was just as eager to reach shelter. It was fully dark now. They could see nothing of their surroundings, and had to trust the mules to follow Dick Frey and Michael Redbird across a narrow wooden bridge.

Just beyond that, the sheer relief of finally coming to a stop. No more jolting and clinging to creaking saddles. They sat for a moment, the quiet settling about them like downy feathers. Only then did they notice the purl of the running river, the breath of a breeze sighing in the pines, the pulsing of a galaxy of stars.

The Ranch of the Ten Elders, at long last.

Before them was a one-story stone cottage. Long and low, it seemed to have grown organically from the earth, as though it had always been there and always would be. Small leaded windows, deeply set, shone golden with lamplight. Steps led up to a narrow porch and toward a heavy front door strapped with wrought iron.

Suddenly that door was flung open and light streamed out. Mrs. Evelyn Frey, Dick's mother, came to the edge of the porch. She was tiny, barely five feet tall, with nothing of the physical sturdiness they expected of a ranching woman. She wiped her hands on her apron and spread her arms wide.

"Welcome!" she called. "We're so glad you've come!"

"Evelyn!" Jack dismounted quickly and reached to hug her. "Thank you for having us. I know it's not easy to fit us in at holiday time."

"It's always a pleasure to have you, Jack! But things are quite different this year. Actually, you are our only guests."

"Really? How can that be?"

"I'll tell you all about it inside. But, I assure you, we are more than grateful to see some friendly faces this week."

The rest of the party dismounted stiffly, exhausted. Jack introduced them to Mrs. Frey and she greeted each of them warmly. Corax jumped onto the porch and received special attention.

"You're a lovely dog, aren't you?" she said to him, and he circled happily to show his delight. "And how was your ride, everyone? A bit long?"

They groaned. They actually did. It was rude, but they did.

"We ... we've never ridden mules," said Anya, trying to be tactful.

Robert was more direct. "I feel like I've been bouncing up and down on top of a brick wall!" Mrs. Frey laughed and tousled his hair. He caught himself smiling back at her. Wow, that feels odd, he thought. Very odd – him smiling, for nearly the first time all week. All month, really.

"Now," called Mrs. Frey, "take your bags, everyone, so Michael can stable the mules. Dick, light the lanterns and show them their cabins, will you, honey? You just have time for a quick wash up, folks. Dinner's almost ready."

Dinner. The word made them realize that they were ravenously hungry.

"Come this way," said Dick, leading them around the main lodge and up a hill. The light breeze, rolling off the high canyon walls, showered them with incense of pine and pinon. Dick stopped, scraped a match, and lit a lantern that sat on a stone post next to the walkway. "Keep your dog close, Anya. A leash is a good idea after dark. Girls, you are in the first cabin here." He opened the door to a tiny stone guest cottage. "When you're ready for dinner, just go straight back down this path to the lodge. Jack and Robert, you'll be in the big cabin further up the hill here."

The men went on up the path and Anya and Hattie entered their cabin. They stood for a minute, admiring. Dark wood-paneled walls. A pair of wing chairs near the window. An oil lamp burning low. A fragrant slow fire burning in a cone-shaped fireplace in the corner. Another unlit lamp between the beds. The room was full of shadows, yet warm and so cozy that both girls sighed with happiness. Simple curtains were trimmed with little painted turkeys, the ranch's logo.

"Isn't this beautiful?"

"Maybe I'll stay here forever."

Corax danced here and there, examining everything.

Hattie threw herself onto the bed. "The beds are nice. Look at the embroidery on these pillow cases. More of these cute little turkeys."

There was a bowl and a pitcher of water for washing up, and a pile of sweet-smelling towels. Dick had informed them that only the kitchen had running water. They washed, and unpacked warm sweaters. The night was already cold.

"I'm starving! I could eat a ...." Hattie stopped. "Hey. I'm actually hungry. I haven't been hungry in, gee, I don't know how long."

"Let's go eat! I'd better put a leash on the dog. Are there wild animals here, do you think?"

"I expect there may be. Who knows what's out there? It's so dark, I can't see a thing."

"Maybe I'll let Corax sniff around a little. You go ahead, Hattie. We'll be down in a minute."

"Don't go far, okay? Stay near the path."

Corax discovered secrets to investigate and news to read from undreamed-of sources. Strange strange creatures of mysterious origin had passed here. He wanted to know about every single one. Furred creatures, feathered creatures, oh, this was indeed the best night of his life!

Anya walked him slowly down the lantern-lit path. It was so soothing to hear the river rushing along out there, though she couldn't see it in the dark. She stood gazing down at the stone lodge. Laughter bubbled up, and she could hear the rattle of plates and pots in the kitchen. The smells made her stomach hurt, she was that hungry, and soon Corax, too, was overcome with curiosity about where these aromas were coming from.

He trotted ahead of her down the path. Suddenly, only a few feet away, a pair of eyes shone out from the dark, reflecting the light from a garden lantern. Anya stopped. Yellow eyes focused intently on Corax. Her dog backed up and snarled low in his throat.

Then Anya heard the crunch of stones behind her. The creature, whatever it was, heard it too, and fled into the night. Anya whirled. Above her on the path was a dark figure, a tall man. He was bigger and more muscular than her dad. It wasn't Robert or Dick Frey. She shrank back. He kept coming, closer, looming above her, and the closer he came, the more she panicked.

Corax scuttled to safety behind her legs. She tried to step back and nearly tripped over him.

Who? Who was this? Some other guest?

"Hello, Anya."

She froze, wishing her dad, Robert, anybody was beside her. Corax stiffened too, but then, with a yelp, he bounded around in front of her, leaping and barking excitedly. Was he defending her?

His leash tore from her hand and he jumped straight into the air. If he was defending her, that seemed like an odd defense.

The man bent toward the dog and the light from a lantern lit his face.

Anya's own face split into a grin. She nearly sobbed with joy.

"Hugh!"

Hugh Durant opened his arms and she buried her face against his waist. Weeping, cavorting like a jackrabbit on laughing gas, Corax begged to be included.

"I thought I'd never see you again, Hugh!" Of all people to be here! Hugh Durant, a friend who had once helped her and Corax just when they needed help the most.

"Well, I really thought I'd never see you, and I searched for days last summer! And look at Corax! You're a big guy now, aren't you, eh?" He wrangled the dog's head back and forth. "You remember me, don't you?"

"Of course he does! Hugh, what are you doing here?"

"Your dad asked me to do the photographs for his book. I got here last night. I think he wanted to surprise you."

"Your photos are going to be in Dad's book?"

"That's the idea."

"You came all this way with Clodhopper? Clear across the country?" The last time she had seen Hugh, he was living on the back of a wagon, trying to keep body and soul together by selling portraits for a dime apiece. His ancient horse Clodhopper pulled him around the countryside of New York State, stopping in little towns here and there. At that time, Hugh was selling portraits, photographing people from all walks of life, and they waited in long lines to buy his work.

"I'm done with horses, and no more wagon," Hugh laughed. "Old Clodhopper has been put out to pasture. I sold him to a farmer. He might pull a couple of wagonloads of fruit to the train station now and then, but that's about it." He took Anya's hand.

"Let's go inside. It's getting cold out here. And we do not want to miss any of Mrs. Frey's dinner, let me tell you. The food here is amazing."

Corax led the way down the path. Anya was in a state of bliss, so happy to see her old friend Hugh. And to think that he and her dad had struck up a friendship!

Oh! When they stepped into the main lodge, her happiness was complete, even though her nasty cousin Robert was in the picture. This lodge – what a beautiful place! Like her cottage, the walls here were paneled in wood darkened by age, rustic yet homey, and with every comfort, it seemed. Anya decided this place had everything a home should have. Bookshelves, paintings, a piano, a grandfather clock, beautifully colored rugs in strange bold patterns, and big plump chairs.

The Ranch of the Ten Elders had no electricity, but there were oil lamps beside every chair, casting their soft mellow light. The room –  Mrs. Frey called it the living room – was huge, with the biggest fireplace Anya had ever seen. Everyone was sitting near it now, glad to warm themselves at the roaring pinon-wood fire. Corax nosed each person affectionately. Then, much to Anya's disgust, her dog threw himself down beside Robert and yawned mightily. He had missed a number of naps today and Robert, sitting on the floor near the fire with his back to everyone, made a good pillow.

"So you two found each other?" said Jack, as Hugh settled down beside him. "I told you I had a nice surprise for you, Anya."

"Oh, Dad, it's the best."

"I want you to meet our friend Hattie," Jack said to Hugh. "Hattie, this is Mr. Durant."

"I remember Anya talking a lot about you," Hattie said.

"And Anya's cousin Robert."

"Nice to meet you," Hugh said. He looked sideways at Anya, his eyebrows raised. She rolled her eyes, as if to say 'yes, *that*

Robert'.

The Grandfather Clock interrupted, ringing the hour, and promptly came the call they were waiting for.

"Dinner is ready." Mrs. Frey opened the double dining room doors. There were several tables in the room, but, as they were the only guests, she had set the long table for them. Candles sashayed down its length, and their swaying flames set the silverware gleaming. Pretty handmade plates were painted with the ranch logo and sprigs of pine nestled at each place for decoration. Dick set bowls of soup in front of them as they took their seats.

Hattie leaned over her bowl and sniffed. "Yum. What is this?"

"Posoles, basically a corn soup. We'll have a little bowl of this to start. Help yourself to our good bread. It's made right here, and so is the butter. The main course for tonight is brook trout, squash, and roasted potatoes. Wine for you, Mr. Durant?"

After a long cold ride, everything tasted fabulous. They saved talk until every scrap of food was gone.

"That was excellent," Hugh Durant said to Dick when he came to clear. "Who do you have in the kitchen, making all this wonderful food?"

"Jemmy and Mrs. Snow cook most everything."

Mrs. Frey came in with coffee.

"Thank you for this, Evelyn. It was lovely, as always."

"It's our pleasure, Jack."

"Do we get to meet Jimmy?"

"Jimmy?"

"The chef. I'd like to thank him, too."

"Ooh! Jimmy." She laughed. "Yes. Come. I don't think you've ever seen the kitchen, have you?"

"Can we see it too?" asked Anya.

"Sure. Come on."

They trouped through the kitchen door, Robert first, followed by Hugh, Jack, the girls, and the dog too, until Mrs. Frey booted him out.

Once through the kitchen door, the male members of the group showed no interest in the room itself. They took no notice whatsoever of its huge iron cookstove, or the pile of wood over in the corner that was constantly fed into its maw. The stacks of plates handmade especially for the lodge also escaped their notice, as did the shelves of colored glassware. The hanging copper pots were ignored. The wide stone sink received not a glance.

The chef, who was brining chickens at the moment, turned as they came in. Robert stopped short. Hugh ran smack into him and never felt a thing. Jack, banging against Hugh, had to force his gaping mouth shut. The girls looked at the three of them, perplexed.

"May I present our chef?" said Mrs. Frey. "Jemmy. Not Jimmy. Jemmy Snow."

Jemmy was beautiful. An equally fine-featured older woman, working at the counter in the corner, laughed. "Jimmy?"

The men were still speechless, gawking. Jemmy was a young Native American woman, classically beautiful. Black hair, pulled into a bun, emphasized her tawny cheekbones. Her black eyes had a slant that looked exotic, and her mouth – well, not one of the men could have thought of a word to describe that mouth.

Jemmy sighed, shook her head, and smiled. More alike than different, men were.

"Hello," she said, and turned back to her chickens.

"We just – the reason – sorry to bother – it's just – your food – we really enjoyed it," spluttered Jack. Hugh, never very eloquent, could not utter a word. Even Robert couldn't take his eyes off Jemmy.

"Thank you," was all Jemmy said in answer. She plunked another chicken into a crock of brine.

Robert finally motivated his feet to move toward Jemmy's worktable. He watched what she was doing, fascinated. "Will you cook those for dinner tomorrow?"

"We will." At least the boy could speak intelligently. She smiled at him. "Do you like to cook?"

"I would, if I could cook like you." He groaned inwardly, wishing immediately that he hadn't said that. Cooking? Everybody would think he was a complete ninny.

"Our chickens were raised right here." Jemmy spoke mostly to Robert. "They'll rest in the brine all night and tomorrow we'll roast them. You'll see how tender it will make them. And my mother, over here, is making – Mother! I told you not to overmix – "

"You mind your chickens and I'll take care of the biscuits."

"Don't do it that way! Do I have to come over there and mix them myself?"

"Spare me your lip, Jemima!" The woman turned to the guests. "Hello, everyone. I apologize for my daughter's rudeness."

"My rudeness, Mother? You're the one –"

"Let's leave these two to their work, shall we?" chirped Mrs. Frey. She herded the men ahead of her. Still agape, they shuffled backwards to the door.

"Wow," said Jack softly to Hugh, when the kitchen door closed behind them.

"Yeah."

"Definitely not Jimmy."

"I know," said Hugh. "Indeed." He looked like he'd been whacked on the head with a six gallon soup pot.

Robert looked wistfully at the two men, wishing he were ten years older.


They drifted back to the fireplace.

"Mrs. Frey has a little library here, girls. She lets guests borrow her books. Maybe you can find something," Jack told them.

Anya and Hattie went immediately to the shelves. Hattie selected *The Last of the Mohicans*. She settled into a chair and was soon lost to New Mexico completely.

"Do you have any books about Bandelier?" Anya asked Mrs. Frey.

"We don't. We can hardly wait for your father's book to come out. How about Mark Twain, Anya? Have you read any of his?" Mrs. Frey pulled out a book. "*Huck Finn* would be a good one to start with. Do you want to try it?"

"Thank you." Anya found a chair and Mrs. Frey turned up the oil lamp for her. Corax, sighing deeply, settled at her feet.

Robert was poring over a map that hung on the wall.

"See anything interesting?" his uncle asked him.

"Eh, I dunno."

"I've asked Michael Redbird to take you on a little tour tomorrow." He pointed to the map. "Down this way, along the river. Hugh and I have a lot of ground to cover this week, so we'll be off hiking into the back country. But Michael is a great guide. I think you'll have fun with him."

"I want to see this place." Robert put his finger on the map and squinted with his nose up close. "I saw it on your map, Uncle Jack. You can hardly read the name here. It's half scraped off or something. Are there lions here?"

"Ah, the Stone Lions," said Mrs. Frey. "That is one place Michael will not show you, I'm afraid. It's sacred to his people and they want to keep it private."

"But I want to go there."

"I'm sorry, Robert. Michael refuses," she said. "He never tells anyone how to get there. He even tried to remove the label from that map."

"He can't stop me. It's not his land."

"Well, he believes it is, actually, or his people's land, anyway. He believes his ancestors were the first to live in this canyon, before they moved out some six hundred years ago."

"I thought you owned all this place."

"I wish I did own it, but I am only leasing it. It's government property, though now the Pueblo people are fighting for ownership. As are the cattle ranchers. And the loggers."

Hugh got up and threw some wood on the fire. "I did some tramping around today," he said. "I think you'll find plenty of other interesting places to explore, Robert."

"Yeah. Right." Robert looked back at the map, trying to memorize the trails. How stupid, somebody telling him he couldn't visit a part of a national monument. It wasn't like he was going to ruin the place by standing in it. He sat on the floor, again with his back to everyone.

"Have you made any progress with the government people, Evelyn?" Jack asked.

She shook her head. "They know they can't throw me out. But they insist we move our house farther down the canyon. They are going to build us a new lodge and tear this place down."

"No! Please tell me that's not true! Not this lodge? It's so beautiful. And historic."

"It's too close to the ruins, they say. When the new park opens, they want people to get a sense of what it was like here six hundred years ago. This house didn't exist then, of course, and in their opinion it doesn't belong within view of the ancient sites."

"Oh Evelyn, I'm so sorry to hear this!" said Jack.

"I said we could plant trees out in front to hide the lodge. I begged and pleaded with the new manager but he has his mind set and will not back down. I don't mind admitting that I have sworn an oath to hate that man for the rest of time. I will never forgive him. It really pains me to say that, but it's true."

"They'll tear all this down? That is tragic. You built *all* this."

"I'm heart-broken, Jack. We worked so hard on this place for more than sixteen years. Guests love coming here. I love living here, though it hasn't been easy. I've made gardens here, an orchard. I hope that I've finally trained most of the ranchers to keep their cattle from wandering into the canyon. We've done a pretty good job discouraging vandals." She pointed to a rifle hanging above the fireplace. Ornately carved, it had been made for the last Russian tsar, but never delivered. "I've personally scared off many people who were looting the ruins. But while Hoover was president he decided the place should be opened for tourists, and presto! Everything we've built will be swept away and next year, droves of people will be paying to come in here."

"It's all decided?"

"All settled. It can't be undone now."

"Just like that?"

"Life turns on a dime, doesn't it?"

Hattie's head snapped up. Life did turn on a dime. That much she had learned this fall.

"When does all this destruction begin?" Hugh asked.

"Next week."

"Next week?"

"As soon as Thanksgiving is over, they're bringing two hundred men to tear the place apart."

"They really mean business! No wonder you're not taking more guests."

"They'll start by building temporary housing for themselves. And a road."

"A road!"

"Still, it's good to know that the work will give two hundred hungry men an income," said Hugh, who, in these hard times, knew whereof he spoke. "Forgive me for bringing up an old platitude, but one man's loss can be another man's profit."

"And this time it's my loss," said Mrs. Frey. "The Ranch of the Ten Elders will soon be gone, I'm afraid. You are our last guests."

They sat still, stunned and hardly believing. The Grandfather

Clock whirred and boomed the hour into the silence.

Jack sighed and looked around the room. "We're very lucky to be here this week, aren't we?"

Evelyn reached out and took his hand, unable to say anything.

"Will you play something for us tonight?" Jack asked, gesturing to the piano.

"I shouldn't try to play when I'm upset."

Jack covered her hand with his. "It might provide some comfort. For all of us."

"All right. Maybe I will. Chopin, I think. I feel like some Chopin tonight." Mrs. Frey sat at the piano. She bent her head for a minute. Then, softly, she touched the first two notes of the Nocturne in E Flat. She faltered, and stopped. Collecting herself, she began again, playing with a sense of longing so acute that no one moved until the last note disappeared.


Outside, in the deeps of the canyon, the lodge sits at the bottom of a river of stars. The moon is afloat in the pewter sky. It swims the short passage from one side of the Frijoles canyon to the other, and lights Coyote with her silver beams. He is sitting, his head cocked, at the edge of the cliff, listening. His intense yellow eyes gleam within their pencil-thin linings of black. Ensorcelled, he is caught in the net of music. The notes of Mrs. Frey's nocturne rise like bubbles to the top of the canyon and sail off downwind.

Coyote's mate comes from behind and noses his shoulder. He turns quickly to look at her, then back, bending his head to catch every ripple of music. She sits obediently, until the last note is swept away. Then together they slip down into the canyon, to hunt, to rest, to dream coyote dreams. High above, wind surges through the magnificent yellow pines. Gently, it breaks over the pair like a tide, and, near dawn, finally sings them to sleep.

TRICKSTER, DESTROYER

Tuesday

Jack and Hugh were at breakfast before it was light the next morning. After putting away a stack of berry pancakes, eggs, and sausage, Jack rose from the table.

"We should get going, Hugh. It's warm outside. With any luck we'll have fine weather this morning."

"Right. I'm ready." Hugh was slurping the rest of his coffee when Jemmy came in with a fresh pot.

She smiled. "More?" Hugh's cup clattered clumsily to its saucer.

Jack answered for him. "Thanks, but no more coffee for us, Miss Snow. Great pancakes!"

"Please, call me Jemmy." Michael Redbird came in behind her. "A cup for you, Michael?"

"Sure."

"Keep those kids in line today, Michael," said Jack.

"I'm sure there won't be a problem. You come back tonight?"

"Oh yes. We have no intention of missing dinner here!"

Jack and Hugh decided it would be easier, since they would be hiking into unfamiliar back country, to travel without a mule. Hugh's camera equipment was heavy, though, so Jack shared the load. The going was rough and there were times when they wished they didn't have a large tripod, two heavy cameras, big lenses, and backpacks to carry.

After a couple of hours, Jack stopped walking to consult his compass. "I found some jasper points right around this spot last year –"

"Jasper points?"

"Stone arrow heads. Near a side canyon. I didn't have time to explore it then but I'm guessing, if weapons were being made here, we might find signs of human habitation nearby. If we're very lucky, we'll find cliff dwellings." He forced his way through a cottonwood thicket and Hugh followed. "It'll be easier going along this creek. I wonder how the kids are doing."

"You know, Jack, I was watching your nephew Robert last night," Hugh began. "He seems like an unhappy kid."

"Yeah. My sister is a little flighty and I'm sure my mother, his grandmother, hasn't encouraged him to act like a normal kid. I haven't met his new step-father, but he'll have his hands full with Robert."

Hugh stopped abruptly, one hand up in warning. He looked back the way they had come. He listened, then shook his head. "I thought I heard an animal. Anyway, I can imagine Robert being difficult. I only know Anya's side of her story, but now that I've met him, I think she described him pretty accurately."

"He gave her a lot of trouble last summer, that's for sure."

"Anya said he has never known his father."

"Ha! He's actually better off for that. His father's a crook."

"He deserted your sister and nephew?"

"My sister left him, the smartest thing she ever did. She was only married to him for two weeks. I don't know if the man is even aware that Robert exists."

"Aw, that's too bad. It was good of you to bring him along on this trip. And, speaking of that, I want to thank you again for giving me this work, Jack."

"I was happy you were available."

"When you wrote, I was really scraping the bottom of the barrel. I was wondering where my next nickel would come from. Like many another man these days."

"Hard times these past few years, and no end in sight. I've been lucky, thankfully. I'm almost afraid to admit it, but I've actually made money since the Panic."

"Want to tell your secret?"

"A man named Clarence Birdseye. I invested in his frozen food company. It's – what?"

Hugh held out his arm. "Look!" He pointed to some rocks embedded in the ground. Overgrown with brush, the ring of rocks could easily go unnoticed. Their circular placement did not appear to be natural. Hugh's first find! Excited, he knelt to move a branch aside. "What is this? A grave?"

"I don't think so. It looks like it's marking the location of a food pit. We won't dig it out, but if we could, we'd probably find pottery jars full of seeds and dried roots. Maybe corn. We should cover it again." Jack replaced the branch to conceal the pit.

Hugh pointed at a cliff farther down the nearly-dry creek bed. "Look! Do you think someone from up there made this pit?"

"Up where? Oh wow, Hugh. I didn't even see that. Now you know why I brought you along."

"It's a cliff dwelling, right?"

"It certainly is. I was so hoping to find something like this."

They both turned at a sound from behind. But, though they stood still for a long minute, they heard nothing more.

They ducked through a thicket of willow to get a closer view of the houses tucked high up under the cliff.

"I can't believe this! People lived way up there?"

"The best I can tell from here, maybe ten or twelve families."

"It looks like there are paintings on that one wall."

"Your photographer's eye doesn't miss much, does it?"

"But the question is, can my photographer's feet get me up there?"

It took them the better part of an hour to scramble up the cliff and work their way over to the place where a tiny village lay hidden under an immense shelf of rock. They stepped out onto a broad courtyard protected by the cliff that arched overhead. Several small block-shaped houses were tucked against the back wall.

"This is awesome!" Hugh stood in the center of the courtyard, hands on hips, just soaking up the wonder of the place before he set up his camera. "Amazing! If you lived here, you'd be completely safe from enemies. And protected from the elements."

"You'd only be vulnerable if you had to descend to look for food."

"I never, ever imagined a place like this."

But Jack, after peeking into each dwelling, was disappointed. "Either someone has robbed the place or the Old Ones left nothing here. These pictographs are interesting, though."

"Jack, come here a minute," Hugh called. "Look through this opening in the rocks. Use your binoculars."

"It's another cliff dwelling! It must be – what would you say? A mile up the creek from here? Did they signal each other from this opening?"

"It looks like they could have –" Hugh tilted his head back, squinting suspiciously. He spoke in a whisper. "Wait a minute. Smell that?"

"What?"

"Cigarettes." Hugh sniffed the air. "Do you smell them?"

"I don't. It could just be some of these old dried wooden

beams."

"I could swear it was cigarettes. Oh well, let's try to get a picture of that place from this view."

"Ah! Here's a trail, Hugh. It's heading straight toward the other cliff dwelling. Are you up for another couple of miles of walking?"

"That's what we came to do."

The trail to the next spot was well-worn, though once again they found it difficult to climb up to the dwellings. But it was here that they found wonderful things. Together, they found and photographed several pots and grinding stones, a collection of spears, a feathered prayer shaft.

"This pot has got to be very old. Basketmaker, I would think, by the color. Can you get a shot of this one, Hugh?"

"Sure I can. I have never in my life touched such ancient things!"

Jack had never in his life heard Hugh emote so much.

"And to think we may be the first ever to find these pieces, right Jack? Don't you think? Do you ever get used to it?"

"I certainly don't."

"We could be the first people to set foot here in ages, maybe centuries, right? Did you find something else?"

"Turquoise." Jack fingered a necklace strung with animal claws and turquoise stones that had lain hidden in a depression on a high slab of rock. "Turquoise is not found in these parts," he said thoughtfully. "I would say that this proves they were doing some trading with tribes further west."

"Is that good?"

"This is just the kind of thing I was hoping to find. It tells us something about their habits and lifestyle. They weren't living in isolation here. They were trading with each other, visiting, maybe feasting together."

"Can you bring that neck piece out here so I can get a picture?

It's really clouding over. I'm losing light."

"It's getting cold too."

They photographed everything they found, working until a nasty wind slashed through the canyon and it began to rain. They packed the cameras into waxed canvas bags and Hugh dropped the film into metal boxes. Thankfully, by the time they were ready to descend, there was a break in the clouds and the sun peeked out again, though it was still cold.

It was when they came back down to the creek bed again that Hugh found two cigarette butts on the shore, near the place where they had crossed.

"These were not here before."

"This better not be what I think it is," Jack said, swearing angrily. He picked up one of the cigarette butts and sniffed. "It is. French cigarettes."

Hugh looked at him warily. He had seen Jack's temper once before, and he could tell he was furious now.

Jack hurled the butt to the ground. "I don't believe it. We've been followed."


Earlier, just after Jack and Hugh left the lodge that morning, Anya and Hattie and Corax stepped out of their cabin. The air felt warm, though the sun had yet to ride above the cliff tops.

"Mmm. I smell breakfast," said Hattie. 'Look, Anya! Wow! This is incredible! Look at this place!"

The full drama of the canyon, cloaked in darkness last night, took their breath away. Across the Rio Frijoles was a broad shore with the ruins of what looked like an ancient circular apartment house of many rooms. Beyond that rose the walls of the canyon, strange beyond imagining. They were pinkish in color and so pocked with holes and outlandish rock formations that the girls ran down to the river to get a closer look.

"How weird. Are we on another planet?"

"Did you ever see rocks so full of holes? Like Swiss cheese."

"What do you suppose made them? I mean, look how strange! How was all this formed?"

"There's Dick. Let's ask him."

"Dick!" Hattie saw him coming toward them, a big basket of eggs on his arm. I'm just going to act normal, she vowed to herself. No big deal. She could not stop herself, though, from smiling idiotically. Not exactly normal behavior for that girl, but Anya did not dare point this out to her. She knew well the old saying about rushing in where angels fear to tread.

"Good morning!" Dick called. "Your first view of the canyon? Pretty amazing, isn't it?"

"What are all those holes?' asked Anya, pointing across the river.

"Some are natural, due to erosion. That pinkish stone – it's called *tufa* – is so soft it can be carved, even with primitive hand tools. See those deeper holes up higher? They have all been dug out by hand. The Old Ones, the people who lived here, were able to make small caves up in those cliffs."

"Caves for what?"

"They lived in them."

"But they're so small."

"They were a small people, apparently."

"How did they get up there?"

"We know for sure they used ladders, but old lore says these people were like human spiders. It's claimed that they could crawl straight up a rock face. They did cut holes into the rock to make trails for ascending the cliff. They're called hand-and-toe trails."

"How did they get their stuff up there? And their little children?" asked Anya.

"They were very agile, I guess. And see those holes all lined up in a horizontal line? Those held roof beams for the houses that were on the ground."

"Look, more caves down there." Hattie pointed.

"Yeah," answered Dick. "All the way down the canyon."

"How far?" Anya asked.

"They're scattered here and there all along the river. Michael is going to take you to the Alcove House this morning. Wait til you see that one."

"I never imagined such a place," said Hattie.

"You're so lucky to live here," Anya added.

"I know. Hey, I'd better get these eggs to Jemmy or she'll have a fit. You coming in? It's almost breakfast time."

Michael Redbird was sitting at the table when they entered the dining room. Another beautiful person, thought Anya. Is it the air here? She ignored Robert, who was just finishing his pile of pancakes. Jemmy came in and poured Michael another cup of coffee.

"You'll need to bring warm clothing today," Michael told them. "You never know what the weather will do here. I hope you're ready for a walk."

"Sure, Mr. Redbird."

"Wear boots, if you have them. The place we're going to is a couple of miles away."

"We're going to a cave?" asked Hattie.

"It's more than just a cave. You'll see."

"I'd rather go to the Stone Lions, Mike," said Robert.

Michael frowned. "I'm sorry. I cannot take you there," he said. "It's a sacred place, a place of such great power that people from other tribes are afraid to go anywhere near it."

"That's dumb."

"I'd advise you to heed this warning. Even our own medicine men take the time to prepare themselves carefully before setting foot inside the shrine.”

“Really?” Anya and Hattie were intrigued.

“And some of the plants that grow there are good for medicinal purposes. Our women like to be able to gather them without being ogled.”

“Mike,” scoffed Robert. “Who's going to ogle a bunch of old ladies?”

“Anglos,” Michael said, a dark look on his face. “Since you asked. Gawking Anglos make the women uncomfortable. So no, we won't be going there.”

“Come on, Michael,” said Jemmy. “Robert just wants to see the place. Don't be such a stick-in-the-mud.”

“No, Jemmy. We can't have outsiders wandering around there, breaking the harmony. The Stone Lions are not for display, they're for worship. Too bad you can't appreciate that, Jemima.”

Jemmy looked at Robert. “Don't feel bad,” she said, though she could see that he did. “If it were up to Michael, nobody would ever mess with tradition or change a single thing. He's just an old fart.” She gestured toward Michael Redbird with her coffee pot. “Maybe one day you'll join the twentieth century, Michael.”

Michael bit his lower lip. “Just stop it, Jemima. You make such a big deal of being more modern than the rest of us. It just kills you to follow the Pueblo way.” He rose from the table, stopping her from answering with a gesture. “Let's go, folks. Everybody about ready?”


Michael sat on the porch, waiting for them. The morning was warm and fine. “Is Robert coming?” he asked, when the girls appeared.

“He should be.”

“I hope your dog is obedient,” Michael said to Anya.

“I think he is. Will there be wild animals?”

"They do live here. It's their world too," answered Michael, "but they're not likely to bother us."

Robert sauntered up, taking his time.

"You have a jacket, don't you, Robert?"

"Nah. I don't need one. It's warm."

"I suggest you take one."

Robert shrugged. "I don't feel like carrying it."

"Suit yourself."

They set off down a trail. Robert did not want to walk with Anya, so he slowed his pace, lagging behind. Michael made a point of walking with Hattie.

"Are you Mohawk, Hattie?" Michael asked her.

"I'm Onondagan," she said. "Wolf clan. And you, Mr. Redbird?"

Michael smiled. He liked her polite deference. "We're from the Pueblo di Cochiti. Cochiti means 'people from the mountains'. We belong to the Calabash clan."

"How about Miss Snow?"

"Jemmy? Well yeah, she is Calabash clan too. You know she is my sister, right?"

"Sister?"

"Half-sister. Did you meet our mother in the kitchen?"

"Mrs. Snow is your mother?"

"She is. My father, John Redbird, died and Mama remarried and had Jemima. For better or worse."

"Ah." Remarried? It suddenly struck Hattie that her mother, now a widow, might remarry someday, though widows in the Onondaga Nation did not often do so. That wouldn't be right, if she did. Not right. Hattie wouldn't like that at all. And Robert — wow, she hadn't thought it through before, how he must be struggling with both a new father and a new home. How could he bear it? Parents should be required to stay always the same. They shouldn't confuse things by changing. Or dying. She wondered how Mr. Redbird felt about that. "Were you a little boy when your father died?"

"I was three. So Jim Snow was the only father I really knew."

"Oh." Hattie was quiet for a minute. "My father passed on recently."

"I pray the gods have welcomed him to the Afterlife, Hattie."

"Well, I don't know about any of that. I'm sorry but I've never noticed any god having much of a hand in anything."

"No? My people see gods everywhere."

"Yeah, but ...." She shook her head and they went along in silence for a bit.

"Your father was Onondagan, too?"

"Oh yes. Very traditional, both my parents."

"Good. That's good." Michael saw a tear slide down her cheek. "Was that a problem for you?"

"A little, yeah. My dad and I didn't always agree on things. He didn't like me working off the reservation, especially doing what I do. He thought it was very wrong."

Alarmed, Michael said, "Do you mind my asking – is your work ... dishonorable?"

"Dad thought so. He thought it was ruining me, making me unmarriageable."

Michael tried to picture Hattie in some unsavory job, but he couldn't. She seemed like such a nice girl. "I don't want to pry. Is it okay if I ask what work you do?"

"I help my uncle, my dad's brother."

"Is he doing something dishonest?"

"Oh," Hattie smiled, "no. He's an airplane mechanic."

Michael burst out laughing.

"What?" Michael's laugh was infectious. "What's so funny?" She was almost laughing herself.

"I was picturing you – er, in a job – much worse." They both giggled. "But a girl working in an airport, alongside men?"

"For me, it's better than getting dragged off to residential school."

"Ah, I understand. Still, a job like yours – this would be difficult for some fathers. You don't disrespect your parents, I hope."

"Not too often, but it's hard sometimes, you know?"

"Yes, but you have to understand that our ways must be preserved, Hattie. We must live in the Indian way. We don't want to be part of the changes in the world. Our traditions have served us for hundreds of generations, so if something is working well, don't change it! That just tempts the gods to punish you. Right?"

Hattie half-nodded and shrugged.

"That was surely a concern of your father's. A girl must listen to her parents. Please, don't be like that smart-mouth sister of mine!" He shook his head. "Better not get me started about Jemima. It will ruin our walk."

They ambled along the narrow bottom of the canyon, following the Rio Frijoles. Sunlight flickered through the tops of the bare cottonwood and box elder trees that grew along the river. They passed low waterfalls now and then, their music a gentle counterpoint to the lightest of breezes. Their footsteps were the only other sounds to be heard, until a tiny cactus wren shattered the silence with an operatic swell of song.

Now and then Michael pointed out small cave houses hidden in the cliffs, once homes to two or three families. They saw strange plants clinging to the steep canyon walls, yucca and saltbush and cholla cactus. It was indeed a world different from their own.

There was something else here, too. Something ... something that gave a lift to their spirits. Maybe it was the exercise and fresh air. How else to explain it?

Anya wouldn't speak of it because she was afraid of sounding childish, especially in front of Robert. Hattie was afraid they'd think she was being melodramatic, so she didn't bring it up.

Robert – well, how could anyone know for sure that Robert even had any feelings?

The sun grew warm and, protected by the cliffs as they were, the cold wind hadn't found them. So the girls took off their jackets and stuffed them into the bags Jemmy had given them for their lunches.

"There's the Alcove House, up ahead." Michael pointed. "No, up. Look up."

"Up there?" "People lived way up there?"

All three of them stopped, heads thrown back as far as they would go, and gaped upwards.

A hundred fifty feet above the river a horizontal gap in the cliff yawned like a wide-open mouth. It was eighty feet across, and from below they couldn't tell how far back it went. Leading up to it, there was a series of frighteningly long ladders climbing at almost vertical angles. All around the base of the cliff were the oddest cone-shaped rock formations they had ever seen.

"All this rock is volcanic stone from an eruption in the Jemez Mountains from a time way back," Michael Redbird told them.

"But those mountains look so far away from here."

"They are far from here. It was a very large eruption, or so I've read. It blew some rocks all the way to Iowa. Now, are any of you afraid of heights? If you are, it's best to wait down here. You're sure you're all good? Okay. We don't want to leave the dog down here alone, though. Robert, can you lift him into my pack basket?"

After the dog was settled with his head peering from Michael's backpack, they began the ascent.

"I can't imagine using these ladders every day," panted Anya. Maybe she should have admitted that the climb terrified her. Hattie and Robert were high above her.

"Take your time," said Michael, behind her.

Four very long stout ladders and many stone steps later, she finally stepped shakily onto the broad empty courtyard of Alcove House. Hattie, Robert, and Anya stared. It was a wonder of a place. Far back under the cliff and against the back wall, a row of block-shaped houses had been built, one or two stories high, though many were now crumbling with age.

The very air up there seemed heavy with ancient secrets. The silence felt charged with the sound of movements that were just below their range of hearing, and visions just outside of the visible spectrum. Corax, released from Michael's pack basket, stood without moving, waving his nose in the air. They all stood stock still at first, mouths open, listening, their eyes flicking from doorways to hidden corners, expecting to see somebody, when of course, there was no one there. It was a strange sensation.

They took a few cautious steps and spoke in whispers.

"Let me show you something that I keep secret." Michael beckoned them to the back, and he pointed at a small niche hidden against the wall. There were three pottery vessels there, painted with black and white designs. "Those two pots were for cooking and this one is an *olla* for carrying water."

"These are old?"

"Oh yes. Made by my people many times ago."

"They're beautiful."

Curiosity finally got the better of them. Darting here and there, peeking into doorways, gazing out at the views up and down the canyon, they felt, for just a few minutes, like three friends on holiday.

Even Robert was struck by the atmosphere. "This place is empty, but it feels like ..."

"There's something ..."

"*Something.*"

"Or somebody."

"This is incredible! Imagine living here!"

"A whole village of people walking around up here!"

"Their children must have loved it!"

"What a perfect hide-out. You can see everything from up here. Why would anyone want to leave this place?"

"How did the people get inside these houses? The doors are so tiny."

Anya had to drop to her knees to reach into a doorway and pull Corax out. He was reluctant, sniffing curiously.

"Please do not go in," Michael asked her. "Some of the buildings are unstable."

"I won't, but look! Peek inside here. Look what the dog found." She backed out and pointed.

"What is it?"

"It looks like a shoe. A small shoe."

They gathered. "Don't touch it." Michael put his head inside the doorway. "It is, it's a child's shoe."

"My dad would love to see that," said Anya. "Is it old, do you think?"

"Oh, I think so. The air is so dry here that things don't deteriorate as quickly as elsewhere. How very fortunate that you were shown this, Anya," said Michael. "You can think of it as a gift, truly."

"I know. But really, Corax found it." She knelt again, wondering how this one little shoe had been left behind. "It's perfect. It looks like someone dropped it last week. Do you think it is a hundred years old, Mr. Redbird?"

"Your dad would know better than I, but I suspect it's much, much older than that. This place was abandoned six hundred years ago and no one has lived here since. Promise me, everyone, that you will not mention that you found this shoe? We don't want vandals stealing it."

The girls promised. Michael looked at Robert. "Agreed, Robert?"

Robert felt himself singled out and became the old Robert again. He shrugged. "Who would care about an old shoe?"

Michael turned away.

"What's this thing, Mike?" Robert asked him. "Looks like a swimming pool." At the lip of the alcove was a large deep circular structure.

"This is the kiva. You'll see others like it throughout the canyon."

"What is it for?"

"The kiva is very important to our culture. This one had a roof at one time. It is a place to purify ourselves so our prayers will be carried up to the Creator – no, Robert. No, please. Do not go inside."

"Why can't I? You gonna to tell me I'm an outsider again?"

"Yes, for one thing. You have not been initiated. And you are also being disrespectful of my ancestors." Michael was not surprised to see Robert sneer. "Also, this is a very old and fragile structure. I'm sorry to have to remind you of that. Now, look. Do you see, down there at its center? See those seven broad stones? One represents our Creator, one is for the Earth, one for all living things, one for each of the Four Directions, North, South, East, and West. When our people have all gathered inside our kivas, we heat the stones and pour water over them. The rising steam cleanses us, erasing our past mistakes and our heartaches. That way, we can come before our Creator with a clean mind, clean body, and clean life."

"That sounds kind of nice," said Anya.

Crazy, Robert thought of saying. Steaming away your mistakes?

Michael ignored his snicker.

"Hey, look!" Hattie moved to the edge of the cliff and pointed down the canyon. "There is a really big bunch of cows down there."

Michael followed her pointing finger. "Oh, not again. The

ranchers know they are not supposed to bring cattle into this canyon." He saw three men riding alongside the herd that had stopped to graze. "It's not a big herd. Still, I'll have to go down to speak to them."

"This has happened before, Mr. Redbird?"

"Many times. The ranchers know very well that it's illegal. Their cattle walk all over our ruins. They do a lot of damage. And besides, it's not their land."

"What are they doing here, then?" asked Anya.

"They claim the park is nothing but a waste of good grazing land. Come on, we'll have to go back down. We shouldn't stay any longer anyway. It looks like the weather might be turning."


Descending was actually more difficult than going up, but they finally made it down. By then, the cattle had come even farther into the canyon.

"Listen, I'm going over there to ask them to turn around. Hang on to the dog, would you, Anya? It would be best if you all just waited here. Stay quiet. If the cattle are spooked, they'll cause even more damage. Robert, no! Robert! I said to wait."

"I just want to have a look at these cowboys. I've never seen a real one!"

"Not so loud! Come back!" Michael Redbird hissed. "The slightest thing – "

Robert trotted toward one of the cowhands. "Hey! Hey, cowpoke!" he yelled.

The man turned and put up a hand and shook his head.

"Are you guys real cowboys?" shouted Robert. "With lassos and all that?" He swung an imaginary rope.

"Stand back, kid! Stay still! Don't. You'll spook 'em!" The cowhand turned in his saddle. "Oh, holy crap!"

The cattle nearest Robert were huddling together in fright,

trying to move back, lowing and snorting at this alarming newcomer. They shook their heads, eyes rolling, and kept trying to back further away, pressing against others in the herd.

Danger! Their alarm was transferred so quickly to the other beasts that a wave of terror swept almost instantly through the entire herd. There was suddenly a roar like an earthquake. A volcano of panicked motion erupted. The signal had been sent: get out! The herd's only thought was to flee to somewhere safe. In one enormous body they wheeled and spiraled and tried to run every which way.

A stampede! Robert, his hands to his forehead and his face contorted in panic, heard the cowhand swear an unholy oath. He swung his horse around. Robert backed away, trying to run, the next instant finding himself flat on the ground. He had tripped backwards over a log and he fell, way too near the thundering feet of the herd.

Pounding hoofs, panicked animals, just a few yards away from him!

Now the cattle became a massive sea of bucking creatures. Terrified, they struggled to move, willing to mow down anything in their way. A  hundred confused beasts jostling and shoving. They needed to get out, go back, get away, but they were packed too tightly in the narrow canyon. They collided with the cattle in front of them, yet still they used their immense weight to push stubbornly forward.

Over the din, Robert could hear the cowhand calling to them, trying to soothe them, but his voice was lost. Every bellowing steer had his tail in the air. The dirt and stones they kicked up rained over Robert in waves. He raised his hands to shield his face, sick with disbelief.

These were big cows. Immense! He hadn't really thought it would take so little to scare them. He had only been fooling around!

The cowhands on the far side of the herd pulled out their pistols and shot into the ground right in front of the cattle, trying to slow the runaways by turning them. The leading cattle swerved to the right to avoid the guns. The men kept firing at the ground. Stones sprayed up into the animals' faces. In full panic now, the rest swerved right as well. They were turning, now running back, against the oncoming herd. If the canyon hadn't been so narrow, they would have run til they dropped, or until they slipped down a riverbank, or thundered over a cliff.

One of the cowhands nearly fell off his horse when it stumbled in front of the herd. The man pulled his mount up and only barely saved both of them from being trampled. Mooing, bellowing, shaking the very earth with their massive weight, the herd swept over anything in their path.

Finally, a little way down the canyon, the cowhands managed to get them milling in a circle. Still rearing, heedless of any who stumbled, it eventually dawned on the animals that there was nowhere else for them to go. They slowed up, unsure, but still restless. The men spoke and sang softly, to quiet them. When one animal finally bent to nip at some grass, the men watched others take up the idea. Almost as quickly as the fear had set in, the cattle seemed to have forgotten it, and the cowhands could finally relax a bit.

But that young kid who started all this – where was that mindless idiot?

Robert hauled himself up off the ground and saw, right in front of him, a horrible sight. Two animals, trampled upon, struggling, terribly mangled and bloody. They writhed in pain, unable to get up.

This was my fault, thought Robert. He was afraid he was going to be sick.

Hattie ran to him to pull him back.

"I never thought cows were that stupid," he gasped. "I really never thought – "

"It's okay, Robert." She tugged on his arm. "You didn't know."

"Yes, he did know. I told him." Michael stood behind them, furious.

Robert hardly dared to look at the maimed animals. He began to back away. One of the cowhands was riding slowly toward them. Robert watched as he stopped to look at the wounded animals. The man's shoulders sagged and he shook his head. Slowly, he pulled out his gun and shot them dead.

Anya's hands flew to her ears. "What's he doing?" she screamed.

"There was no help for those two. He had no choice."

"But he shouldn't – "

"They were suffering. He had no choice," Michael repeated.

The cowhand, sitting on his horse, turned to look at the the two girls, the man, and the dog. They were huddled together, watching him, afraid to even imagine how angry he must be. He moved his horse toward where they stood.

"Great. Now Mrs. Frey is going to be blamed for this," said Michael softly, as the man came near. "And you know that guy's going to want someone to pay for those dead animals, right, Robert? Robert?"

At the sound of the gunshot, Robert had turned to run. It wasn't his fault that cattle were such cowards! He hid behind a rock and buried his face in his arms, shaking.

"Where is that jackass?" the cowhand demanded.

Robert peeked over the rock.

"Where's the blockhead that started this?" The cowhand was yelling at Michael. When the man looked in Robert's direction, he ducked behind the rock again. Would the man come after him? If that happened, what should he do?

He had to get out of here. Where could he hide? The trail. It was just behind him! He crawled toward it, then got to his feet, crouching low, hoping he wouldn't be seen. He'd go back to the lodge by himself. But what if that man came to the ranch? How could he explain what he'd done? Confused, panicked, he got up and ran as fast as he could up the trail.

Finally, after speaking with Michael, the cowhand pulled his horse around and went back to his job.

"Come on, girls," Michael called. "Let's start back. We can stop and have something to eat beside the waterfall."

"That was so terrible," said Anya. "I really don't feel like eating."

"You'll be hungry by the time we get there."

"Where's Robert?" asked Hattie.

They called, they searched.

"Where could he be?"

"He probably wanted to be by himself," said Michael Redbird. "We'll see him back at the lodge."

"But what if he gets lost?" said Anya. She was a little worried about him, she had to admit. He was so impulsive! She would have run away too, if she had caused a stampede. But then again, it seemed to her that Robert was never ashamed about anything he'd done.

"How can he get lost?" said Hattie. "All he has to do is follow the river. Don't worry, Anya."

Michael,too, had his doubts about Robert. The kid couldn't be all that smart. He had left his lunch behind. And he hadn't brought a jacket, even when reminded.

"I'm not so sure," he said, "that he has the sense to keep to the river trail."

"Well − ." Suddenly Hattie wasn't so sure, either, about Robert's skills in the woods. "He'll be fine," she said, without conviction. "Don't worry. He'll be fine."

The trail going back through the canyon was uphill. Robert hadn't been aware of the slope when they came down the trail. Now, panting heavily, he was very aware of it. He ran until his side cramped up. It slowed him down and doubled him over. But he kept staggering along until he remembered the side path he had seen earlier that morning. He had wondered, when he noticed it then, if it was the one he had seen on the map, a path that would lead directly to the Stone Lions. He had been wanting to go there, though Michael Redbird had told him he couldn't. Now maybe he would go, if he could find the path. Sure, why not go there if he wanted to? Mike would never know. If he did find out, who cared?

The Stone Lions would be a good place to hide out for a couple of hours. That's what he'd do. Everyone would wonder where he was, but – well, fine. Let them worry for a while. Maybe that way they'd be glad to see him when he got back, instead of being mad at him.

Anyway, why should I care about what happened? he asked himself. It wasn't his fault that cattle were so ignorant. But still it gnawed at him, the thought of those two maimed cows. He couldn't get that sight out of his mind.

It made him feel sick to his stomach. It would have been better if he hadn't done what he did. If only he had thought first. If only he had listened to what Mike said to him. How he wished he had never come to New Mexico. He wanted to go anywhere but back to the lodge.

He had always, before now, been able to ignore his own transgressions. Just forget about stupid things. A couple of dead cows? Really? Who cared? But his pride! If only this humiliating thing had not happened in front of the girls. And Mike Redbird.

The bright flame of his cocky defiance wavered. Really though, he tried to tell himself as he hurried along, it was no big deal, and who cared? His cousin despised him. Mike already disliked him. What had changed this morning? Nothing.

And then his mother's exasperated voice sounded in his ear. His mother, always pleading with him. Why, Robert? Why are you always going off without thinking? Whenever she started scolding, he tried to let her know he was ignoring her. And yet, this time ... a stray thought wormed its way into his head. A small niggling feeling that he had been very, very stupid. Forget that! What difference did any of this stuff make?

Ah. There, across the river, on the left. That had to be the path he was looking for! He would go that way. So he could get away from everybody. So he didn't have to see angry looks on their frowning faces. The river was narrow here. He splashed across a shallow place, trying to jump from rock to rock, but ending up with wet feet. The path before him climbed steeply and he started up. He was worn out when he got to the top.

Huh. There was nothing up here but a steely cold wind. No lions that he could see. The trail went further, steeply downhill again. He sat for a minute, catching his breath, then followed the path as it descended the wall of another canyon.

At the bottom, out of the wind, it was eerily quiet. He wandered off the path for a way, to see what he could find. There were no landmarks to be seen. He didn't like it down here, so desolate and grey.

He eyed the cliffs, like fortress walls above him. The day had turned dark, the sky heavy. All the running he'd done had made him thirsty. Too bad there was no water down here. Nothing to see in this canyon, either, and nothing remotely resembling lions.

Now that he thought about it, he didn't even know what to look for. Were the Stone Lions actual statues? That seemed unlikely. Lions, out here? Maybe they were just boulders that had been named for lions. Come to think of it, how did the ancient native people even know about lions? Robert slowed, beginning to have doubts. He stood at the bottom of the canyon, thinking.

He could go back.

No. Impossible. He couldn't. Well, he could but he wouldn't.

Right at that moment, the moment he let that small opportunity slip by, Robert's trajectory was radically altered, though whether for good or ill makes no difference whatsoever.

Maybe, he thought, if he hiked to the top of that next cliff, he'd find something. He began to climb again. It was another steep trail and his legs were feeling like rubber. He stopped, leaning over a boulder so he could catch his breath. The thought came to him that he should have turned around.

That is when the coyote crossed his path.

The coyote had been running after something, either that, or away from something. Who could tell? He didn't see Robert until he was almost in front of him. The boy shouted in alarm and tried to scramble to the top of a boulder.

The thing is, according to Pueblo people, if a coyote crosses your path, it's a sign. A bad sign. Don't go on! Turn around immediately. Now, if Robert had known that, things might have been different. But he did not. And who knows if he would have respected that old piece of lore if he did know it. What use did he have for other people's stupid advice?

He froze, staring at the coyote. The creature's back arched and the fur stood up on his neck. A wild animal – Robert had neither seen one in real life, nor ever sensed an animal's terrifying power. He was completely defenseless. His stomach began to quiver.

Then, abruptly, the coyote's attention snapped away. He had heard something. He raised up on his hind legs, ears erect, taking a look down toward the bottom of the canyon. Alert, every fiber of his being a receptor of signals. He was ignoring Robert altogether. One short instant later, he turned and dashed up over the rim of the canyon. Between one breath and another, the coyote was gone.

An experienced hiker might have deduced something from this, but again, it was another sign that Robert missed.

He was relieved. He relaxed. He'd been spared.

Then the rain started.

He shivered. This place – it was horrible! He had no coat, not even a sweater. He had to find shelter. He was closer to the top of the cliff than the bottom. Hurry, get up there. Find a tree! Find a rock! Something, anything he could hide under.

It began to rain so hard that he could hardly see the path. The trail was turning to mud. He slipped, scrambled clumsily to stay on his feet.

The rain turned bitter cold. He hated this! He hated this whole place. He never should have come. His foot slid backward on a loose stone and he slipped again. His feet flew out from under him. He put out a hand but smashed down hard on a boulder and banged to the ground, hidden for a moment from sight, if only he realized it. Hidden from any other creature that might be approaching.

He lay there, pain clamping his body. The rain beat against his face. His arms could not move. He could not even raise a hand to shield his eyes.

He had landed on his side. For a minute, he couldn't even take a breath. Aw, his ribs. One arm was twisted under him and his shoulder hurt like fire. He rolled over and struggled to sit up.

Then the rain turned to icy, hard-driving snow.

His fall had landed him on rocky scree. He could hardly get to his feet. He'd wrenched his shoulder. With every move, bolts of pain seared his ribs. He finally managed to find his footing, swaying a bit until the pain settled. He took a step. Oh, his side! That hurt. The snow clung to his body, covering him, every inch, with white. He could barely walk. He had to find shelter! He floundered his way up the path, and the wind drove the snow at him, layering it thick against his face.

But there, up there! What was that? Near the top of the cliff. If only he could see well enough to get up there. A shape, barely visible in the storm. A small box of a place, like a little hut on the edge of the mesa. Whoever lived there would let him come in, would help him find his way. Somebody had to help him, because he was wet and freezing and everything hurt. Shielding his face against the wind, trying to run, he had trouble keeping his balance. Slipping and skidding, he stumbled onto the flat ground of the mesa's rim. He called out as he ran, to whoever was in the house.

"Hey! Hey!" No one answered. No door? There had to be a door! Running around to the back, he was suddenly powerfully afraid to go near the place. Something evil in there. He felt a strong urge to back away. Frightened, he stumbled and almost fell. He had startled a hare, had just about tripped over the thing. It bolted right at his feet and Robert swerved. Whether he wanted to or not, he practically fell through the open doorway of the hut. Gasping and in pain, he crawled inside.

Shelter. Thank goodne – Aaah!

A terrible commotion outside, something thundering past the doorway! Robert froze in shock. Something huge. Enormous power, the extraordinary power of pure muscle. A cat?

It was! A large cat bounded right past the hut, flying over the snow.

A cat, moving with unbelievable swiftness. Robert scrambled to move backwards, away from the doorway. So there were lions here – mountain lions! Tawny gold, sleek as a lightning bolt, the cat tore across the snow in front of the hut. The poor hare, the one Robert had spooked, saw the cat coming. He zigzagged in panic. There was a wild skirmish. Vicious snarling! Snow kicking up in a high white cloud! A brawl of fur!

And then the cat stood alone and the silent world drew a wary breath. A limp hare hung clamped in his jaws. He blinked and surveyed the whitening mesa, then trotted with his prize back along the edge of the canyon.

He was gone.

It had happened so fast! Death, released like an arrow from a powerful bow, had driven deep into its target and stilled a beating heart. The struggle was over. It couldn't be undone.

Robert felt his whole body trembling and he could not stop shaking. A lion? So close behind him? Had it been following him? If it weren't for the hare, that lion would have found him! Turned on him!

He would be dead by now. He, not the hare, would have been fighting for his life in the snow out there. And he would surely be dead.

He stood petrified in place. Silence glistened like crystal around him.

A miracle.

The hare, this hut – just when everything seemed against him, he had been saved. Finally, for once luck had favored him. A wave of relief washed over him with such force, he almost sobbed. Every muscle in his body slackened. Gently, like a falling leaf, he drifted to the floor.

And here, now, the real miracle: something like gratitude, one tiny pinpoint, pricked open inside him. Gratitude, the key to countless other doors.

He looked around, still trembling. He tried to brush snow from his shoulders and hair. This place, so eerie, so small and dark, no window. Who lived here? He saw no furniture, nothing.

Spooky. This felt like such a spooky place, but if he hadn't found it, what then?

Robert curled into a ball and lay shivering on the floor.

Out of the snowstorm. Saved from being torn apart by a lion. But trembling with cold and pain.

And lost. Hopelessly lost.

Nevertheless, alive. So glad to be alive.


"Robert? No, I haven't seen him," Jemmy told the girls when

Michael Redbird brought them back to the lodge. "Did you check his cabin?"

"I'll go up," said Michael, obviously disgusted.

"We can look," offered Hattie. "We have to get dry clothes anyway." They too had been caught in the rain, just as they came within sight of the ranch.

They checked the men's cottage. No one was there.

They ran back down to their own cottage to change their clothes. Corax, too, was soaking wet. With what seemed a spectacular effort, he shook fountains of water from his coat.

"Hey!" Hattie and Anya cried out, pulling back.

Corax smiled at them, all innocence. HEY WHAT? WHY DON'T YOU GIRLS JUST DO AS I DO?

Anya poked her head through the neck of a warm sweater. "Robert will get lost, for sure. He thinks he's so smart but I know he'll get lost. What do you think we should do?"

"There's no sense in us going to look for him. We don't know our way around here." Hattie perched on the edge of a chair.

"He's not here, but we never passed him on the trail. We never saw a sign of him. That doesn't seem too good, do you think, Hattie?"

"Maybe he heard us coming and hid."

"Yeah, he probably would do something like that. He's such a dummy! Why did he have to go running off like that?"

Hattie shrugged. She'd been thinking about Robert. "Maybe he ran off for the same reason I ran away from the residential school three times." She studied Anya, waiting for the proverbial penny to drop. "Maybe for the same reason you ran away from home last summer?"

Anya blinked. "I was afraid." She saw Hattie's eyebrows go up and she looked away.

A little later, down at the lodge, Anya looked up from her

book, thinking she heard someone coming. Yes, it had stopped raining. But no, there was no one there.

At three o'clock Jemmy came in to ask them if they'd like some cocoa.

"No Robert?" she asked.

"Nope. No Robert."

With grave authority, Grandfather Clock creaked, whirled his air governor, and struck the hour.


Robert lay in a fog of misery. He curled up, trying to stay warm. When he could finally stir himself, the snow had stopped. He must have been lying on that floor for quite some time. His clothes, soaking wet before, were only damp now. He struggled to sit up. His shoulder and side were throbbing.

This place, made of some kind of rough bricks, what was it? Nothing inside here, an empty doorway but no door. He dared a cautious look outside. No neighbors? Why would someone build a house out here, when no one else was near? He knew he wasn't safe here. There must be other wild animals out there, hungry creatures, too strong for him to fight, even if he weren't hurt. He backed away from the door.

The Sun peeked out then, and She looked askance at the boy sitting slumped in the little hut. Look at you. You're a fine specimen, aren't you? She beamed a finger of light into the doorway and lit one corner of the hut, so he could see what was there. Look, foolish boy. See? This could have been you. This should make you think a little.

Suddenly, he sensed that he was not alone.

No, he was not. There was someone back there, in the corner. He had felt that presence before, hadn't he? Now he saw someone staring at him. Two black eyes. He got to his knees and crawled a little closer.

Beginning to tremble all over again, he strained to see, then fell backwards in horror. They *were* eyes, or had been. A skull. Wait, a whole skeleton. One arm bone had fallen out of place but the rest of the bones seemed intact. The hands lay pressed together under the head. Not animal bones. A human. A very small person, curled into a fetal position.

Some dreadfulness kept Robert from moving closer. He bent so as not to block the light.

This must have been a child. A dead child? Shocked, Robert could hardly put those two words together. They were like a cold hand on his heart. He and everyone he knew had been born to health and plenty. He had never seen a dead child.

When had this happened? Had this boy been left behind? Lost, like him? It was a boy, Robert felt certain. Did he die alone in this very place? Like I almost did, thought Robert? The way I almost did.

It pierced him deeply, the unexpected agony of this other boy's pain. He sensed that pain with such intensity that his breath stuck clamped in his throat. Was it possible that this boy, this other person, might have felt the same kind of fear that he was feeling right now? Robert had never had a thought like that before. He swayed, crouching to the floor.

Dizziness, panic. The shadows in the corners – he felt them yearning to grasp him by the arms and crush him. He was muddled, confused. He couldn't keep his balance. Time space twining spinning swirling about until here before him, he could find only one still point. A boy. This little boy, much younger than himself.

He saw him clearly. Eyes – shining eyes that smiled up at him. Robert smiled back, all feeling of dread draining away. For several moments, he and the boy were of one heart. Then the eyes closed, the connection withered, and Robert was as alone as ever. He was as insubstantial as the dead boy. A nothing, nobody.

He sat back, bitter, his head heavy, his whole body leaden. But was that boy really nothing? He didn't feel like nothing. What did it mean, to be something? This question had finally come to Robert. But there was no one here to answer it.

His eyes brimmed with tears. He pressed his lips tight between his teeth; then put his arm on his knee and buried his face against it and wept.

After a while, he struggled to push himself to a sitting position so he could wipe his face on his shirt tail. He hadn't noticed the blood on his shirt before. He should get it cleaned off somehow. His shoulder, his ribs. They hurt worse than anything.

He was probably going to die. Right here beside the boy. He would die, after all. He stared at the little boy, curled up against the wall. Then something caught his eye.

A small carved figure, hardly two inches long, was wedged between the bricks right above the boy's head. A long-faced figure with a wide-open mouth. Carved from a lovely blue stone, it was. Turquoise? He should take it home for a souvenir. Maybe it would bring him luck. He reached for it.

Something stayed his hand. Stopped it in mid-air. But he wanted that carving. It was probably valuable, maybe very old. Something about that little figure made it seem special. But what? Why was he so intrigued by it? He was surprised to find himself actually wanting it badly, as though it were a treasure. Maybe the carving was some kind of talisman, charged with mysterious meaning. He reached for it again. He wanted to keep it.

But no. No. He tried, but could not bring himself to touch it. Whatever it was doing here, he must leave it to do its work. For the boy. Someone had put it there for the boy.

Robert sighed. Then again, his mother's maddening voice in his ear. "It's time to stop fooling around and get your head on straight, Robert. It's time you started thinking about a plan."

Yes, okay. He should. He probably should smarten up. It must be getting late. If I'm still out here when it gets dark, I'll never find my way back.

He realized that he had changed his mind about getting back to the lodge. What a good idea it seemed now, a wonderful idea. How far away was it? How much longer could he last out here alone, freezing, hurting? And to think Mike had tried to warn him. What ever made him ignore Michael Redbird's advice? Bring a coat. Stay away from the cows. What had he been thinking?

His insides tightened when his mind replayed those terrible events. You're a stupid moron, he told himself. And very cold. Awfully hungry. Why did these bad things always happen to him?

He thought of his cousin then. Last summer, so she could avoid being punished severely for something he himself had secretly done, Anya had run away from home. When they finally found her, she was halfway across the state. Just a kid, wandering on her own for days. How had she done it? He hadn't been on his own for even one day, and look at the mess he was in.

He studied the little boy one more time. He was so sorry to leave. Robert hated to abandon him. It seemed so heartless. Like leaving a little brother.

Listen to yourself, he chided. You don't have a brother. What, are you crazy? You're just afraid to go outside again, that's all. It's disgusting, how afraid you are. You're acting like a coward. Pull yourself together.

All right. Say good-bye to the little boy. Start walking. Find the ranch.

He left the piece of turquoise untouched and turned to the door, having no idea, yet, that the Robert who had come in was not the same as the Robert who was leaving.

He studied the landscape carefully, then crawled out of the hut and stood up. No animals around, that he could see. Cold wind out here. The shivering started again, now as much from fear as from cold. The sun was near the horizon already, the shadows on the snow a bright blue-violet. The canyon he had climbed out of a while ago yawned before him again. That was the way back, through the fearsome canyon. The path he had taken before was now covered with a thin layer of snow, but he was able to follow it back down the steep cliff side.

Go carefully, side-step the steep parts. Take it easy. Keep your eyes open. The exertion helped warm him.

He could not afford to fall again. He tried to put his worries aside because it took all his will to concentrate on where to put his feet. Down, down to the bottom of the canyon, slowly crawling, literally crawling back up the other side. He suddenly began to wonder if this really was the same canyon he had traversed earlier. He stopped near the rim. Was it the same? His head felt thick. He was confused. He couldn't tell.

The sun was low, the wind sharp. So quiet out here. There had to be wild animals around. And they knew how to be quiet. So quiet, you didn't know they were behind you. Stalking you. He looked over his shoulder. Don't panic, he told himself. Think.

He raised his head. Was that – had he heard voices? Uncle Jack? Coming to find him? He was hearing voices, the voices of men. Yes, Jack! His uncle! His best hope for a rescue. Robert tripped and skidded along the canyon rim. Maybe it was foolish to leave the path. But voices! They were coming to find him. He knew Jack would come for him!

He stopped. Down there – a tent? Almost hidden on a shelf of rock. Tied behind the tent, a mule. Men inside, arguing. Shouting at each other. So, it wasn't Uncle Jack. Robert crouched and listened to what they were saying.

"You are such a greedy man! Try be reasonable, would you? Nobody's trying to cheat you!"

What was that about? Robert was afraid to go closer. What if these were criminals hiding out here? But oh! Possibly they had food – thoughts of food made him put aside his fear. Maybe these men would give him something to eat. Anything. He was so hungry. He crept closer.

Wait! *Was* it safe? Who were these men? He saw movement from the corner of his eye. The mule, tied to a bush, was swishing her tail and looking at him with big dewy eyes.

Just then, the shouting in the tent grew furious. One man burst outside, rummaged in a bag and yanked out a rifle. Robert tried to duck behind some rocks but he wasn't quick enough.

"Hey! You!" screamed the man. The mule bellowed in fear. "What are you doing? Get yourself out here!"

Robert rose slowly, terrified to see the rifle pointed at him. Then, greatly relieved, he saw who held the gun.

"Hello?" he said in a meek voice.

Snyder Ravilious reared back in surprise. "What are you doing here? You filthy dirty little brat! What do you think you're doing? Are you spying on us?"

The tent flap was thrown open and Ouisel stepped out. He took in the situation, sighed in disgust, and pulled out a pack of cigarettes. With one arm folded across his belly, he rested the other elbow on that hand, a cigarette between his fingers.

"Spying? I'm not spying!" Robert cried. "No! No, I got lost. You have to help me."

"Don't give me that pigswill! You're lying! Who's with you?" If Ravilious noticed the blood on Robert's shirt, he didn't react.

"No one's with me! Honest! Please, I've got to have something to eat. Can you – I was hoping you could give me something."

Ouisel cleared his throat. "You want to know what I think, Snyd? He's snooping, that's what he's doing," Ouisel claimed, his high voice squeaking in anger. He waved his cigarette in front of his face. "What else could possibly have brought him here?"

"I'm not snooping! All I want is some food. That's all."

"Who sent you, huh?" demanded Ravilious, stabbing the air with the rifle. "Your uncle put you up to this? Did he?"

"No! Nobody! I got lost –"

"Oh, please," peepered Ouisel like a soprano. "That is a big load of caca. You can't expect us to believe a word of it. Snyder, I beg you. Don't just stand there waving the rifle around."

"I'm handling this, okay?" Snyder Ravilious spread his hands. "What do you want me to do, throw him over the cliff?"

"Well, give me a teensy moment to think this through." Ouisel chewed his thumbnail. "Look. A silly boy doesn't just show up here. Somebody sent him. Somebody knows we're here. Now that's not a good thing, is it? No, it's not." He flicked a hand at Robert. "You're going to have to do something about him."

Robert stared at them, practically in shock at their cold-heartedness.

Snyder lowered the gun and glared at Ouisel. "What? I'm not about to shoot a kid, fer crissake!" He gestured roughly. "Go on, you lousy brat! Get out of here."

"No no no, Snyder!" Ouisel's voice rose higher. He stamped his little foot."

"Then you think of something!"

Ouisel shook his head primly, the hand with his cigarette following the motion. "Do I have to spell it out for you? Really, Snyd?"

Ravilious grimaced in disgust. "Geezis, Ouisel, you really take the cake. Kid, beat it, will you? Go on, get outa here."

"Snyder! Just shut up and –"

"Shut up? You shut yourself up!"

"Okay, I have had just about enough! Here! Give me the damn rifle!" Ouisel made a grab for the weapon.

"Keep your paws – " They ducked and wrestled, about as energetic as rattlesnakes that had recently swallowed a couple of marmots whole.

"Snyder, must I remind –"

"Gimme that –"

"Stop it! You'll rip my –" A shot rang out. The mule brayed in panic. Robert, shaking so hard he could barely take a step, was trying to edge past the struggling men.

"That shot could have killed somebody, you stupid Frog!" Ravilious screamed.

Fat little Ouisel wrenched the rifle from the big man's hands and, with the butt, jabbed him hard, twice, in the abdomen. "Call me a Frog again and you're a dead man!"

Cowering low, Robert took a few hesitant steps.

"You better beat it, kid!" Ravilious motioned furiously, holding his midriff. "This guy is whacko!"

Robert lurched toward a path through the boulders. He looked over his shoulder. Now Ouisel was pointing the rifle at him. He panicked, turned and stumbled for several steps, slipping in the muddy snow. He lost his footing, and the next thing he knew, he was tumbling head over heels off the edge of a steep bank. Bang, he hit his shoulder again and kept rolling. Bang, another sharp pain bolted through his ribs. He plummeted, bouncing, crashing down toward where the narrow path made a switchback. The last thing he heard was Ravilious swearing from far above him.

Up by the tent, Ouisel picked up the cigarette he had dropped in the dirt and fished a piece of tobacco off his tongue. "Well. There now. I guess that takes care of him. Can we forget our little spat now, you and I?"

"Honoré! Did you see that?" Ravilious was frantic. "I did not do that! I did not lay a finger on him! He just went flying over the edge! Geezis! He might have broken his neck."

"Was that not the whole idea?"

"Are you crazy? You want to be arrested for murder, Ouisel?"

"Oh, he'll rot down there before anyone finds him. Anyway, he had no right to be here. What's it called here – trespassage or something?" He yawned. "Whew. Sleepy-time for me. I need a nap."


Robert opened his eyes. It was nearly dark now. How did he end up flat on his back? He couldn't even shake his head to clear it. His arm was excruciatingly painful. He could hardly get up. Aiy. He swayed with dizziness, and realized that he was on a path. Was it the path to the ranch? All he could do was follow it. He started down, barely able to shuffle now. Was he hallucinating? Or were those lights down there?

He was so dizzy he had to drop to his knees. Get up, he told himself. You have to keep going, make it back to the ranch.

He would get there. Yes. He had to.


"Dad?" Anya knocked on the door to her father's cottage.

Jack opened the door. "Hey, how was your day?" he asked Anya.

Anya had seen her father and Hugh trudging up the path to their cottage, just as they arrived back at the ranch. Hugh was bent under a load of camera equipment. Her father carried Hugh's big tripod, and a pack for food and extra clothing. She picked up her coat and ran after them.

Both men looked worn out when she entered their cottage, but she had to let them know.

"What's the matter? What's up, honey?"

"Dad, Robert ran off and we haven't seen him all day. Not since this morning." She told them what had happened. "He doesn't have a coat and he forgot to take his lunch."

"Missing since this morning? Are you serious? I don't even know where to begin to look for him," said her father. "There must be a hundred trails and canyons he could get lost in."

"Maybe Dick Frey could help."

They hurried back to the lodge and found Dick.

"Robert hasn't come back?" Dick ran his hands over his face. "The sun has set already. Okay. He'll need a coat, if we do find him. Is there any chance your dog would make a good blood hound?"

"No harm in trying him," said Hugh.

"We'll need lanterns, a first aid kit. And I'll get some water from the kitchen. Bundle up, it's getting windy out there. I'll tell Jemmy to hold dinner."


Anya and Hattie watched anxiously as the men set out. The wind was howling, tugging at their lanterns so they swayed beneath their outstretched arms. Over the bridge, up the trail, bending into the slope, laboring up the slippery path in the cold night wind. Only Corax was relishing the experience, prancing ahead so merrily, you'd think he was going to a birthday party.

Then they were lost to view. Hattie sat down to wait and Jemmy, her dinner duties delayed, came in and sat beside her.

"Come sit with us, Anya." Jemmy patted the seat next to her.

"In a minute. I will in a minute." She stayed by the window.

"You're worried about your cousin?"

Anya shrugged.

"He's not one of her favorite people," said Hattie.

"You don't get along?" Jemmy asked.

Anya couldn't answer. She wasn't proud of her feelings toward Robert.

"He caused her a lot of trouble in the past," explained Hattie.

"Ah, family. It's always something with family."

At that, Hattie shrank into herself.

Jemmy turned to her, concerned. They began a soft conversation. Jemmy talked about her half-brother Michael, and

Anya heard Hattie briefly mention her father, but she couldn't pay attention to what they were saying.

The machinery heart of the big Grandfather Clock, ticking the seconds away, murmured and stuttered incoherently, finally assumed some measure of dignity, and chimed the hour.

Outside, the dark pressed against the windows and the wind wailed. Wild Boreas, purple-winged god of the north wind, had mounted his ice-steed and he rode, shrieking in fury, down from off a storm cloud. He tore through the canyon, shaking and rattling every door and window in a fit of cold rage.

Anya leaned on the windowsill, almost sick with worry. She was glad she wasn't out there tonight. She knew well what it was like to be lost and alone. Anything could be happening out there. The minutes of waiting dragged by so slowly.

The quarter-hour chimed, the half hour. Then Grandfather Clock's internal workings felt the call of the cosmos. His fan fly flew. His rack-and-snail mechanism scraped. He sang out the hour, oblivious to the villainous wind that clamored at eaves and chimneys, unconcerned with worries and apprehensions that did no one any good anyway. With the brio of the late tenor Enrico Caruso, he sang out the hour, a clear and simple rebuke from He Who Rules Time.


Robert trudged doggedly down the path. It wasn't easy in the dark. It was his will, not his legs that held him up now. The wind had risen, slamming out of the north with such ferocity that it nearly knocked him over. Fortunately, his hands and feet were just big lumps that didn't feel the cold at all anymore. But he couldn't keep his balance. He cradled his hurt left arm in his right. Something was badly wrong with that arm.

Keep going, keep going. Oh, that poor little boy back there in the hut. It's not a good night for him to be up there. All alone. No blankets.

Watch where you're going. Keep walking.

He's cold, I bet. I shouldn't have abandoned him, but ... but ... I wish he had come with me. He should have. It would have been so much better if we were together. But instead, he gave up. We could have helped each other. We could have been friends.

He'd be alive today, rambled Robert, if he had only come with me. Then he frowned. Wait, could that be true?

The tail of his shirt billowed in the wind, except where the blood had dried the cotton to his ribs. The cold blew right up his back. He lurched along the trail like a drunken person. Those lights – those are lights down there. I think. Aren't they? No. Just his imagination. They disappeared, came back. Wishful thinking. Was he losing his mind? They moved around a lot. They could not be the lights of ... huh – where? He was trying to get to somewhere. Somewhere far away. Those lights made no sense. Lights in houses didn't move around like that.

All of a sudden his legs gave out. He stretched out his stronger hand to keep from falling, but it impacted so hard with a boulder that it made him cry out. He collapsed, hitting the ground with a painful jolt. Aaw!

Maybe he should rest. Rest until the hurting eased, rest, just for a minute. He struggled to sit up. I'll just lean against this rock for a bit. Freezing cold rock, hard against his wounded ribs. He wanted so much to go to sleep. So much.

Lights again. Far down the trail. Maybe someone .... He tried calling. A wisp of sound blew off into the night. No one answered. He rested his head against the boulder and gathered the energy to shout. Help me, he called. Or thought he did. He was sliding, slipping. He fell over. His shoulder hit the ground again. Sharp jab of pain.

Please. Help.

Corax's ears perked. He stopped in the path, nosing the wind. He took a step. Head up, neck craning, he stopped again to listen. He bounded forward. Yes, something ahead, something on the trail up there.

HERE!

He sniffed the body excitedly and whined in recognition.

THE BOY! IT'S THE BOY! GET UP, GET UP! WHAT'S THE MATTER?

He barked.

THE BOY IS HERE!

He sniffed him all over and barked again.

SOMETHING'S WRONG. SOMETHING'S VERY WRONG!

He licked the boy's motionless face.

Jack and Hugh hurried to kneel beside him, and Dick whooped with relief.

THE BOY! THE BOY IS HERE! Corax danced around the men. SOMETHING IS WRONG WITH HIM! YOU MUST HELP HIM!

They wrapped Robert in his coat, being as careful as they could with his arm. They saw immediately that it was hurt by the swelling and its ghastly color. Robert groaned, barely conscious. They lifted him onto Dick's back. A nasty wind prodded them all the way down the trail, howling threats of more snow. They had to go slowly, picking their way with care. Jack and Hugh went first, holding the lanterns so Dick could see where he was going. Hugh took a turn carrying him, and then Jack. They tried to hold Robert without hurting him, but knew it could not be very comfortable for him.

Corax lead the way triumphantly to the lodge.

I FOUND HIM. I FOUND THE BOY.


"I see lights!" Anya cried. She hadn't left the window for even a minute. They were coming back! She ran to the door and out into the storm. They had stopped on the bridge. What was going wrong? She feared the worst. She could hardly run, battling the wind, trying to get her leaden legs to move. Why had they stopped?

Robert lifted his head as they came to the bridge over the Rio Frijoles.

"Can I – " He gasped some words.

"What, Robert?"

"Walk."

"You want to walk?" They helped him to the ground. He gyrated alarmingly.

"Whoa! Are you sure?" asked Jack. "You don't have to be a hero, son."

"… th' bes'. Nummer one …." He mumbled, staggering.

"Number one? I've heard that before. Your grandmother's favorite line," said Jack.

"Is he alive? He's okay?" Anya cried, as she pounded over the bridge. Hattie followed, and brought her a coat.

"He's in one piece," said Jack.

Robert had to stifle a sob. What? He was? In one piece? Well that was good news! He'd never felt so brave! Look at everybody! Everybody out here, all here to see him?

He stumbled. They managed to get hold of his good arm just as he was about to topple into the river.


Where was he?

Somewhere soft. Still so cold. Except where the hot water bottles pressed against his arm and chest. So cold. He could barely summon the energy to turn his head to see the person beside him.

"Who –"

"It's Mrs. Snow, Robert. I work in the kitchen, remember? Here, take a sip of this."

Warm drink. Too tired. Can't sit up. Arm – all padded? What? It wouldn't move. Ribs, aw, his ribs hurt.

"Have a little more." Mrs. Snow held his head up and tilted a cup to his mouth. This tasted kind of … kind of ….

Anya opened Jemmy's bedroom door a crack so she could call her dog. How had Corax gotten into the room with Robert? Robert was lying on his back, his bandaged arm taped across his chest. He was sound asleep.

"Come," she whispered, beckoning to the dog. Corax hunched stubbornly on the rug beside the bed where Robert slept. He dropped his head to his paws and looked at her from the corners of his eyes. He didn't come when she called.

"Don't you want to go out?" Corax wouldn't look at her. She slipped into the room and took him by the collar, but he refused to budge. She straightened, surprised that the dog would not obey. Then she heard a sound from the bed. Robert was looking at her. His face was pinched and troubled.

He mouthed a word at her.

"What is it?" She bent closer. "Do you need something?"

So softly that she wasn't sure she heard right, he whispered a word, then abruptly turned away. He fumbled the sheet up over his face.

Anya blinked rapidly. She stood very still. She must have misheard. It was so unlike Robert to say something like that.

Should she answer? Should she say something?

She patted the bed. "Come on," she said to the dog. Corax leapt up and settled next to Robert on the bed. He leaned against the boy and looked at Anya with warm brown eyes. She stroked his head and went out, closing the door quietly.

The dog, here beside him? Who was that next to his bed? Was it Uncle Jack? Yes, Mr. Durant and Uncle Jack.

"You missed a great dinner, Robert. I brought you some

leftovers. Here, can you sit up?" Jack sat down on his bed (Somebody's bed. Whose was it?), and put a fork into his bruised right hand. "Try the chicken."

Food. The best he'd ever eaten in his whole life. He wanted to eat everything, but after three bites, he was too tired.

"You can have the rest later. You're going to sleep in Jemmy's bed tonight. I've hired Mrs. Snow to be your nurse. She'll keep an eye on you. Just sleep now. Shh. Just sleep."

Drifting ... wait. Tell them. "Uncle Jack." His throat was so sore, it gave him a raspy voice.

"What is it?"

"The little boy."

"I can't hear you."

"Little boy."

"What boy?"

"I saw him."

"No kidding."

"Up there."

"Uh huh."

"All alone."

"Sure. You need to rest, Robert. We'll talk tomorrow."

"He was so ...." His voice faded. His eyes dropped closed.

Jack looked at Hugh. "He's in pretty bad shape."

Mrs. Snow came in with a pot of her special tea, wrapped in a towel to keep it warm. "Will you get that dog off the bed? What is it with you white people and your animals?"

Jack laughed and pulled Corax away. Mrs. Snow shooed him out the door.

"Robert is pretty loopy. I can't understand what he's mumbling about," Jack told her.

"I can assure you he'll feel better tomorrow."

"Is that a remedy for fever?" Jack pointed to her tea pot.

"This? It's good for whatever ails you. It once cured a monkey who almost died from eating glue."

"A monkey?" Hugh and Jack asked at the same time.

"Yes." Mrs. Snow proclaimed slowly, regally. She drew herself to full height and looked down her nose at them. "It was a very sick monkey."

"A monkey." "Here in New Mexico."

Mrs. Snow fastened them with a dangerous warning look. "Did I say it was my monkey?"

Jack wished he could take back his words. "I – I – I'm sure that – that your tea is –"

"I think we can trust," interrupted Hugh, pulling Jack toward the door, "that Robert is in exceptionally good hands here. We'll look in again in a little while, Mrs. Snow."


Robert woke again an hour later, whimpering.

"Why aren't you sleeping?" Mrs. Snow asked him. She had given him some more of her secret recipe, enough to knock out a grown man for hours. "Close your eyes."

Oh. I'm here? I'm here?

He clutched at the blankets, so afraid. Why was he trembling? He tried to get Mrs. Snow's image into focus.

"I have to tell you, uh, Mrs. –?"

"Mrs. Snow."

"There was a boy," he rasped at her. "Did I tell you before? I can't remember. A boy up there. I saw him."

"Did you?"

"All curled up. Sleeping."

"I see."

"All alone. Five, six years old, only."

"Yes, well, close your eyes, Robert."

"Too young, too young to be alone."

"Maybe you only think you saw a boy."

"I did see him. He's been there for a long, long time."

"Where was this?"

"In a house where nobody lives. Nobody anywhere near."

"Ah. Was it a boy, Robert, or the bones of a boy?"

"Not just bones." He frowned. "I don't think." He paused. "Was I dreaming?"

"Maybe not. There is a skeleton in a field house up there."

"You've seen him?"

"Yes, I have."

"What happened to him, Mrs. Snow?"

"Nobody knows, Robert. Nobody remembers."

"It made me ... feel ... so bad."

"Well, Death is a teacher of great wisdom, isn't he?"

Robert stared, blinking.

"Don't you think, Robert?"

He nodded. "Maybe," he whispered.

"You should sleep now. Go to sleep."

He awoke with a start, panicked and crying. "What? Watch out! What?" Oh! He wasn't alone. Thank goodness. Uncle Jack, and Mr. Durant too.

"Easy there, easy."

"Uncle Jack!" Robert wept. "The boy. Did I tell you? First there was this big lion, then this boy."

"Huh. Really."

"Yeah. You have to go find him."

"Find ...?"

"The boy."

"A boy?"

"Up there. In this sort of hut."

"What? Are you saying you left a boy out there today?"

Robert nodded, his lips trembling. "I had to." He snuffled.

Jack handed him his handkerchief and felt his forehead. "I hated to leave him."

"Maybe you imagined –"

"No!" He mopped his eyes. "No, he's up there."

Jack rose quickly. "A boy? Alone? I wish you'd told us before. Was he hurt?"

Robert nodded again.

"And you left him there?"

"He was dead."

"Dead?"

"I think so." Robert hiccuped. "Maybe a long time ago. Just a little kid." He crumpled the handkerchief in one hand, then mopped his eyes again.

Jack sat down. "Can you tell me where you found him?"

"You should go to see him, Uncle Jack. Nobody knows what happened to him."

"I see. Yes, we'll have to find him. Here. Drink some more of this." He held a cup for Robert, then pulled the covers up around his chin. "Don't worry. Just sleep now."

Mrs. Snow came in again.

"He's all upset about a dream he had," Jack told her quietly. "He thinks he saw a dead child."

"He probably did. The remains of a child, anyway."

"Remains? Left lying somewhere?"

"Oh, he, or she, has been there for generations. Nobody I ever knew will go near him, much less get close enough to bury him."

"Why not?"

"Taboo. A strong taboo since olden times. He was Navaho, my grandmother told me. Our ancient enemies. The Navaho say that the spirits of the dead can harm the living. So no one will touch him." She looked at Robert, sound asleep, and bit her lip. "I hope this one didn't get near him."

"Where are they, these remains? Do you know?"

"I don't know how to get there from here. We were forbidden to go there when we were young, so of course we all had to go running, daring each other to take a look. But once only. We worked ourselves into a terrible state. Scared us out of our wits. If you absolutely must go there, Dick could probably tell you how to find him. Just don't get too close."

Jack and Hugh left Robert in Mrs. Snow's care. They went back to the lodge and found Dick gathering a load of firewood from the porch.

"I'll carry some," Hugh offered. They each took an armload and stacked the logs near the fireplace.

"Dick, before you go, can I ask you something? My nephew was all upset about a boy he said he saw today. 'Up there', he said. In a hut of some kind."

"A boy? He saw someone?" asked Dick.

"He was obviously feverish, but he seemed very sure."

"Mrs. Snow said she knew what he was talking about," said Hugh. "The remains of a Navaho child, maybe."

"Oh! I bet I know. Robert might have sheltered in a field house."

"What's a field house?"

"The Old Ones ran some irrigation and grew corn up on the mesa. They built *tufa*-brick structures so a couple of men could sleep up there in the summer. And it gave them a place to shelter if they got caught in a storm. Mostly they wanted to guard their crops, or so Michael Redbird tells us."

"You know where these field houses are?"

"Oh, I bet I know the exact place he's talking about. I found a skeleton up there when I was a kid. Scared the pants off me and my buddies. I'm kind of surprised it's still there."

"It seemed to have quite an effect on Robert."

"It sure affected me. It was the first time I realized that kids could die. I behaved myself for at least a week afterwards."

"Can you show us where it is on the map?" asked Hugh. "I'd like to try to get a photo."

"Maybe I can do better than that. I have to take Mom into town tomorrow. But if you're willing to leave early, I can guide you at least part way."

"The thing is, Hugh and I had planned to go to the Alcove House tomorrow. Anya found something interesting there."

"You can easily do both. The field house is only an hour, maybe an hour and a half from here."

That same night, Ravilious opened the flap of his tent and looked out. The weather was nasty. This was ridiculous! Why hadn't they taken a hotel room? The last thing he wanted to do tonight was to go stumbling around in the dark. They had stealthily followed Jack Netherby and his photographer that morning, and were ready to return to that site and do some collecting tonight. They had rented a mule and were loading her with picks and shovels, lanterns, a small crate to carry the treasure, warm clothing.

"This is too much work. There has to be a better way to get what we want," he whined to Ouisel, practically yelling over the wind.

"Come now. We mustn't be foolish. All we have to do is show up. Show up and grab the loot."

Ravilious swore and crossed his arms over his chest.

"Look, I'm telling you, Snydie. They've done the hard work for us," coaxed Ouisel. "We'll find the place again and make off with whatever they were photographing. There must be a lot of stuff. They were up there for a long time."

"Oh sure. Finding the place in the dark, and in all this wind. That'll be easy."

"We were just there this morning. We've got the map."

"I can't hear you."

"I say, we've got the map, haven't we."

"But this wind is hideous! And it's scary out here tonight. Didn't you hear that howling? Some animal –"

"Oh now, Snyder."

"Could be wolves or something."

"Never fear. I'm quite a good shot."

That thought hardly comforted Ravilious. "But if a whole pack of wolves –"

"Come on, now. Be a big brave boy. Think of the profits. And be good enough to hold this mule while I tie up the crate."

Grave-robbing was illegal in the Southwest. In fact, removing any artifact, no matter where it was found, was illegal. So naturally, someone dreamed up a way to break the law with the least risk of getting caught. They called it night-hawking. You secretly tailed an archaeologist, marked the spot where he was working, and returned at night to vandalize the site. It was easy, and saved a lot of research, not to mention useless digging.

Night-hawking will make me rich, Ouisel speculated to himself, or at the very least get me out of debt. Ancient objects from the Southwest were just becoming popular among collectors. Prices were skyrocketing in Europe, higher than in America.

Yes, all right, grumbled Ravilious to himself. That bum Ouisel was correct. He had to admit that much. Their efforts would bring in a lot of money. And if they made money, well, that obviously justified everything. Justified breaking the law, justified putting up with the horrible weather, sleeping in a tent, traipsing all over this miserable desert. Money could make anything bearable. Even putting up with fat-headed Frenchmen.

Their hike through wind and rain was sheer misery. The mule was mutinous and had to be dragged along the trail. Stones rolled like marbles under their feet and they stubbed their toes against boulders. Ravilious tripped over twisted saplings and twice stumbled against the fiery barbs of cholla cacti. Willow branches slashed their faces when they reached the creek, and they slipped and scrambled and cut up their hands on the climb up to the cliff dwelling. Though they searched for an hour, they did not find a single artifact.

In the dark, they never spotted the second cliff dwelling, either. They had been nearby when Jack and Hugh found the first cliff dwelling that morning. Assuming it was full of treasure, Ouisel and Ravilious hadn't hung around very long. They had missed seeing Hugh and Jack continue on along the creek bed to the second cliff dwelling. The first settlement was barren, though the second was rich with artifacts. They came back to the tent empty-handed, cold, wet, and angry.

"What a disaster!" Ravilious moaned.

"Very disappointing, yes indeed."

"How, after all our careful preparation, after going to all this damn trouble, how is it we found nothing?"

Ouisel shrugged. "Maybe they cleaned the place out, took everything." He bent to shield his cigarette from the wind.

"I doubt that. No, that's not what's going on." He glared at Ouisel. His rant was rousing no spark of argument, and Ravilious felt very much like having an argument. "I can tell you what's happening here."

"Really?" Ouisel blew a puff of smoke. "Do tell. What's happening here, Snyder?"

"It's the Coyote."

"The what?"

"The old Indian legend. Coyote the Trickster. We're purposefully being led astray."

Ouisel tsk-tsk-ed and rolled his eyes. "That is simply one big pile of horse manure."

"You never know. This is the wild west, after all. Coyote country." Ravilious tried to keep the tremor out of his voice.

Coyote the Trickster. That's what the natives claimed. Always on the prowl, slipping from one disguise to another. Today, smashing and disrupting everything a man tried to do. Tomorrow, changing the rules, changing his disguise yet again.

But on this night, infuriatingly, he was Coyote the Dreaded Destroyer.

If Ravilious was sure of anything, it was that Coyote was working against them. But that stupid Ouisel! He really was a bit thick, the fat dufuss. He just didn't get it. Ravilious wanted to press his point, trying to make this bean-brain understand.

"Honoré, where do you think these Indian legends come from? They don't just make these things up, these old stories," Ravilious whined. Now he was sure he was bugging Ouisel, but he couldn't make himself shut up. "That Netherby boy today, that was a sign. I tell you, that was solid proof. We're jinxed."

"Are you talking about that little cry-baby from the train?"

"Did you see him fall? I did. I saw him. We may have killed him, Honoré."

"Snyder, my dear man. Kids fall down and take tumbles all the time."

"How did he ever find our campsite, anyway? It makes me nervous, really nervous, wondering about all that."

"Well quit worrying. You're driving me the tiniest bit cuckoo."

"You're not from this country, so you don't know these legends. That kid was the start of our bad luck. Don't you get it?"

"No. I don't believe any of it."

"He could be dead, lying down there, the stupid trouble-maker. We could be murderers."

"So he's dead. How on earth would anyone tie his death to us?"

"I don't know. There is too much weird coincidence here. Somehow the kid finds us. And we find nothing. It's some old Indian curse, I'm telling you. It's got to be a curse."

Ouisel finally flared up, turning on him, hissing softly. "That's enough! Button your lip! You're going to send me to the dumps, and believe me, you do not want to see Honoré in the dumps!"

"You mean *down* in the dumps."

"Wherever, it's not a pretty sight." Ouisel dropped his cigarette, ground it into the dirt, and ducked into the tent.

Ravilious squeezed his two hands against his mouth. Good grief, that Netherby kid. He may be dead, who knows?

And for himself, no treasure. An entire day wasted. Some evil force was at work here.

The Destroyer. The Trickster.

Ravilious dove into his sleeping bag and buried his head inside, desperate to hide from – to hide from whatever.


Up on the mesa, not far away, Coyote tips his head back and lets loose a long howl of triumph. Hahaaa! The Trickster has reeled in another believer!

Coyote's entire family hears the news and rolls on the ground, laughing, yipping with glee. Another poor sucker!

And tomorrow? What merry pranks shall we have for tomorrow?

TRICKSTER, TRANSFORMER


Wednesday


If Ravilious and Ouisel had been awake at dawn on Wednesday, and had been spying on the Ranch of the Ten Elders as they had planned to do, they would have seen Hugh and Jack leaving with Dick before it was fully light outside. But the two men in the tent had been out until the wee hours, night-hawking. They had crawled, exhausted, into their sleeping bags and were still snoring away at dawn. By the time they awakened, everyone at the ranch, except for Robert and Mrs. Snow, was long gone.

Dawn was slow in coming. The sky was dark and threatened snow when Dick set off with Hugh and Jack. He showed them the path to the small field house that Robert had found, then left them and turned in the opposite direction so he could meet his mother at the stable. They were going to drive into town to do some grocery shopping for tomorrow's Thanksgiving feast.

Walking along, Dick heard a faint sound. Like snoring, men snoring. That is how he found the tent in a hidden spot just below the rim of the canyon.

Dick called a hello. A mule looked up from her empty feed bag. He called again.

Surprised to have been discovered a second time, the two men staggered out of their tent. They weren't fully dressed. They looked sleepy and perplexed this morning, but then, saggy underwear and haystack hair will tend to take the luster off any man's style. Ravilious went cold with fear. That kid yesterday – maybe he hadn't been killed. Maybe he ratted on them.

"Good morning," Dick said politely. His eyes flicked around the site and over their persons. He had encountered trespassers before and was wary. Sometimes these thieves carried weapons, though not usually in their underclothes. He did see picks and shovels lying on the ground. Yes, and a rifle leaned against a wooden crate. It was obvious what these men were doing.

"You men are aware, aren't you, that you are not allowed to camp or dig in the park? If you've found any artifacts, you must turn them in to the sheriff. You will also have to pack up and leave immediately."

The tall man did the talking. He seemed nervous. "Oh, we're not digging." His eyes slid over to the digging tools and quickly flicked away. "We're just enjoying nature. Not hurting anyone – er, anything, I assure you."

"Still, it's against the law to be here."

"You're here. Why is that all right? Are you in law enforcement?"

"I live at the ranch. If you don't move out immediately, I will have to call an officer of the law."

"Come on. What cop is going to be bothered coming all the way out here, when no crime has been committed?"

"If you wait around to find out, you'll end up spending the night in jail."

"Yeah, we'll take that risk," snapped the tall man. "Why don't you just go on about your business?"

Dick narrowed his eyes. He'd better leave any confrontation to the authorities. There was the threat of that rifle over there. "Okay. Don't say I didn't warn you."

As soon as he arrived at the stable to meet his mother, Dick used the phone there to call the sheriff. He told Sheriff Alvarez exactly where to find the tent.

The sheriff had ties to the pueblo community. His maternal grandmother was a Puebloan, so he felt strongly about grave-robbing. He wasn't about to let those characters get away with it. Granted, he was thirty miles away, but he could drive as fast as he wanted, right? He was the sheriff. Nobody would dare write him a speeding ticket.

Unfortunately, by the time he hiked to the spot, Ravilious and Ouisel had moved their campsite and he never found it.

Ouisel had insisted on moving. They could not afford to get caught.

Ravilious started to complain that moving the tent was a waste of time. Then he thought of that Netherby kid. He hiked down the trail for a good distance but found no sign of him. Did this mean the kid had squealed on them? Okay, maybe they should move the tent.

When he got back to the camp, Ouisel had already begun packing up. This guy is really getting to be a pain, thought Ravilious. He's taken charge once too often. The little weasel is turning out to be too clever by half. I'll have to keep a really close eye on him from now on.

Even earlier the same morning, back at the ranch, Corax was up and eager.

GET UP! THE GIRLS ARE GETTING UP! THE LEASH, THE LEASH! OUT WE GO!

TURKEYS TURKEYS TURKEYS.
WHERE DID THEY GO?
WHAT GOOD FUN!
THIS IS GOING TO BE SUCH A WONDERFUL DAY!


WAIT--ING. NOW WE'RE WAITING. TALK TALK TALK.
BLAH BLAH BLAH CORAX BLAH BLAH BLAH STAY.
WHAT? HERE? NEXT TO THE BOY'S BED?
CONFUSION. PANIC!
A PAT ON THE HEAD. THEN HIS GIRL WALKS OUT.
WITHOUT HER DOG.
HERE WE GO AGAIN. (BIG SIGH.) ABANDONED!
HEAD ON PAWS. HEART SAD. HURTS VERY MUCH.
NOT ALONE. AT LEAST THERE'S THAT. THE BOY IS HERE, ASLEEP ON THE BED.
WAIT A MINUTE. BED?
GOOD IDEA!
AAH, NOW THIS IS BETTER.


It was later that morning when Robert awoke, feeling as though he had to fish his brain out of a sea of mud. He couldn't bear to open his eyes. He wished he could just erase the day, the whole week. Hot tears slid down his temples. He used the sheet to wipe them. The dog stirred next to him. He felt his hot breath against his ear. Corax, the only person who liked him.

Mrs. Snow came in to help him get up.

"What's this animal doing on the bed again?" she demanded.

Corax slunk to the floor. ANIMAL? WHAT IS THAT SUPPOSED TO MEAN?

She helped Robert with his pajama shirt and robe. He was still weak, and he had to lean on her arm as they made their way down the path to the lodge. Last night Jemmy had slept on the couch so Robert could have her bed. He had had a restless night and kept waking in a panic. Mrs. Snow had to get up four or five times to attend him. Now she and he minced down the path, Robert a little unsteady, Corax trailing behind with his head, tail, and spirits all drooping, pouting over Mrs. Snow's scolding.

Today Dr. Tomillo was coming to look at Robert's arm. It would have taken two and a half hours out of the doctor's day if he had to make the trip both ways by mule. But Michael Redbird had long ago declared that there were two outsiders worthy of the honor of using the cable car to get down to the ranch. The doctor was one of those people. The sheriff was the other. You could hardly expect people with such important jobs to spend hours on the back of a mule. So Dr. Tomillo arrived before mid-morning.

Robert had already wolfed down two waffles and a gaggle of sausages, but he had to put his toast and jelly aside on a table in the living room so he could be examined.

"You did a good job with this splint," Dr. Tomillo told Mrs. Snow. "The arm is definitely broken, but this helped keep the bones in place." He held Robert's bare arm and bent to peer through his bifocals. "I am going to have to check the fracture, though, Robert. It might hurt a bit."

He probed. Robert writhed.

"Hang on. Just a minute more. I'm almost done. I think that does it. Good."

Robert was white and panting. He lay back on the sofa, exhausted. He could barely muster the energy to speak.

The doctor checked the pulse in his wrist, then in his neck. "You were very lucky. No broken ribs, as far as I can tell, but some nasty fractures. We'll keep you bound up. On the arm, I found only one closed fracture. If Mrs. Snow hadn't immobilized it, it could have been much worse. Let's put a cast on it so that bone doesn't move. I'll give you a sling. Be sure to have someone look at the arm as soon as you get home."

After the doctor said good-bye, Mrs. Snow bent over Robert.

"I have to get the pie crusts made for the holiday tomorrow," she said. "Will you be all right on your own for a while?"

Robert nodded weakly. Corax came to sit beside the couch. He rested his head on Robert's shoulder.

"Where did the girls go?" Robert mumbled, as Mrs. Snow headed for the door.

"Jemima took them for a long hike." She didn't mention their destination.

"They didn't take the dog?"

"They thought you'd like some company."

Robert frowned, unable to process what she was saying.

"They felt badly that you had to stay behind. I'll be in the kitchen if you need me."

Robert stroked the dog's head. I'm very lucky to be here with you today, Robert's eyes told Corax. I could have been eaten by a lion. Are you glad that didn't happen? You would miss me, wouldn't you, buddy? Wouldn't you?

Corax swept the floor with his tail. GOOD DOG?

The two of them weren't on quite the same wavelength, but they communicated the essentials.

There was a beautiful blanket, woven by a Hopi woman, on the back of the sofa. Robert pulled it over himself and fell instantly asleep.

Corax sat up. He looked around. They were alone.

Was ever a dog born who felt the slightest qualm about giving in to temptation? That plate of toast just at eye level – gone, every crumb. Jelly – gone in a lick. He looked at the boy sleeping on the couch, looked at the blanket.

SHHH. NOW IF I COULD JUST SQUIMMEL MYSELF IN BETWEEN HIM AND THE BACK OF THE SOFA ....

AHH. THIS IS BETTER. (SIGH.) ALL HUMANS SHOULD NAP AT LEAST ONCE A DAY.

Corax leapt off the couch. He woke Robert with his barking. The sound of horses out front, then heavy footsteps on the porch.

The dog ran to the door, crying to be let out. Robert dragged himself off the couch and crept to the window. He peered from behind the curtain. Oh no! He was afraid this would happen. Those cattlemen! They had come for him!

Someone pounded on the door. Robert backed away, his heart hammering. He did not want to answer it. What if they were mean? What if they .... He didn't have time to think. More pounding. A man's face, peering in the window right beside him. He backed against the wall so he wouldn't be seen.

Mrs. Snow was the only person here besides Robert. He was scared. If she came out, he'd have to explain about the cattle yesterday. He hated the thought of doing that. He didn't want her to know. How could he get rid of these guys? He spotted the old rifle that hung above the fireplace. He pulled an ottoman over, and climbed up to get it.

He took his hurt arm from the sling and went to the door. He waited. Maybe they'd go away.

"I know you're in there! Open up!"

Robert opened the door and Corax shot out onto the porch. WHOA! BOOTS! MEN IN BOOTS – TROUBLE! The dog ran back to Robert, half wanting to hide behind him, half aware that he had a duty to fulfill as Guard Dog.

Robert raised the rifle as high as he could. It was much heavier than he expected, especially because his broken arm was weak and shaky.

"Hey! Watch where you point that." Two men backed off the porch. One was the cowhand Robert had seen yesterday. The other was a large fleshy man. His stomach strained his buttonholes and sagged over his belt. He was the better dressed of the two, wearing a fringed leather jacket and decorated cowboy boots.

"This is the kid?" he asked his companion.

"That's the one, Boss," said the cowhand.

"Get out of here or I'll shoot," said Robert in a trembling

voice. He stepped barefoot onto the porch. Yesterday, he had been the one at gunpoint. Today, he had the gun. Which, surprisingly, did not provide him with the bravado to go with it. He tried sighting down the rifle like the guys in the movies. In the back of his mind, he noticed the sound of a motor. A thought flashed through his mind and then was forgotten: a motor? But there were no cars down here.

The large man held out his hands and spoke in reasonable tones. "Calm down, kid. I came to get what you owe me. That's all I want. No trouble. Just payment for my two animals. You can't expect me to forfeit my profit just because – "

"I don't have to pay anything. You weren't supposed to be there."

"Listen, you little twerp. Everything would have been fine if you hadn't made a mess of things. Now somebody has got to pay."

"I said get out or I shoot."

The rancher leaned down and made inviting clucking sounds to the dog. Corax crouched, fearful. The man grabbed him around the belly and scooped him swiftly into his arms. One hand held tight to the skin on the dog's neck. Corax writhed helplessly, trying to get away.

"You put him down!"

"I will when you put the gun down."

"No!" His arm was really shaking now.

The rancher held the dog under his elbow, drew a pistol, and held it up for Robert to see. "You see we have a stand-off, don't you?" he sneered. "You get what I'm saying? If you shoot me, you go to jail. I shoot your mutt, I go free as a bird. You see who's got the advantage here? Now put the gun down and get me my money, kid."

"You put the dog – "

The rancher fired. An incredibly loud blast! Robert jumped in horror and nearly dropped the rifle. Corax, unhurt, struggled to get out of the man's grasp.

"My money," said the rancher, raising an eyebrow. "Or your mutt. Your choice. But I'll aim this time."

Mrs. Snow came running from the kitchen. "You!" She glared at the rancher. "What are you doing here? And what are you doing with that dog?" she demanded. Robert's eyes bugged at her fierce tone.

"Well looky looky. If it isn't Blossom Snow, the pueblo princess." The rancher laughed evilly.

"Spare me the snide remarks, Clement. Just put that dog down and get out of here, will you please?"

"Now you ask that right prettily, Blossom. But I don't ...."

Behind the ranchers, a third man spoke up. He had just stepped off the cable car.

"Did you hear what the lady said? Put the dog down, Mr. Clement." He spoke softly. "And holster your gun."

The rancher turned.

"I said to put him down." Sheriff Alvarez stood behind them, aiming his Colt six-shooter.

The rancher, without bending, opened his arm and dropped Corax to the ground, unconcerned when the dog yelped in pain. Robert knelt and comforted him.

"And holster your gun."

The rancher did so.

"Now, dadgummit! What is all this fuss about?" whined the sheriff in disgust. He lowered his gun. "I don't much like walking in on a passel of trouble before the day's hardly got started."

"I got good reason to make trouble, Jim. This kid started a stampede yesterday. My men had to shoot five head of cattle."

"Two!" Robert bleated. "You shot two!" He could feel his neck crawl under the look of surprise that Mrs. Snow turned on him.

"This happened on the open range, did it?" asked the sheriff.

"They were on park land!" Robert insisted. He hated that he

sounded like some little eight-year-old with his raspy sore-throat voice. "Mike – Mike Redbird said so. Near that place – the Alcove House. They weren't supposed to be there." Robert suddenly realized that, not only must he sound crazed, but he must also look utterly ridiculous standing there barefoot and in his pajamas. Mrs. Snow was staring at him like he was a criminal. His stomach was suddenly too full of breakfast. Perspiration started gathering along his hairline and he leaned against the door frame for support.

"Well now," began the rancher, "truth be told, them cattle were there by accident. My men didn't know – "

"Bull puckey. You know very well you aren't supposed to be up here," said the sheriff.

"All anybody had to do was ask my men to leave and they woulda been gone. I still want my cattle paid for."

"It's not going to happen, Clement. You'd feel the same if someone were trespassing on your land. Now get on outa here and –"

"Listen, Jim –"

"No, you listen. If this happens again, I'll have to charge you."

The rancher turned his hot glare on Robert and stuck his thumbs in his belt. But when he raised his eyes to Mrs. Snow, his face contorted. Robert could tell they knew each other somehow.

"I find this kinda strange, don't you, Sheriff?" said the rancher. "Pretty strange that you don't mind having a filthy Indian on the property, but a decent white man gets run off." He pointed. "Yer just lucky the sheriff came along when he did, *lady* -- I think that's what he called you, though I never done, in all these years." He locked eyes with Mrs. Snow and in smoldering silence, she stared right through him.

"That's just about enough outa you, Clement," the sheriff warned quietly.

"You're defending that –"

"E-nough!" Sheriff Alvarez roared so furiously that Robert

jumped again.

The rancher shrugged. He pointed a finger like a loaded gun. "You and I both know exactly why he is favoring you, don't we, Blossom?"

She spoke without obvious rancor. "Yes, we do. And we both know what a blow that was to your pride, way back when." Her eyes bored holes in his. "Apparently the wound hasn't healed even now."

Robert looked from one to the other.

Aiming carefully, the rancher landed a gob of spittle near Mrs. Snow's feet. "That was a long time ago. And I've come up in the world a good deal since then. Not sure you can say the same. Come on, John. Let's get on outa this hole."

And off they rode.


The sheriff holstered his gun.

Mrs. Snow sighed and rolled her eyes. She put a hand on the sheriff's arm. "Thank you, Jim! And not for the first time."

"My pleasure, Blossom. Any day." Sheriff Jaime Alvarez beamed in delight, stepped closer, and tipped his hat. "I'm very sorry you were treated like that."

Now what, Robert wondered, brought on this guy's gooey smile?

"How did you know those men were here?" Mrs. Snow asked.

"I didn't. I was just coming down here in hopes that I'd see you today." He threw a quick glance at Robert, wishing the kid would get lost.

"Oh? Well come in, now that you're here."

"Okay. Thank you." That smile of his – a pimply tuba player in a high school marching band would smile at a blonde cheerleader in just the same way. And with about as much effect. Blossom Snow breezed into the house and never seemed to notice.

The sheriff took off his hat and floated after her. He frowned at Robert, who, he saw, immediately pretended to take a great interest in that dog of his. The kid was afraid to look him in the eye. Good, he thought. Maybe I can get him to disappear. Might have to put some fear and trembling into him.

Sheriff Alvarez tugged at his waistband, frowned down at Robert, and crossed his arms over his barrel chest. "You, boy!" he growled. "What do you think you're doing?"

"N-nothing."

"Stand up here. Good grief, gimme that weapon. Come on! Snap snap!"

Robert handed over the rifle. Oh man. Really in trouble now.

"Visitors to *my* county are supposed to surrender their firearms. Where's your license to use this?"

Robert sagged visibly. Why me? he asked himself. Why am I'm always the one who gets in trouble? Again, he felt the indignity of standing there in his pajamas. "I – license?"

"Jim, don't give him a hard time. Look at the carving on the stock of that rifle. There's not another like it. You know perfectly well it's Mrs. Frey's."

The sheriff put out a hand. "Blossom, just let me do my work. Answer me, boy. Do you have a license to use this?"

"Uh – no." Did a person go to jail for this?

"Did you fire this weapon?"

"N-no!"

The sheriff pulled the bolt. "Then how come there is a spent shell in the magazine?"

Magazine? Robert shrugged and shook his head.

"You pointed a gun at someone, without knowing anything about firearms, didn't you?"

"There's the, uh – trigger."

"You think," he shook the rifle in Robert's face, "this is a toy?"

Robert's arm, his whole body, was firing big darts of pain. He couldn't even think of an answer.

"Handling this weapon when you don't know what you're doing was wrong in every way."

Robert's legs gave out. He dropped into a chair and put his head on his hand. He was so tired of being hammered on by everybody. He used to be able to bully his way through any situation. He ran his hand through his hair. He must be losing his touch. Where were the smart-mouthed remarks he always used to have at the ready?

The sheriff snorted, figuring now the brat would get out of his way. He looked smugly at Blossom. "Maybe he should go to his room and think about what he's done."

Mrs. Snow patted Robert's back. "Don't fret, Robert. He's just giving you a hard time. Come on. Put your robe on and we'll all have a cup of tea. Come into the kitchen with us, Jim."

She prodded Robert from his chair. He just wanted to hide somewhere but she kept her hand on the back of his neck and guided him to a chair at the kitchen table. She filled a teapot with hot water from the stove. "You didn't tell me why you're really here, Jim."

"Dick Frey called early this morning and asked me to check out a couple of guys. He suspects they're doing some looting here. He told me where they were camping, but they were gone when I got here. So I just thought to myself, well, what I'll do is, I'll go on down and see how Blossom's getting along." He smiled, rosy-faced, and took the mug of tea she offered.

Robert looked up eagerly. "Those men? I saw them, too."

The sheriff ignored him completely. "Actually, though, I was banking on the off-chance that I – and you, Blossom – maybe the two of us could take a little walk or something?"

"You're very thoughtful, Jim."

"What I was really hoping – "

"James." Mrs. Snow spoke sharply. "Please don't embarrass

me in front of the boy."

Robert started to get up. "I could –"

"Sit down, Robert." Mrs. Snow plunked a mug of tea in front of him, looking down her nose at him until he sat.

Jim Alvarez looked at Robert and scowled. Yes, he really wished the kid would disappear. He turned to her again, imploring in his little-boy voice, " But Blossom! I came all the way down here only to see –"

"And just in time, too. We sure are grateful for that." Blossom Snow shone a smile at him. Robert noticed, for the first time, where Jemmy's good looks came from. Mrs. Snow had to be, what? Close to forty? For such an old lady, she was very beautiful.

The sheriff didn't give up. "Blossom, I just saved your skin from Sam Clement this morning. Don't I get special thanks?"

"You sure do. Have a cookie." She passed him a plateful. "And we do thank you, don't we, Robert?"

Robert had been sitting with his head hanging. He looked up and nodded. He took three cookies from the plate and devoured them. He couldn't decide whether he felt sick or hungry.

The sheriff rose. "All right." Stalling, he pushed in his chair. Cleared his throat. Fingered his hat brim. Hemmed. Hawed. "You won't forget that I did you this favor?"

"How can you ask me that question, James? Did you ever know me to forget anything?"

"Oh, come on! You're not bringing that up again? I wish you would just forget that, Blossom."

"I know you do."

"All right." Deflated, the sheriff shuffled toward the door. "I'll go on back to town then." Robert knew that tone – trying for some pity, one of his own techniques. "Michael told me I could use the cable car. At least he appreciates me."

"You're a good sheriff, Jim. We all appreciate you. Will you visit the pueblo to see your grandmother this holiday?"

"Yep." He twirled his hat. "Sure I will."

"Say hello for me."

"Sure, sure. Will do." Still he lingered.

"Shall I see you to the front door?"

Jim tipped his head from side to side. "Okay, then," he sighed.

"Wait right here for me, Robert." Mrs. Snow beckoned and Sheriff Alvarez followed like a puppy on her heels, silently cursing the boy at the table.

Robert cowered in his chair. He felt so miserable. His whole life was in the trash can. He'd had a lot of bad stuff happen, but never this much all at once. Ever since the end of the summer, when his mother had gotten married, trouble at home, trouble at the new school. Now this stupid, stupid New Mexico trip, which was not his idea.

He'd been like a fly trapped in a jar for months now. A fly, buzzing frantically and unable to get free.

He was slumped over the table when Mrs. Snow returned. She put one hand on her hip and the other on the back of his chair. "It sounds like you got yourself into a big heap of trouble yesterday."

It was a long moment before he answered. "You think I'm awful, don't you?"

"Well, I'll tell you." She put her fingers to her chin. "Whenever folks feel like you do right now, my people tell a story about a tree growing on the mesa. Up there, year by year, a tree gets bent by the wind. Twisted, all crooked. Fighting every day to hold its place."

Robert lowered his head, blinking rapidly. So he was that bad? Crooked and twisted?

"Here's the thing, Robert. Anyone might think that tree is worthless. What is it good for? Nobody's ever going to get a single board out of that tree. Everybody likes the straight tree. Ah, but it's the straight tree that gets cut down young and ends up as boards. The crooked tree will be untouched, allowed to live a long and beautiful life."

His back was hunched like a beetle's. He stared at the tablecloth, so confused.

"Yes, you've got a few twists in your nature. You're full up with bad feelings, aren't you? But, like that twisted tree, you've still got a good long life ahead of you. What you've got to do right now is learn some rules."

"I just –! I don't know how! Every – ohh!" he blurted, propping his forehead on his good fist. "Everything's such a mess!"

Mrs. Snow lifted her eyes and studied the thin air for a minute, chasing a thought. "You know," she finally said, "in my clan, when a kid misbehaves, he's expected to make up for it. We give him a task to do, some kind of work to benefit the whole tribe. When he gets that finished, no matter what sort of stupid wrong thing he's done, everyone in the community tells him how grateful they are. And that makes the kid feel better. That's the way we get rid of bad feelings in our pueblo."

Robert looked up at her with a hang-dog face. "So, what are you saying?"

"What do you think I'm saying?"

"You mean – me? Doing some work?"

"Exactly." She waited, then shrugged. "That's what I'd suggest."

Robert brushed his hands over his eyes. "Like what kind of work?"

"Like helping me with the baking for tomorrow."

"Baking! When?"

"What do you mean, when? It's for tomorrow."

"So, right now?"

"Yes, right now."

"But my arm!"

"If you can hold a rifle, you can get a pie ready for the oven."

"I don't know how to bake!"

Mrs. Snow chuckled. "When I get through with you, you can be darn sure you'll know a thing or two about baking. Come on. Help me make lunch. Then, we'll bake."

And in that moment, Robert felt the heaviness crack. Hanging out in the kitchen? Would that be so bad? He could think of plenty of worse things.

Robert suddenly knew what Tom Sawyer felt like, the day he got all his friends to whitewash the fence. Something shifted inside him, like a rock loosening in a canyon wall. He felt ... he felt as clever as clever, he did. Though where that phrase came from, he could not remember.


The night before, when things had calmed down after Robert's return, Jemmy Snow had said to them, "Girls, I'm hiking up to the Stone Lions tomorrow. I've taken a couple of people there in the past, and it meant a lot to them. I'd like to take you two, if you want to go."

"I'd like to," Hattie had answered right away.

Anya nodded. "Me too." Two of us, she wondered? Not Robert? He'll be so mad.

"But Mr. Redbird doesn't like outsiders to go there. Won't he be angry?" Hattie asked.

"Mr. Redbird can just stuff it," said Jemmy, smiling. "And I told him so already. I could have lied and said we were going somewhere else, but I kind of enjoy riling him up a bit." She laughed. "I should warn you, though. This will be a pretty long hike."

"That's fine with me," said Hattie.

Anya worried. She might not be able to keep up. She'd done some strenuous hiking last summer, though, hadn't she? Not for pleasure, but she had covered a lot of miles.

"I'll do the best I can," she said.

"I always leave before dawn, at first light."

The girls nodded.

"I can knock on your door to wake you up."

"Sure."

"One more thing. I fast the morning that I go there. No breakfast. It's kind of a ritual, you know? I do pack a good lunch, though. Will that be okay for you?"

"Sure."

"I'll see you tomorrow, then. Good night, girls."

"'Night, Jemmy."


In the dark of Wednesday morning, Anya took the dog out for a walk. Then, thinking of Robert being left behind, she let the dog into the room where he slept, patted Corax once on the head, and closed the door.

Outside, she found a world heavy with silence. Jemmy was waiting for them at the bridge. They could hardly find her in the dark. She carried a backpack that Anya hoped was filled with good food. She also hoped there was a lot of it. She was hungry already.

Jemmy led them across the bridge and down to the bank of the river on that side.

"I have a couple of things I like to do, little rituals to prepare me for visiting a sacred shrine."

"I wouldn't think you'd care about rituals, Jemmy," said Hattie.

Jemmy smiled. "I'm actually fine with rituals, a person's own private rituals. It's rules I seem to have trouble with. Do you want me to show you what I do?"

The girls nodded. Jemmy could start yodeling; she could mambo like a crazed one-legged turkey – it would all be fine with them. They would follow her anywhere.

"This might seem a little odd to you," Jemmy said. "It's

something my grandmother taught me. It was her morning ritual. First, I hold my hand in the river. Like this." They crouched and let the water run through their fingers. The river was clear and icy cold.

"She said the river is like Time. Flowing away from our fingers is the last of what has just passed. Flowing toward us is the first of what is to come. Right where our hands touch the flow, that is the present moment. Our past and our future will always flow on around us, a river of Time, but we are not swept away by either. We stand only in the present moment. And for this moment, I am grateful."

Jemmy looked at the girls' expectant faces. She paused. "I just like to remind myself of all that before I go."

Jemmy stood. "Now, there is another thing I'd ask, and I hope you don't mind. I'd rather we didn't talk on the way. I just like to be quiet, you know? The paths we'll be following are haunted by old ghosts, and we're visiting a sacred place. My grandma always taught me to listen, to find out what this place knows of me that I don't know about myself."

The girls looked at her, trying to understand. "Okay, Jemmy."

"And the last thing I like to do is find a pretty stone to leave at the shrine."

"I like that idea," Hattie said immediately. They bent over and searched along the riverbank, selecting and discarding stones as well as they could in the dim light, until they each found one that seemed right.

"Look at this one," said Anya. She held up a smooth black stone, shiny and glassy and chipped into a roughly rectangular shape. It had a hole in it.

Jemmy exclaimed and held out her hand. "You know what this is? It's an obsidian pendant. It may once have been part of a necklace."

"Obsidian?"

"The Old Ones used this stone for arrowheads and to make cutting implements. They made obsidian knives that were actually much sharper than any surgical steel today."

"Not really!"

"I'm not kidding you. That's the truth! But this piece looks like an ornament. Anya, you're so lucky to have found this. You realize it has to stay here, though, don't you?"

She wished she could keep it. "Can I leave it at the shrine?"

"That would be a beautiful gesture." Jemmy smiled. "This is a favorable omen. It will be a good day. Shall we get started?"


They set their feet on the path, the day not looking all that promising, not to Anya.

Maybe it's the quiet. It weighs, it presses. Their world is hushed, wrapped in grey velvet. Grey river and rocks, grey sky. An empty world, seemingly. The wind, silent. Maybe snow is coming. Anya tightens her scarf. Single file, Jemmy, then Hattie, Anya last. Their quick boots crunch on the stones. Anya panting, trying to keep up.

A shattering burst of birdsong, as though someone has just opened a music box. A canyon wren's descending cascade of notes splits the heavy air like an obsidian knife. And here, the delightful little singer himself, speckled and long-billed, flittering nervously on a rocky outcrop.

A short walk on flat land before descending into another canyon. Down here, a spectacular stretch of white *tufa* walls; black obsidian stones glitter in the nearly-dry stream bed at the bottom. Pines moan when the dark wind comes up, and the rising light of morning is barely perceptible. In the half-light, it almost feels to Hattie that they are being watched. A figure catches her eye. She looks again. No. Only some trick of the eye, putting shapes together that don't belong to each other.

A difficult climb out of the canyon, hats and scarves off and jackets open, rewarded at the top with a view of the mountains.

Here and there a small cave house hidden in an alcove in the rocks, some of the walls painted with fantastical figures. Then another canyon, and another, the land here being riven with deep fissures. It begins to feel strange, so many signs of human habitation, but every one deserted. In one canyon, seemingly devoid of life, the steep rock walls are banded in pink and white, deposits from separate volcanic eruptions that happened more than a million years ago. Hattie turns more than once, thinking she sees something out of the corner of her eye. Old ghosts? No, again nothing. Only a few swallows swooping and diving at them, taking offense at trespassers.

Hattie and Jemmy climb over the canyon rim and Jemmy breaks the silence to point out the Cochiti Pueblo, her birthplace, far in the distance. Anya, red-faced and sweating and the last to clamber out of the canyon, finally joins them. They drink some water; Jemmy presses on, and they follow.

Suddenly, for no reason she can fathom, Hattie's eyes are drawn upwards. She does see someone. This time, she is sure. She stares. Of course there could be other hikers out here. Why should she have to convince herself of that? It's odd though, how he just stands and stares. She turns to Anya and gestures at the figure standing on the opposite side of the canyon, watching them. Anya, mystified, nods, thinking that Hattie is only warning her that here is yet another deep canyon to traverse.

Hattie turns back. But the other hiker has moved on. When they finally reach the opposite side, they stop again for a silent drink. Hattie searches the long flat terrain. That person she saw a half hour ago, how could he have disappeared? She looks in every direction. He is gone, the entire flat landscape empty. She must have imagined him, conjuring the shape of a man in all the emptiness, only because her eye is so used to seeing that shape.

Still so quiet. They stand for a minute to catch their breath. Almost complete silence. Only a pedal tone of wind thrumming the pines that cling to the canyon walls below. It lifts a raven, like a black rag, aloft into the heavy sky, and she wheels and dips, spying on the interlopers. They watch the bird for a minute, then Jemmy turns to go on. The walking is easy now.

When Hattie stops abruptly, Anya almost runs into her. Hattie squints into the distance at a dim shape. The same person again, a man, watching, seeming to wait for them. She turns to point him out to Anya. We'll surely meet up with him soon, Hattie thinks, but when she turns back, again there is no one there.

This is disturbing, thinks Hattie, now a little spooked. Where did that guy go? Is he sitting down somewhere? Is he hiding in some dip in the landscape? She walks more slowly, wary, her eyes scanning the horizon.

Jemmy leads them across the empty mesa, her pointing finger reminding them to avoid the sharp spines of cactus. A lonely terrain, fairly level, with shallow dips here and there. They stop at the bottom of one low area and Jemmy points to some rocks arranged against the slope. They surround a hole that forms a low doorway.

"A pit house. Long, long ago the Old Ones lived in these," Jemmy tells them briefly.

They bend to peer into the dark opening. It is eerily strange to think of living in a hole, and Hattie and Anya pull back, feeling powerful reluctance, for some strange reason, to go closer. Even Jemmy keeps her distance. Now Hattie feels even more deeply a sense of dread. She turns quickly to look over her shoulder. No, no one there.

Finally ahead, the low circle of stones that marks the shrine of the Stone Lions and the entrance to the Underworld of the Old Ones.

And he is there. The man is standing just beyond, waiting.

He nods once. He raises a hand. Hattie knows him now, of course. She starts to wave back, wanting desperately to run to him. She hesitates. Not believing. This can not be possible. She must be hallucinating.

She stares hard. Is she seeing what she wants to see? Or is she seeing what's there?

She is unable to take a step forward. Her breath catches in her throat. She turns with furrowed brow, gripping Anya's arm, wanting her confirmation. But when she looks back, again he is not there.

Gone. Nowhere.

Shocked to her core, she hunches, shivering, clinging to Anya. "What is it?"

Hattie cannot answer. Still holding Anya close, she follows with child-like steps as they thread their way carefully through the cacti toward the stone circle.

Several stones have fallen from the rough rock ring of the shrine. Inside the circle, the mountain lion sculptures face east-southeast. They are life-size, so very old that erosion has rendered their shapes almost unrecognizable. The ground around them is littered with hundreds of decorated pottery fragments, with obsidian, with mineralized stones of every color. Anya and Hattie approach cautiously, Hattie looking, searching everywhere. They leave their stones on the wall, and back away, waiting outside the ring while Jemmy, without entering the shrine, goes to kneel at the entrance.

Hattie and Anya keep their distance. Standing with bowed heads and linked arms, Anya notices something on her coat sleeve. Wet spots, tear drops, Hattie's tears. She puts her hand over Hattie's where it rests on her arm, and Hattie grips it firmly and shakes her head a little. Anya knows what she is thinking about, and her heart hurts for her. Then Hattie wipes her cheeks and raises her face to the sky for a long moment.

Now she realizes that she has been blessed. She has touched the past.

Finally, she turns to smile down at Anya with such a clear gaze that Anya smiles back with immense relief.

They are still standing, leaning silently on each other, when they feel a stir in the air, a freshness. The wind has changed. A soft breeze pirouettes down from the mountains. Long barges of grey cloud are sailing away, leaving a wide blue ocean of sky. The Sun comes out and they feel her warmth immediately. Jemmy, kneeling beside the stone ring, feels it too. They turn their faces and the Sun's warm hand, like a benediction, rests on each of their heads.

Still silent, they turn to go back, Hattie like a sleep-walker at first. Finally she stops, face to the Sun, breathing deeply. Then she strides more swiftly and begins to run. Arms out, laughing, she looks back at the other two.

Anya speaks softly to Jemmy. "Hattie was acting so strange back there. She kept pointing to things where, I swear, there was nothing."

Jemmy raises her eyebrows. "Really?" She nods and smiles. "Good, good."

"Good? I was worried. You wouldn't call it strange?"

"Well, I don't know what to call it," Jemmy shrugs, "but our old people would say it's the mystery."

"Oh." Anya turns away, shaking her head. "People always say that when they don't have an explanation."

"Do we need an answer for everything, though? Maybe we will never be able to touch the mystery. Maybe we're meant to let it be."

Turning that thought over, Anya stares up into Jemmy's eyes. Then Jemmy takes her hand. "Come on!", and they have to run hard to catch up with Hattie.

When they come to a broad flat rock, Jemmy declares it's time for lunch. She sets out a box of enchiladas filled with beans and sweet potatoes and pickled jalapenos, and another of fajitos stuffed with red peppers, melted cheese, and broiled mushroom caps chopped with basil. She pours rich dark hot chocolate from a thermos. They sip their steaming mugs quietly, the Sun still smiling warm on their faces.


The sun was half-hidden by the rim of the world when they climbed out to flat ground again. One more canyon to go after this. Hot with the effort of the climb, they were grateful for the cooler air. Suddenly Jemmy Snow put out a hand to stop them. She put her finger to her lips and listened. They heard it too, some distance away. Chopping sounds?

They hurried down the trail until they came to the rim of the last canyon. They peered over the edge but could see nothing. Quietly, they began to descend. Jemmy pulled them down behind some boulders. They could hear easily now, the sounds of digging. Stealthy, they moved to see better.

Two men, digging near one of the small cave houses they had seen. A mule, panniers strapped to her sides, waited nearby, shifting from foot to foot.

"What?" hissed Hattie.

Jemmy shushed her. "Treasure hunters," she whispered back.

"They aren't digging for –"

"Yes. They are stealing from graves! Erasing the footprints of my people!"

If she hadn't just come from visiting a sacred place, if she had not seen what she saw there, Hattie might not have responded so angrily. But with a lunge forward, she croaked, "I'm going down there!"

"No!" Jemmy grabbed her arm hard, pulling her back.

"It's not right, Jemmy! How can we let them do that?" This

afternoon, while they stood at the doorway to the Underworld of the Old Ones, Hattie had been given one precious glimpse into Time's vault. After that, witnessing this destruction seemed especially horrible. It made her sick.

Jemmy put her finger to her lips. "It's too late. The damage can't be undone."

"Oh yes it can!"

"No! We're helpless, don't you see? They have a rifle."

"I don't care!"

"You do not want to get shot!"

"What if this were my father's grave they were digging up?" Hattie cried, low and fierce. "I have to stop them!"

"Hattie, no! You don't mess with these people."

"Hattie?" whispered Anya. "You know who that is down there? It's those two guys! Those two from the train!"

They watched as Ravilious reached into the hole he had dug. He stood, and proudly held aloft two skulls, one larger, one very small. Hattie growled, her face crinkled in disbelief, and Jemmy silenced her again. Then Ravilious reached into the hole and brought up a small board with straps attached. A tiny pile of bones slid from the board, back into the hole.

"A cradle board!" Jemmy hissed. "It looks like a mother and her infant were –"

Hattie stood. Framed against the indigo sky, she screamed at the top of her lungs. "NOOO!"

Jemmy forced her back down but her wail ricocheted back and forth off the rock walls, and Ravilious dropped his prize.

He crouched in terror. "Did you hear that?"

Ouisel nodded and lifted his eyes to search the cliffs. He leaned on his shovel.

"I'm getting out of here!" exclaimed Ravilious.

"Don't be a fool, Snyder!"

"It was her! I know it was her!" Ravilious pointed to the grave.

"Pull yourself together, man! They're very very dead. Do you think they care what you do to them?"

With trembling hands, Ravilious laid the skulls inside a pannier. "You stay if you want. I don't like this place!" He reached again for the cradleboard.

"STOP!" screamed Hattie again, but the echoes stirred her word to an indecipherable howl that flitted from rock to rock and cliff to cliff until it faded.

"Oh good lord! Wolves!" wept Ravilious. "Get the rifle! Those are wolves!" He crouched to the ground, then began crawling, fumbling, in a panic to collect his tools.

Ouisel picked up the rifle, his eyes searching the landscape. *"Nom d'un chien!"* he swore, his voice cracking. He was disgusted but, actually, he didn't much like this either. "All right, Snyder. It's getting dark and we've got enough loot, anyway. Let's go."


As soon as the girls returned to the Ranch of the Ten Elders, Jemmy stormed into the kitchen. She was chagrined to see Robert there.

On their hike back to the ranch, Anya and Hattie had told her about Robert, about the suspicions they had about him and those two grave robbers. A couple of days ago they had seen Robert come out of the men's compartment on the train. Now he might be communicating with them. Maybe he had peeked at Jack Netherby's maps. Maybe he was somehow giving Ravilious information about where to dig. Anya had said she would put nothing past Robert. So Jemmy was wary of speaking in front of him.

When she entered the kitchen, Mrs. Snow was peeling a pile of sweet potatoes and Robert was rather clumsily, with one hand, ladling corn muffin batter into pans. Michael Redbird sat at the little kitchen table with a cup of coffee, amused to see Robert obeying a steady stream of orders from his mother.

But Jemmy, as soon as she burst in, interrupted them. "Michael, I'm so glad you're here. I need you to do something."

"And I'm pleased to see you too, Jemima. I hope you're well today."

"Oh, cut it out. I have something serious to tell you. We just got back from a hike to the –" She paused and glanced at Robert. " – to the Stone Lions."

Robert banged his mixing bowl onto the counter. "The Stone Lions?"

"I know you wanted to go, Robert, and I'm sorry. But really you're in no shape to be hiking anywhere."

"That's not fair!"

"It isn't, I know. You missed out. I'm sorry. But Michael, listen! On the way back this afternoon we caught two men digging in a grave. They took skulls, a cradle board, who knows what else."

"Those two are still here?" stormed Michael, sitting up. "Dick Frey warned them off this morning, and called Sheriff Alvarez."

"Well, they are still here. Anya said they came in on the same train you arrived on, Robert." Jemmy watched him carefully, gauging his reaction.

"Them?" cried Robert. "Yeah, I found their tent when I was lost. They threatened to shoot me and chased me away!"

"What? Are you serious?"

"They thought I was spying on them. But I was only begging for something to eat."

Odd, thought Jemmy. Roberts' reaction didn't square with what the girls had said about him.

"You didn't confront those men today, I hope, Jemmy?" Michael asked.

"They had a rifle. So no, but ..."

"But what? Did you do something stupid?" he asked her.

"No. Well, Hattie was so furious, she stood up and yelled

before I could stop her. But don't worry, they never saw her. And actually, hearing her scream scared them off. One of them was really spooked. He was sure he was hearing wolves."

"Hmm." Michael ran a finger over his chin. "Spooked."

"We've got to get rid of them, Michael. What was Sheriff Alvarez thinking? He should have arrested them."

Mrs. Snow turned from the oven. "He tried, Jemmy. They had moved out by the time he got here."

"How do you know?" asked Jemmy.

"Alvarez came down this morning." Mrs. Snow glanced at Robert. "He got here just in time, too. Sam Clement was here making trouble, mad as a hornet."

"Mother!" cried Jemmy. "Not that creepy slob? And you were here all alone? Was he bothering you again?"

"Robert defended us. He gave Clement a real hard time. And then, by good fortune, Jim Alvarez came along to help."

"Robert! How brave!" cried Jemmy.

Mrs. Snow exchanged a long look with Robert. He felt his face grow hot. She had covered up the real reason the ranchers were here. He took a quick glance at Michael, dreading to hear what he would have to say. But Michael apparently had other things on his mind.

"I am so fed up!" Michael complained. "Everybody wants a piece of this canyon. The ranchers, the United States government, vandals, looters. Nobody cares that our people were here first and should have first rights. We have ancestors buried here. Can't they respect that? Ancestors that should be given the privilege of resting in peace."

Jemmy nodded. "By next year we'll have something else to contend with, too. Tourists. This place is going to be over-run."

"In the meantime, we've got to get Jim Alvarez to arrest those grave robbers," said Mrs. Snow, "before Mrs. Frey finds out. She'd shoot them first and ask questions later."

"No, wait," said Michael thoughtfully. "You know your favorite saying, Mother – it takes cunning to defeat cunning?"

"I say a lot of things. But this is something for the sheriff to handle. Not you, Michael."

Michael stood up. "I'm going out right now to look for those grave robbers. Then, I think I'll head down to the pueblo. There are some things I may need there. I'll be back in the morning."

"Michael!" moaned his mother. "It's nearly dark. It's not smart to confront men with guns –"

"I won't confront them. Those two will never see me. I'm just going to soften them up a bit. I do a pretty convincing wolf howl."

Robert tried, with his good hand, to untie his apron. "Can I come, Mike?"

"No, definitely not."

Robert's shoulders slumped. Nobody trusted him.

"Michael," Mrs. Snow mouthed silently, her eyes flicking meaningfully to Robert's back.

"Well ...." Michael looked down at Robert for a minute, speculating. This kid, he thought. He craves something, badly. And yet he doesn't want anyone to know. He probably doesn't know himself. "What are you doing tomorrow night, Robert?"

"I – " He looked at Mrs. Snow. Her face held a warning. "Nothing, right?" he asked her.

"Michael, I didn't mean for Robert to be in on anything –"

"Don't worry, Mother! I wouldn't let him come to harm." Michael thought for a minute. "Is there any chance we can move the Thanksgiving feast to early afternoon tomorrow? Instead of evening?"

"It's up to Jemima."

"Why, Michael?" asked Jemmy.

"I need to go out bird hunting tomorrow night. Do you want to come, Robert?"

"Bird hunting?" queried Robert.

"Looking for night hawks. Grave diggers."

"Cool!" Robert grinned at Mrs. Snow, who vented her disapproval with a disgusted sigh.

Michael put a hand on Robert's shoulder. "But ... hey, look at me, Robert. What we're going to do, yeah, sure, there will be some excitement. But listen to me, kid. And listen good this time, will you? This won't be a game tomorrow night. If you come with us, – are you listening? If you do come with us, I'm going to lay down some rules. Got it?"

Robert withered. Rules. Mrs. Snow had spoken about rules. He revolted against rules. He could never figure out why other boys followed them.

"Y'hear me, Robert? You'll do exactly what I tell you." Michael's hand moved to grasp a handful of Robert's hair. He pulled hard, tilting Robert's head back. "Cuz if you take one step out of line – *one step* – I have a large knife that simply longs for a white man's scalp. Got it?"

"Okay, Mike."

"Also, geez, kid. Let's get something else straight. I expect good manners, okay? Is that too much to ask?"

"Manners?" Robert tried to stretch taller to ease the grip Michael had on his hair.

"Manners. Respect your elders. To you, I'm Mr. Redbird."

Robert blinked and tried to nod. "Mr. Redbird."

"My mother is Mrs. Snow and my sister is –"

"Just Jemmy." She batted her eyes teasingly at Michael and waved an empty iron skillet in the air. "I defy anyone to call me Miss Snow."

"Okay. My sister is a little weird, but you get my point." Michael let go of Robert's hair and slipped into his coat. "I'll be here for dinner tomorrow. You and I will talk then, Robert. We'll work some stuff out. What do you think, Jemmy? Could we plan on a one o'clock dinner?"

"Sure, Michael."

"Okay. I'm off to see what trouble I can stir up. See you tomorrow." Michael waved and left.

Robert didn't move a step after Michael Redbird left. His fingers gripped the heavy cast that bound his arm.

Jemmy went behind the counter, put an arm around her mother, and pressed her nose against her head. "Are you sure that awful rancher didn't hurt you, Mama?"

Her mother nodded and smiled. "I'm glad I wasn't here alone, though."

Jemmy left and Mrs Snow turned around to see Robert standing at the counter, bent like a crippled person and looking very dejected.

"Robert?" She folded her arms. "You gonna stare into space or get the rest of those muffins into a pan?"

"Uh. Yeah," said Robert. "Muffins."

"Well, hop to it."

With a show of reluctance, he went back to his workspace. Mrs. Snow sure had a way about her. Robert had never known a woman like her. His mother – he could always get the better of her; his grandmother – she was so bossy she was practically a bully, but he could even get around her whenever he wanted. But Mrs. Snow – well.

Without hesitation, Robert hopped to it.


Jemmy left the kitchen and went to her cabin to wash and change her hiking clothes. On impulse, she knocked first at Hattie and Anya's cabin door.

"I just told my brother about the men we saw. He's got some plan to get rid them. I don't know what he has in mind."

"Wow, that's good!"

"And you know what else? Robert was in the kitchen just now.

I mentioned those men. I think you may have misjudged him. I don't think he's involved with them at all."

Anya sniffed. "Believe me, I wouldn't put anything past him."

"We saw him come out of their compartment on the train," said Hattie.

"That doesn't prove anything," countered Jemmy. "I watched him very carefully. He seemed sincere. He said he met those same two men when he was lost yesterday and they threatened to shoot him."

"Shoot him?" Hattie and Anya looked at each other, frowning.

"Yeah, I bet," claimed Anya. "So he says."

"I don't think he was lying," said Jemmy. "He was out there yesterday with no coat, blood all over him. And those men never offered to help him? They wouldn't even give him anything to eat."

"Well," Hattie said, turning to Anya, "we could be wrong."

Anya narrowed her eyes and bit her lip. "Maybe," she conceded grudgingly, with what she considered to be generosity.

After Jemmy left, Anya griped to Hattie, "I don't know why Robert had to come along on this trip."

"I thought his mother was away in Europe."

"Still, I wish my dad hadn't said he could come."

"You would want your dad to turn away his own nephew? He is not the type of person who would do that, Anya. You should be glad he's not."

Anya sat down on the edge of the bed. My dad really isn't that type of person, she realized. No. He wouldn't turn someone away.


At dinnertime, Jemmy brought a steaming pot of green chili stew into the dining room and cleared a place so Mrs. Frey could serve it. Jack Netherby and Hugh Durant sat on one side of the table, Anya and Hattie on the other. Corax was banished to the living room, where he languished unhappily in front of the fire. THE HUNGRIEST DOG IN THE WORLD.

ALLOWED ONLY THE SMELL OF FOOD.

TORTURE OF THE UTMOST CRUELTY.

SMELLING IS AS GOOD AS TASTING— BAH! PEOPLE ALWAYS SAY THAT.

BUT NO DOGS, EVER.

Hugh looked at the empty place at the other end of the table. "Robert isn't well enough to join us?" he asked.

"He is better than well," said Mrs. Frey, just as Robert came in with a basket of corn muffins. "He's been busy in the kitchen all afternoon." She didn't mention that he was atoning for misdeeds. "In fact, these corn muffins are his handiwork. Try one!"

Robert stumbled into his chair amid a flurry of compliments. He felt a small swell of gladness. Maybe Mrs. Snow was right. Maybe helping in the kitchen did get rid of bad feelings. And then he realized he was still in his pajamas. Oh no! He would have to leave his apron on. Maybe no one would notice. But then, everyone would make fun of him for wearing an apron like some kind of sissy. He felt stupid.

As everyone knows though, or ought to, you take a little home-made butter. You take a warm corn muffin. You put them together, and not a soul will spare a thought for either pajamas or aprons. Anyone who does not know that should make every attempt to test the theory.

"We're having a light supper tonight," said Mrs. Frey. "I want everyone to be good and hungry for tomorrow's dinner, which, I have been told, will be happening at one o'clock." She began ladling stew into bowls. "We'll eat as a family. Mrs. Snow and Jemmy will be joining us. And Michael too, I think."

Hugh bent his head to hide the smile that he felt bubbling up.

Hugh smiling, Robert cheery – such a lot of euphoria on the night before Thanksgiving.

Jack turned to Hugh and found him grinning at his bowl. He gave Hugh a nudge. "Hey."

No response.

He elbowed him again. "Hey! Do you want to leave tomorrow after dinner so we can get a head start ... Hugh!"

Hugh sat up. "What?"

"I said, do you want to leave after dinner tomorrow? We could get a head start on the hike to the Painted Cave. If we camp overnight on the trail, we can go the rest of the way on Friday morning. Unless you'd rather just stay here for some reason?"

"Uuuh," Hugh sighed. He came thudding back to earth, or maybe the earth rose up and jolted sense back into him. "No. Uh, no. Yes. Oh. Sure. We can leave tomorrow. Maybe we can camp overnight on the trail."

"I just said that."

"Oh."

"So you might expect us back here by lunchtime on Friday, Evelyn."

"Can we go too, Dad?" asked Anya.

"If you don't mind sleeping in a tent, I don't see why not. You really should see this particular place while you're here. It's quite the spectacle. What about you, Robert? Are you up for a hike tomorrow?"

Robert looked down at his stew, not knowing how to answer. This was a turnaround. He'd have to choose between camping with Uncle Jack or joining Michael – Mr. Redbird – in some mysterious scheme. Two options? He, Robert the Scorned and Unpopular, had been asked to join not one but two adventures? On the same day? Why couldn't it always be like this? "I'm not sure," he said, finally.

"No need to decide tonight," Jack said. "See how you feel tomorrow. By the way, have you phoned your mother to tell her about your broken arm? She's gonna be mad at me."

"Mother? No." His mother. She would be back in Montreal by now. He should phone her. They'd always been pretty close, he and she – until the day she went off and married that lame-brained Harvey. Well, that settled it. He had just talked himself out of phoning his mother.

"Hattie, you too. Your mother might like to hear from you."

"Yes. Maybe I'll call her tonight. It's cheaper to phone at night, right?" It would be expensive to call long distance, but there were so many things she wanted to say to her mother.

After dinner, Mrs. Frey sat down at the piano and they listened while she tore at hurricane speed through Chopin's *Winter Wind Etude*. The piece was aptly named, a wild storm of notes.

With rapt attention, Robert leaned forward on his chair, watching her small hands flying over the keys. For the first time, he heard sounds shaping themselves in ways that made sense to him. He didn't move a muscle until Mrs. Frey finished, and he crossed the room to talk to her before she had even risen from the piano bench.

He spoke softly. "That was very –" Magnificent, he wanted to tell her. Was that the right word for a piece of music? He felt ignorant. "That was nice."

"Thank you, Robert."

Robert stood with bowed head and waited to speak while Grandfather Clock, having no wish to be outdone by Chopin, slipped a cog, bizzed with an eloquence quite uncharacteristic of any ordinary piece of machinery, and finally donged the hour.

Robert scratched his head. "I, um. Can I ask a favor, Mrs. Frey?" He held out a five dollar bill. "Could I make a long distance call on your telephone? I won't talk long."

"Of course."

"I think I should call my mother. Wish her a happy Thanksgiving."

"I'm sure that would please her."

"Is five dollars enough for calling Montreal?"

"If you keep it short, yes, that will be fine." What a nice boy, Mrs. Frey thought.

Something almost no other person had said, ever.

Although when you think about it, there is that old saying, isn't there, about the eye of the beholder?


Out in the dark of night, Coyote prowls. He doesn't miss much. It isn't too long after dinner that he, observing the ranch from across the river, watches every window go dark, one by one. He trots across the bridge, fairly certain by then that he would not be in danger of meeting any humans. He has some investigating to do.

He has noticed a ridiculously docile four-foot lately, who seemed to be at the beck and call of a small human. A four-foot so meek that Coyote is embarrassed for him. He has never seen such a creature before this week. He wants to get a whiff of his scent, so he can figure out if he is deathly ill or just plain stupid. Because, unless that animal is tricksier than any coyote, he has to assume that something is wrong with him. When did he give up his freedom, his wildness, all the best things about being a four-foot?

And for what? For what?

TRICKSTER, JOKER

Thursday

On Thanksgiving morning, the November sun barely pierces the heavy clouds above the plateau. Colors are muted and greyed. Coyote, still out from the night before, steals from under a pinon tree and noses among cold rocks and boulders, hoping to come upon some unwary animal and surprise it into providing him with lunch. But most creatures are content to stay in their warm holes and burrows, and provide themselves with lunch. He'd missed breakfast. He had come close to catching a rabbit before dawn, but without success, so he is hungry, very hungry.

He pauses at the rim of the canyon and sniffs the breeze. Ah! Now here was something promising! He knows the smell of that creature. Unmistakable. Oh boy. If there are many of them, he doesn't stand a chance, but if it is a young one, alone, and unwary, he might attempt an attack. He follows his nose, but then stops abruptly and turns away. Bah! Humans. More than one of them. He'll have to make other plans for lunch.

Unseen by him, just below where he had stopped, young

Felicity was ruminating sadly on the good fortune of those more blessed than she, those who have a warm dry home, plenty of food, and someone who cares about them. Signor Rossini sends me out on the worst jobs, she complained to herself, this time slaving for a couple of men who don't even notice that I'm ready to drop from exhaustion.

Look at me, out in good weather and bad. They pile the work on me but do I ever get the occasional kind word, or a little special treatment? No. And today, Thanksgiving Day no less, they make me go without lunch. No lunch! MAMMA MIA! I need some nourishing food. I haven't eaten enough to keep a pica alive today.

How many more days will I be on this job? she moaned aloud. She knew the men couldn't stand to listen to her complaining but her misery finally overwhelmed her and she began to weep. She made a genuine effort to snuffle quietly so she wouldn't annoy anyone, but she could hold back only so much emotion. I don't think I can last much longer, she blubbered. Then, in a flood of self-pity, she let loose a full-throated lament.

I'M HUNGRY! I'M WASTING AWAY!

"Shut up out there!" Snyder Ravilious poked his head outside the tent. "Keep quiet or you won't get dinner either!"

Forlorn, Felicity drooped and whimpered quietly, but she could hardly bear the torment. She longed for the touch of a soft hand, someone to say nice things to her. But instead, she is hollered at constantly. That big man was still angry at her, obviously. The nasty old grump. STUPIDO! CRETINO! He still hadn't forgiven her for the tiny little – well, she would call it a mishap – yes, that PICCOLO PICCOLO mishap that had occurred this morning. Come on! Was that really such a big deal?

That situation, earlier today? Well AI MADONNA, it's not like anything was happening at the campsite at the time. Just a lot of hanging about. Felicity had been bored. She began fooling around, just amusing herself, fussing with a piece of rope, picking at it a little. The men were still in their tent when she was surprised to discover that she had loosened a knot. Oh. Look at that. Well, good. Now she could sneak something out of the food bag. She stopped in her tracks. Someone coming?

An elderly Pueblo man came doddering into their camp. The men came out of the tent when they heard him, and the three of them sat for a while, talking and sketching on a piece of paper. Listening to him, the men got very excited.

When the old man left them, Felicity heard him chuckling over something as he passed her. Some saying about a fool and his money. She didn't know what that was about, but the mood at the tent site had changed. Suddenly everyone was much cheerier this morning. The men were studying the old guy's paper, whatever it was. That's all they were doing. They were just standing around looking at a dumb piece of paper, like it was some prize or something.

So, here was a chance to get them to pay a little attention to her. She stepped demurely, right up next to them, a hint broad enough for even the most ignorant of men. She simpered daintily.

She got no response.

Coquettish, she swayed her backside a little. They paid no attention.

What? Nothing? Her pretty little POSTERIORE got no reaction at all?

She gave the big man a sharp whack with her tail. HEY, PAESAN! WOULD IT KILL YOU TO SCRATCH MY BUTT?

He ignored her completely.

That did it! She whirled and tried to nip at him. She missed him, and got a mouthful of that paper instead. That made the big man furious! He really wanted that paper! He came after her, yelling nasty and untrue things about her, some very cutting remarks too – oh very cutting; words so hurtful that she honestly believed she might be scarred for life by them.

So? Was a girl supposed to overlook that kind of talk? Take those insults? *RIDICOLO!* Felicity backed away, tossing her head, and then, with the paper still in her mouth, she took off, gallivanting across the plain. She didn't go far, just far enough to make her point.

Then she stood still and watched as the big man approached.

*SIGNOR ORRIBILE!* YOU BRUTE! COME ON! BRING ME A TREAT, YOU VILE FLESH-EATER! TRY TO BRIBE ME!

She started to drool just thinking about a nice carrot. The wad of paper between her teeth, wet with saliva, began to annoy her. She opened her mouth wide and let the wind take it.

*SANTO CIELO!* That made the man really angry! What a temper! He came thundering toward her, hollering his head off.

"You stupid, stupid mule!"

Okay. Okay.

Now that right there? That was a mistake.

He should not have called her that. That was extremely hurtful, not to mention entirely wrong and completely inaccurate. One attribute she did not possess was stupidity.

The ball of paper rolled across the plain like a little white tumbleweed. The man chased after it, cursing and grunting. Felicity ran toward him and intercepted him, cutting him off.

NO TREAT FOR ME, MR. SAGGY-*PANTALONI*? ALL RIGHT! NO PAPER FOR YOU!

He dodged left. She stopped him.

He veered right.

The chorus girl in her aimed a high kick at him. Give him a view he'd never forget!

That stopped him in his tracks.

Yeah. She was feelin' sass-ee! She strutted toward him like a showgirl.

AND-A ONE, AND-A TWO, AND A LA-DI-DA!

*PORCA VACCA!* Did that ever provoke him. He didn't like that! No, not one bit!

They faced each other, defiant. By then the paper had blown half-way to the Jemez Mountains. And who should spot it, tumbling along, but Raven. She dived, seized it, and flew off with it.

The man nearly tore his hair!

And that is the reason, true in every detail, that poor Felicity was given no lunch on Thanksgiving Day.


"What are you doing? Why are you bothering to pack those? There's no point now," Ravilious barked later. He sat on a rock holding his head.

"You expect me to dig with my hands?" snapped Ouisel, perching his fists on his bulbous hips.

"If we don't have the map, there is no sense in going out there digging tonight, or going bloody anywhere. Damn that mule!"

"Of course we're going out there. I remember most of what was on the map. All we have to do is find the painted rock. Two diamond shapes. He said the place is very easy to spot."

"We'll never find it without the map."

"We most certainly can! Dear man, this is an opportunity not to be wasted! We're talking about gold! A piece of advice like this is priceless. We were lucky that man came along."

"What do you want to bet there's no gold there? Ha! Two diamond shapes! He just lied, I bet."

"Now now now. Come on, we paid the man good money. Let's not waste it, Snyder."

"We? We paid? No, not we. Me! I'm the one who paid! I paid good money, not you, Honoré! Twenty-five dollars!"

"So let's get these tools packed into the panniers and go find that rock painting."

"I'm not going near that mule. She's just dying to bite me."

"I can't say as I blame her," muttered Ouisel.

"What did you say?"

"I said, don't forget the rifle."


Much earlier that morning. It is not yet five o'clock on Thanksgiving Day. Deep darkness in the canyon of the Rio Frijoles. All silent, quite, quite still. Great Horned Owl glides out of the trees, soundless as a shadow, and lights on a fencepost.

He listens. He can hear what others miss. There are wild things rustling and scuttling about. He can hear the river, of course, still swollen with rainwater as it rushes down to the valley below. But beneath that sound, he can hear the night hunters. He swivels his head. Cottontail Rabbit, nibbling noisily on the last of the parsley in Mrs. Frey's vegetable garden. Coyote, not entirely silent either, though he creeps down the garden path on velvet paws. Either creature would make a nice meal.

Owl's immensely powerful talons could easily snap Coyote's spine, but he decides that Rabbit would put up less of a fight and be just as tasty. His head rotates slowly until his terrible golden eyes sight her soft tender form. He spreads his wings, one instant away from the kill, and then freezes.

A door slams. Owl squats low on his fencepost. Coyote crouches, squinting over his shoulder. Rabbit sits up, her ears working.

Daybreak, a perilous time for the wildlings. Each and every day, when Morning rises and shakes out her tangled tresses, the Night World must scramble to hide under her bed.


Mrs. Snow came down the path and knocked on a door to one of the cottages.

"Robert?" she called softly. "Are you up?" She turned the knob and poked her head in the door. "Time to get up."

Robert groaned and thrashed his covers.

She felt a little odd entering the cabin where Dr. Netherby and Mr. Durant were also sleeping, but that did not stop her. She shook Robert awake.

"Blahhg," he moaned.

Mrs. Snow half-pulled him from his warm bed. "Get dressed," she whispered.

He tried to see his wrist watch, but it was too dark.

She pulled him to a standing position. "Get moving. I need you in the kitchen in five minutes."

It took him almost half an hour. Getting dressed with one arm in a cast was not easy. By the time he stumbled in, Mrs. Snow had gotten the oven heating. The warm kitchen made him feel so deliciously drowsy that he wished he could curl up in front of the stove like a cat. Mrs. Snow didn't say a word as she punched down a big bowl of dough. Robert gaped when he saw what time it was. He put his wrist to his ear. Had his watch stopped? Five o'clock? In the morning? He wound it absently.

In the time it took him to wind his watch, Mrs. Snow had rolled out a piece of dough and was handing him a bowl of melted butter, another of raisins, cinnamon, brown sugar, walnuts. Dumb with sleep, barely able to hold his eyes open, he obeyed her terse instructions for filling breakfast rolls.

Jemmy came in and silently went about her tasks. Only Mrs. Snow spoke, occasional directions to Robert. Cut this up, clean that, get out the table linens, the china and silver, and set them on the sideboard.

No chitchat. Just sizzling, chopping, stirring, the clinking of china. Nearly silent preparations for a day of feasting, and everything well underway.

With a clonk, a protesting twang of springs, and a cranky grind of worm gears, bleary-eyed old Grandfather Clock rang in the day.

A couple of hours later, it was breakfast time. The others came in and took places at the table.

Jack put his head into the kitchen. Mrs. Snow had told him about her arrangement with Robert, that he had agreed, more or less of his own accord, to work in her kitchen for a couple of days. And there, amazingly, was his nephew, on his knees mopping up a spill, one-handed.

"How's the arm today?" Jack asked him.

"Kinda hurts." Robert got up and washed his hands. "Is it time, Mrs. Snow?"

"Open the oven and take a look, Robert. You know what breakfast rolls should look like."

Robert pulled out a pan of sweet rolls and set them on a trivet. Jack came closer.

"Did you make these?" he asked.

"Mrs. Snow made the dough. I just put them together."

"And a fine job you did, too, Robert."

Mrs. Snow came over, inspected, and said without fanfare, "Good."

He grinned. "Thanks." Breakfast rolls – so silly, the astonishing amount of pride a person could take in a breakfast roll.

"Go ahead and sit down, Dr. Netherby. Robert will come right in with the coffee. As soon as you get the coffee poured, Robert, you can put the rolls in a basket and serve them."

That basket was soon emptied and a second one passed around. Even though he made it clear that Mrs. Snow made the dough, all the compliments went to Robert. Even Michael Redbird, when he came in, ate three of them.

Then Michael went into the kitchen and asked if he could borrow Robert for five minutes. They stepped outside and Michael told Robert his plans for the evening.

"I'll come for you around five o'clock," Michael said, "And for pete's sake bring warm clothing this time, will you, Robert?"

"Yeah, sure. Sure, Mr. Redbird."

"After, we can join the others at their campsite for an overnight. And Mother tells me that she won't need you in the kitchen tomorrow."

"What? She won't?"

"I don't know how she roped you into that in the first place."

Robert was too ashamed to say that he was atoning for wrong-doings. Likewise, he could hardly admit something else, especially to a guy like Mr. Redbird: he liked being in the kitchen with Mrs. Snow; going methodically through a set of tasks, coming out with something wonderful in the end. Such clarity. Nothing else for a long time had given him this much satisfaction.

"My mother is quite the boss-lady, isn't she?" Michael laughed.

"Mrs. Snow? She's okay."

"You can see where Jemmy gets her mouthy ways."

"No. She's good, your mother. She's teaching me stuff."

"Yeah, I just bet she is. She once tried to teach me to cook." Michael laughed again. "It looks like you're more patient than I was."

Strange. Robert had never thought of himself as patient. And neither had anyone else, ever.


Outdoors after breakfast, Dick Frey set up a badminton net. Even though the wind was chilly, Hugh and Jack began a game against Hattie and Anya. The first time the birdie came sailing over the net, Hattie lunged after it in her fierce, competitive way. The other three stopped playing and stared at her.

"What?" she asked, her eyes wide-innocent.

"Ah ha. I see what we have here," said Hugh. "Apparently we are not playing for fun." He smashed the birdie back across the net, making her dive for it.

"I call it fun!" She sent the birdie back. Laughing, they battled fast and hard, until Corax captured the birdie and refused to bring it back.

"Oh well," said Hattie. We beat you two anyway, right Anya?"

"You did not!" declared Jack. "We didn't get to finish the game. We were gaining on you –"

That started an argument.

"Let's play Kick the Can," suggested Hugh diplomatically. "The dog won't be likely to steal that."

"We don't have a can," said Anya.

"They must have an empty one in the kitchen," Hugh suggested.

"Hugh, you can be the one to go ask Jemmy if she has a can," teased Jack.

"Wait. Isn't that kind of rude?" Hugh shook his head.

"What's rude?"

"Asking her if she has a can. I can't say that to her."

Hattie and Anya started to laugh. Hugh was blushing.

"One of the girls should go ask," Hugh suggested.

"What's the matter?" "Don't be shy, Hugh!" they taunted.

"You want to come with me, Anya?"

"No," she giggled. "I don't."

It ended with Hugh throwing down his racket and stomping off to the kitchen. He came back wearing a foolish grin.

"What? No can, Hugh?"

Hugh stopped and looked up, puzzled. "Oh. Yeah. I forgot the can." He turned around.

"I'm glad he's on your team, Dr. Netherby. He's not going to be worth much for the rest of the morning," Hattie joked.

"I suggest we make new teams. I'll take Anya. You'll have to do what you can to whip Hugh into line, Hattie," said Jack.

"I certainly will, and we will whip the pants off you two," Hattie cried, forgetting to be polite. But she spoke the truth. Nobody, but nobody got the better of Hattie Fish when she was in a fighting mood.

When that game wore them out, they went inside to sit near the fire and await dinner. Mrs. Frey gave the girls some scrapbooks to look through while Hugh and Jack, a little stiff and sore, took cat naps. Just when everyone felt they could not stand the hunger pangs a minute longer, the doors to the dining room were thrown open.

The tableware glittered and gleamed, and all the tantalizing things they had been smelling were arrayed on the sideboard. Almost everything had been grown and prepared on the ranch. Two of the wild turkeys who often came to sit on the stone wall outside the kitchen door had been shot dead by Mrs. Frey yesterday. She hit both of them right between the eyes. Considering that these twenty pound birds had heads the size of lollipops, that was no mean feat. So not one, but two roasted birds sat resplendent and golden at the head of the table.

An interruption from Grandfather Clock gave everyone pause, precisely the reaction he had intended. His mechanism spluttered and rumbled importantly. Finally he tintinabulated once for the thirteenth hour of the day, following which announcement, for the nonce, he promptly retired.

Jack waited, then lifted his glass to propose a toast. "To our hostess, Mrs. Frey. To our cooks, Mrs. Snow and Jemmy and Robert. And to what will be, I'm sure, the most memorable Thanksgiving ever. Thank you all."

Mrs. Frey had to blink hard to keep the tears back. All she could manage to say was, "You have made my last Thanksgiving, here in this house that I love, very special. So thank *you*."

They got down to serious business then, with plates full to

overflowing. There is a saying about eyes being bigger than bellies, but no one gave that any credence.

When they had had second helpings, and in some cases, thirds, Jack made a suggestion. "You ladies have worked very hard. Why don't you let the men clear the dishes and serve dessert?"

"I'm going to excuse myself," said Dick. "I'll go out to get the mules saddled and loaded for your camping trip. Then I'm off to my girlfriend's house."

Hattie's face corkscrewed, maybe from the news of a girlfriend, maybe from the under-the-table kick that Anya landed on her shin.

"Some people will do anything to get out of a little dish washing," chided Jack. "Seriously though, Dick, we do appreciate all you've done for us."

"You're very welcome. I am glad you will finally be getting some decent weather tomorrow. I've got your tents all set up at a spot that Michael chose. They're only a few miles up the trail, but it will probably be dark by the time you get there. So take lanterns. Make sure you have matches."

"We'll manage just fine. Thank you for arranging all this."

The men poured everyone something to drink, beckoned to Robert, and disappeared into the kitchen.

Hattie watched Dick leave, trying not to be obvious about it. Oh well. As her mother was fond of saying, you win some, you lose some, and some get rained out. She leaned her elbows on the table. "Are you looking forward to moving into your new home, Mrs. Frey?" she asked.

"Most certainly not. I can't imagine a place that will be one whit better than the one I have right here."

"You have to admit, Evelyn," said Mrs. Snow, "that having hot running water and an electric oven will make things a lot easier. They have electric irons now too, for laundry. And washing machines."

"That's all baloney. Our kitchen has worked fine for almost twenty years without all that folderol."

"But just think, Mrs. Frey," exclaimed Jemmy, "an indoor bathroom!"

"With a bathtub," said Hattie.

"You'll be able to take a bubble bath!" agreed Anya.

"Please. I don't have time to waste on things like that. And that other piece in that room. My friend in town has one, but I refuse to have one in any house of mine. You know what I mean. That hideous thing with the wooden seat. It makes the most frightening noise."

Anya snickered. "You mean the toilet?"

"Ugh! Don't want it. Won't have it. I would never get used to it."

"You don't think so?" asked Anya. "It's so much more convenient. It's warm in winter."

"It's so unsanitary!"

"It's not!" argued Jemmy. "And it smells ever so much better. When I lived in Santa Fe last year, I really got to love an indoor bathroom."

"But it's so unnatural!" declared Mrs. Snow. "With a latrine, everything gets returned to the earth."

"I agree, Blossom. That's the way things should work," said Mrs. Frey.

"Well, where do you think everything goes when it leaves the indoor bathroom?" demanded Jemmy.

The two older women looked at each other, perplexed.

"I can't say that I've thought about that. I suspect it, well ... I guess it all just sort of disappears. Lord knows where," said Mrs. Frey finally.

"And he'll never tell," added Mrs. Snow.

"It's white man's magic!" hissed Hattie, half-standing and

waving her arms. "White man's magic!"

They were laughing when the men came in with dessert.

"What's so funny?" asked Jack. "What are you ladies talking about?"

"Well ..." began Mrs. Snow, a little embarrassed.

"Plumbing," Jemmy said. "Magic toilets."

"Jemima! Your manners!" her mother cried.

"Hmm, toilets," said Jack. "Well I'm not sure I could contribute much to that conversation. What do you think?" He looked at Hugh.

Oh crap, thought Hugh, that being the only answer – and a fairly inappropriate one – that came to his mind at that moment. Hopelessly tongue-tied, he glanced at Jemmy, then frowned at Anya and Hattie when they started to giggle.

Hugh was saved from further comment when Grandfather Clock whuzzled, chomped, and once again belched the hour.


Dick Frey had told them that the mules could find their way to the Painted Cave unaided. They can actually smell their way there, he claimed. Whether or not that part was true, after the Thanksgiving feast, the mules took the four campers, the two girls and two men, and Corax of course, to the tent site without once getting lost. Robert told them he had decided not to go with them. It was dark by the time they got there, but Dick had come earlier in the day to set up the two tents, a large one for the men, and a small one for Anya and Hattie.

"Why did he put up such a big tent?" asked Anya.

"You girls are small," Hugh explained, though he knew the real reason. "We he-men need room! You'll have to sleep with the dog, though."

"Maybe Dick is planning on joining us later," said Anya. "That would be nice, wouldn't it, Hattie?"

"Quit it," Hattie said. She managed to keep the smile off her face, but not out of her eyes.

The lanterns were lit and they were about to set a match to the camp fire when they heard something strange. Wary, ears sharpened, Corax whoofed softly. He stared into the night.

From far away, the faint, steady beat of a drum.

"What is that?" whispered Anya, but no one answered. They stood listening, perplexed, goosebumps prickling their arms.

Directly over a small hill from where they camped, Ravilious and Ouisel were standing before a rock cliff, hardly believing their luck. They had found the spot, a minor miracle, they were sure – the very spot the old man had shown them on the map. They were certain it was the right place. By the light of their lantern, they could see ancient paintings all over a tall slab of rock that formed the bottom of a cliff, just as the man had described. Without question, one of the symbols was a pair of diamond shapes.

"There's where you'll find the gold." The old man had told them that those diamond shapes indicated that gold was buried there. "But you must tell no one from my tribe that I have given you this map. No one!"

"Why haven't you dug the gold up yourself?" they had asked him.

He had been quiet for a minute. He had bowed his head, looking very troubled. "I was one of the men who buried the gold there, years ago. I might as well warn you, though. It is cursed," the old man had whispered. "That gold is cursed! It brought so much fighting and unhappiness to me and to my people that we Elders took it away and buried it in a place where no one would ever dare dig for it."

"Why not?"

"I don't want to scare you. But just above where it lies," the old man whispered, " is the Cave of the She-Wolf."

"She-wolf?"

"Oh, they are vicious creatures! But you've picked a lucky time to dig there. They're usually at the caves only while they raise their pups in the spring. I tell you, you would be doing us an enormous favor if you took that gold away from here. It still haunts the minds of our young men and makes them crazy with greed. A lot of mothers will rest easier if they don't have to worry about their sons trying to break the curse." He gazed at them sadly before throwing the last dart. "Take it please. But have a care. Go in, get the gold, and get out as fast as you can. You'll need more courage than the last men who tried to dig there ...." He shook his head and let his voice trail off.

Courage? Ha! They had plenty of courage, and they weren't brainless idiots, either. Privately, Ravilious and Ouisel thought the old man must be remarkably stupid.

As it turned out, that was a remarkably wrong assessment.

So here they were tonight, Ravilious and Ouisel, beside the painted cliff. At their feet, a fortune in gold.

"This is it! Two diamonds!" said Ravilious, nearly trembling with anticipation.

"So hustle those tools out of the crate, Snyd. Let's get to work."

"I didn't believe the old fart. The twenty-five dollars I gave him was well-spent after all."

"You are absolutely right, my friend!" Ouisel unpacked the rifle. "I'll keep this near me." He noted Snyder's sudden suspicion. "Does that worry you? Are you afraid I'm going to shoot you?" He giggled. "I probably won't. I only want to make sure this is close to hand. Now get that other lantern lit. Turn it down. Turn it down low. Come on. Time to stop gawking and shoulder our behinds!"

They tied Felicity the mule to a willow sapling and unpacked their shovels and trowels.

They dug for a while near the rock face, found nothing, and moved out a couple of feet. The second hole they dug was not even six inches deep when they heard it. They stopped digging for a minute, listening.

Far far away.      The sound of a drum.

The moon had not yet risen and the night, though dense with starlight, was darker than they at first realized. They felt a subtle change of perspective. A current of uncertainty flickered over them. They were suddenly sharply aware of the immensity of the heavens. Of the vast empty void of the desert. Of the threat in a drum beat borne on the black wind of night.

Beating   steadily   beating   ceaselessly.

What did it mean?

A finger of fear scratched a claw mark in their guts.

Two white men, trespassing in Indian country. All around, wide emptiness. Hushed, immense, and inscrutable. Some lurking menace out there ... and two white men all at once admitted that they were doing something that was offensive, deeply offensive, to native people. With no safe haven anywhere near. Alone in hostile territory. Two careless, vulnerable men, out of their element, rattled by the sound of a distant drum.

It would put anybody on edge.

Beat     Beat     Beat

Felicity the mule pranced nervously.

"What is that?" whispered Ravilious.

"I don't know. Maybe some tribe is performing a ceremony."

"You think so?"

"Pay no attention. Keep digging," Ouisel's voice warbled noticeably.

Beat   Beat   Beat

Nearer. The drumbeat seemed to be getting closer.   Now softer. Now louder. But steady, relentless.

Beat  Beat

Felicity stomped and snorted in protest.

Ravilious stopped digging again, turned up the lantern and shined it up and down the cliff.

"What is that?" he asked again. Ouisel stopped digging too, his eyes following the lantern light as it panned across the rocks.

Beat Beat Beat  Louder closer.

A drumbeat in the night.

Spellbinding. It had to mean something.

Doom  doom  doom.  The threat, the hypnotic sense of impending doom. It gripped hard.

Someone out there. Or some thing. Coming closer.

"I don't like this," said Ravilious, his heart pounding, his eyes searching frantically.

"Oh, phooey. It's probably some Indian ritual. It has nothing to do with us. Stop fretting, Snyder."

Now, the beating somewhere just above them.

They both grabbed lanterns, held them aloft, and scanned the rocky cliff. The light caught something.

Two yellow eyes.

Two more, and more. Animals. They could make out their ears but that was all.

Up there, in the rocks, the she-wolf and her minions. It had to be! Piercing yellow eyes staring, locked onto the aliens – two slow-witted white men standing in the wrong place, the scent of their fear unmistakable.

The drum, beating, beating.

"Watch out," said Ouisel quietly. He put the lantern down and picked up his shovel like a weapon.

"Are – are they – a whole pack?" stammered Ravilious.

Wolf heads swayed rhythmically from side to side. Back and forth, chanting a low growl with every motion. Threatening, angry.

"Are they real?" Ouisel's voice had risen two octaves.

Faster, louder went the drum. The wolves began to rise

slowly, still with that swaying motion. They rose to standing position on two legs. The horrible chanting intensified. Wolf lips were twisted into snarls; white teeth were shining fangs.

The drum, faster faster.

Four of them. Men. They were men wearing wolf skins over their heads. Their bare arms, chests, legs smeared with black paint. Faces hidden, the snouts of the wolf skins pulled low over their brows. Now more men materialized among the rocks. How many? Men covered with black paint. Large spiky fearsome black headdresses. Their eyes marked out with white. Hanging on their chests, dozens of sharp gleaming white teeth, strings and strings of them. Their terrible chanting swelled, guttural, savage.

In all the commotion, while they stared transfixed from the foot of the cliff, neither Ravilious nor Ouisel saw a slender black shadow slither over to where their gear lay strewn about. The rifle – in an instant a Cochiti boy had grabbed it and disappeared.

The wolf men began to descend through the rocks, swaying from side to side with every step. Bent at the waist, arms holding clubs in threatening position, barking their terrifying chant.

Felicity the mule was screaming and pulling frantically on her rope. It slipped, came free, and Ouisel just managed to get a hand on her bridle. He could hardly hold her. She reared and pulled, shrieking in panic.

Ravilious swore and, unable to stand on shaking legs, crouched in terror.

Hearing the drum, drawn by all the noise, the four campers, Jack and Hugh, Hattie and Anya, had come running to the top of the hill. They crouched in the rocks so they could watch. What bloody horror would they be witnessing? Anya had all she could do to hold Corax back. Her father took hold of the dog's collar and finally managed to control him, but his barking added to the panic. Transfixed with dread, they watched as black-painted men, some covered in wolf skins, danced slowly down through the rocks.

"Get the gun!" ordered Ouisel, trying desperately to hold Felicity. She struggled so hard she was pulling him off his feet. "The gun, you idiot!"

Ravilious, in a panic, looked right and left. He darted here and there. "It's gone! I can't find —" A stone whizzed through the air and he stopped, holding his head.

Ouisel tried desperately to heave his flabby body onto Felicity's back. Finally he got one leg over and, clinging for his life to her neck, he let her have her way. She fled, with him barely able to hang on. She raced for the safety of their tent, back the way they had come. Ravilious screamed and, shouting with rage, got up and ran after. Gradually, gradually, very gradually, his screams disappeared into the night.


The four campers, watching from the top of the small hill, barely breathed, waiting to see what would happen next. The black-painted men came down to level ground. They looked into the crate that had been left behind.

"Nothing here," one of them said in English. He laughed. "But then, we knew there was nothing buried here." He slid the black headdress off his head.

It was Michael Redbird. The other men did the same. They all appeared to be Native Americans. A boy slipped up next to them and handed one of them the rifle.

"Good job, son," the man told him.

The four men in wolf skins pulled them from their heads and the pueblo boy was asked to turn his face away so their identity would remain secret, even though they were part of the same tribe. Michael spoke a few words with them and they left.

The drummer took longer to join them, having to scramble down through the rocks without bumping the precious drum, the soul-stirring drum so revered by the Cochiti people. The drummer wore no wolf skin and no black paint. He had a cast on one arm. His cheeks glowed red with excitement. Michael took the drum from him, laughing.

"A drum normally chooses only one person to play it, Robert, but this one of mine seemed more than willing to work with you."

Robert's eyes sparkled.

"You'd think he was part Cochiti, the way he played," laughed one of the men.

Robert looked from one man to another, pinching his lips between his teeth, trying not to grin.

The wolf men all turned, suddenly wary. They saw the four campers coming over the hill toward them. Corax ran ahead to greet Robert eagerly.

"Hey!" called Jack. "That was quite the show!"

"You saw?" laughed Michael.

"How could we miss it, with all that racket?"

"I was hoping you would. These are my friends from Pueblo di Cochiti." He turned to the black-painted men. "These folks are staying at the ranch, friends of Robert's. How did you like our skin-shifters?"

"Those wolf men? I would hate to meet them alone at night."

"It took me a while to convince them that it really isn't taboo to invoke the wolf for this purpose."

"What is their usual purpose?" asked Hugh.

"Skin-shifters assume the wolf's characteristics for rituals, and for medical purposes. It takes them years to learn the sacred lore and prepare themselves for initiation."

"They were very effective," said Hugh. "I'd love to photograph them."

"No. Sorry. Our people would not like that. They're very secretive and we've taken too many liberties with the skins tonight as it is."

"Of course. I understand. They must terrify the children in

your pueblo."

Michael laughed. "You thought they were scary tonight? You should see them during a ceremony. A skin-shifter can scare you out of a year's growth!"


The men from Cochiti had a car parked on the mesa. While they took the road back to their pueblo, Ravilious was running, whimpering and stumbling through the dark, trying to find the trail. He couldn't remember the way to his tent. What if he came upon a wild animal? What if those terrible wolf men chased him down? His wobbly legs were so uncontrollable and he slipped so many times, he finally had to huddle down between two boulders so he could get his breath, stop shaking, and collect his courage.

Three hours later, when he finally fell shivering into his campsite, Ouisel was nowhere to be found.

Good, thought Ravilious. I hope he's lost out there somewhere. Maybe the wolf men found him. I hope they did. I won't have to put up with the fat little turd any longer. And, he thought greedily, I'll have the treasure we've collected all to myself. First thing tomorrow, I'm taking it to the train station. With that happy thought, he fell exhausted into sleep.


After the Cochiti men left, Robert and Michael Redbird joined the others at the campfire and helped themselves to the supper Jemmy had packed for them.

"Now I see why Dick set up the big tent," said Anya. "It was for you."

"How did you know where Ravilious was digging?" Hattie asked Michael.

"We sent them a visitor this morning who told them there was gold buried near a certain symbol. He drew them a map and told them to look for a pair of diamond shapes painted on the rock."

"Is that what those diamond shapes mean? Gold?" asked Anya.

Michael laughed. "Not at all. That symbol stands for clarity and wisdom. Good joke, right? We told your dad and Hugh we'd be showing up tonight. But you never expected we would look like that, did you?"

"I had to convince myself it was you in that black paint," said Jack.

Anya got up and offered slices of Thanksgiving pie all round.

"We have to get up very early tomorrow," continued Michael, "if we want to get to the Painted Cave and back by lunchtime. There is time for one story tonight, though, if you'd like to hear one."

"A story?" "Oh yes!" "Yes, we would!"

"Good. I need to practice my skills. Because I hope someday," said Michael, "to be named Storyteller for our pueblo. Storyteller must know every tale in the history of our people. I haven't learned them all yet, but I can tell you one tonight. Since this is wintertime, it is right that this should be a story about Coyote, the Trickster. He is one of our winter characters."

They all settled down to hear the tale. Michael's voice was expressive and he pantomimed his words with gestures.

"Long ago, Raven and Coyote were making the world together. They had made the earth. They had made the animal people. They had made the sun, and they fixed it so it would shine all the time. They liked everything they made, and they liked each other. The two were the best of friends, as a matter of fact, until something bad happened between them. Coyote caused some trouble that made Raven furious. She never forgave him. After that, Raven spent her days searching for ways to make Coyote miserable.

"One day she thought of a way to make it more difficult for Coyote to hunt for food. Using her black feathers as a paintbrush, she painted half of the entire sky with black, so for half the time, it would be night and Coyote would not be able to see well enough to hunt. When she saw Coyote so hungry and confused, Raven shrieked peals of ugly laughter.

"But she forgot about the moon. Now that the sky was dark half the time, the moon was much more visible. There it was tonight, rising into the sky, shining big and bright and round.

"But still, Coyote knew the moon would not be there every night. It wouldn't be easy for him to see the small, secretive animals he liked to hunt. He didn't know what to do. He sat down on a rock to think things over.

"On this rock, a small pool of rainwater had collected. And in this pool was reflected the light of the moon. Coyote took a sip from the puddle and his nose, where it touched the reflection, came out covered in shiny moonbeams. He dipped his paw in and collected more moonbeams. Then he dipped his tail in and, using it as a paintbrush, scattered sparkling dots of light all over the sky. Dancing and prancing and flicking his tail, he had soon spangled the entire sky with tiny lights. And he called them stars.

"Now, by starlight, even when the moon is down, Coyote is able to hunt at night. It was in this manner that he learned from his enemy to make the best of things. He never allows anything to trouble him, or not for very long. This is why we call him Clever Coyote."

It was a minute before anyone wanted to break the spell of the story. Who would ever have known that starlight was made of magicked moonbeams? Spread far above their campfire, the awesome Milky Way pulsed and gleamed. Clever Coyote's beautiful handiwork had to be contemplated and appreciated, before anyone felt like speaking.

"Thank you, Mr. Redbird," said Hattie finally. "That was lovely. Do you know what is interesting? My people have stories of a trickster too. Nanabozho, he's called." Turning to Anya, she said, "See? The white man isn't the only one with magic."

Friday

The next morning they had to cross a long succession of canyons and ridges to arrive at the Painted Cave. Like the Alcove House they had visited a few days ago, it also was high above the trail. But there were no houses up there. Instead, its back wall was completely covered with ancient red paintings. Monsters, tall fantastical people with their hair standing on end, elk and wolves, suns and stars, all looking as fresh as if they had been painted yesterday.

They tied their mules and stood staring upward, heads tilted back, mouths open.

"Wow," said Robert. "This was the way they saw the world?"

"It's kind of, almost ...," Hattie hesitated, "terrifying, really. All that red paint, like blood."

"What does it all mean?" asked Anya.

"Was life so very scary back then?" asked Robert. "Look at those monsters." He wondered again about the child whose skeleton he had seen in the hut. What had that poor kid's world been like?

"Those figures are frightening." Anya shivered. "Or frightened. It almost gives me goosebumps."

"You know what's odd? We visited the houses where they lived," said Hattie, "and that was pretty cool. But then you see their art ..."

"You're right. The things they made ...."

"Their art makes you want to know ...."

"... to know about them ...."

"... what kind of people they were."

"Yeah."

"How did they know, way back then, how to make paint that didn't disappear after hundreds of years?" asked Anya. "*Hundreds* of years."

"They knew stuff we don't," Hattie said solemnly. "I think they knew a lot that we don't know."

"That must be why my dad stayed out here for so long," said Anya quietly to Hattie.

"You mean, for all that time you lived with your grandparents?"

"Yes. I had no idea how much there was to learn here. That's why he didn't come home."

"You thought he just didn't care about you?"

"I did wonder. Yes, I did. I'm so glad we came this week."

"Me too," whispered Hattie.

After a pause, they heard, soft as a breath, "Yeah."

The day was beautifully clear and warm. Hugh and Jack stayed to take pictures. Robert, Hattie, and Anya rode back to the ranch with Michael Redbird, Corax trotting happily alongside or riding in a pannier. Michael was hurrying. He had work to do at the ranch, but, as it was to be their last day in the canyon, none of them minded being rushed back to the lodge. And the mules, of course, were just as eager as ever to get back to their barn.

When they got back, everyone was starving. Jemmy made them turkey sandwiches for lunch. She was just sitting down to eat with them when the phone rang.

"Oh, hi Michael," they heard her say. She gestured to them to stop talking. "Go ahead. I can hear you now."

The conversation, of course, was one-sided.

"Really? Right now?" She sounded surprised.

"*Shbiy' ai?*" she said, speaking Keres. "Why are you calling to tell me a hawk is ... oh. *K' apishuni*. A night hawk. Really? Uh huh. The guy is there beside you, right now? He stole one of your horses! You're – *Dyuuni?* Pottery too! That pig! The drums scared him off last night, so he's planning on ... I see what you're saying. Yes, I get it. Yes, yes, we'll hurry. But Michael, wait!" cried Jemmy, her voice rising, "That stupid truck! What if I can't get it started? And even if I do, you know I can't drive it. No, I can't! I never – I can't really, oh nuts –  *Hin' a, hin' a.* 'Bye." She slammed the phone down and they looked up from their half-eaten sandwiches.

"All right. Who here knows how to drive?"


She herded them into the cable car.

"We're not supposed to use this, but today we have no choice," Jemmy explained.

"Wait! My dog!"

"Come on, come on." She opened the gate for Corax and the cable car began its ascent.

"Where are we going?" they all asked at once.

"Nowhere, if I can't get the truck started. Michael needs us at the train station. He said that this afternoon he opened the stable, you know the one up on the rim of the canyon, and discovered a horse was missing. And just then, one of those guys walked into the barn."

"What guys?"

"One of those night-hawking guys we saw digging up the grave. He begged Michael to drive him to the train station."

"Only one of them?" "What happened to the other guy?" "Which one was it?" they all asked at once.

"I don't know who it was," she said. "So Michael told him he couldn't drive him anywhere until he phoned me at the lodge. The whole time Michael was talking to me, the guy was standing right next to him, listening. So Michael had to speak Keres. Our language. I think he was trying to say that one of the vandals has disappeared. He sneaked off and took all the loot with him. It must have been last night or early this morning. Apparently he loaded his mule with a crate full of pottery and walked as far as Mrs. Frey's stable. Then he broke into the barn and stole a horse. Michael thinks he rode to the train station, dragging the mule and the pottery behind him."

"Why is he going –? Oh, he wants to catch the train to Chicago this afternoon?"

"He's taking all the loot with him!"

"Before his buddy catches up with him!"

"So his buddy, who he left behind, wants to follow him and catch him?"

"I guess so," said Jemmy. "One guy is begging Michael to help him nab the other guy, and especially the loot, before the train leaves."

"But why are we going there?"

"Somebody's got to save the artifacts."

"Us?"

"We don't want either of these guys to get them, right? You'll have to help me think of some way to get our hands on that crate." Jemmy stopped the cable car at the top. "Come to the barn with me. I have no idea how to get this old jalopy started."

They went inside. "Look at this wreck!" Jemmy moaned. "I'll

never get it going."

"Where's the key?" Hattie asked quickly.

"In the – wha'dya call it – the keyhole there."

It was in the ignition. Hattie jumped into the driver's seat and turned the key. The motor started but it wouldn't catch. She ran to the front, threw the hood up, and fidgeted with something. "Try it, somebody!" she called.

Robert slipped into the seat and turned the key. It wouldn't start.

"Try it now!" It caught! Hattie slammed the hood down. "Move over, Robert!" she ordered.

"No, you get in the back. I'll drive."

Hattie snapped her fingers in his face and pointed. "Move over!"

Robert muttered a couple of snide comments under his breath, but he did something he never would have done one short week ago. It pained him, though. It pained him.

Hattie slid in behind the wheel. "Get in, you two!" she hollered to Anya and Jemmy. She rammed the stick into reverse, backed out of the barn, changed gears, and roared onto the dirt track.

"We go straight down this road to get to the train station?" she yelled to the back seat.

Jemmy nodded, gripping the front seat in terror. "Yes, but – slow down!"

Hattie lowered her head and gunned the engine harder. In twenty minutes, enveloped in a cloud of dust, they were at the train station. A stray mule, nosing among the sagebrush, looked up in alarm as Hattie swerved recklessly and stopped near the tracks.

"Where should I park?"

Jemmy pointed. "Hold it a second. Stop! That's Michael's truck. He must be inside. With that grave-robber, maybe?"

"What should we do?" They all sat for a minute with the

engine running, perplexed.

"Okay, let's figure this out," said Hattie. "The guy who stole the loot is probably on the train already."

"Ravilious, I bet."

"Yeah, I'm sure it's Ravilious, trying to double-cross the fat little French guy. So the Frenchman is probably with Mr. Redbird."

"Mr. Redbird didn't tell you what to do when we got here?"

Jemmy shook her head. "No! The guy was standing right next to him while he talked to me on the phone. But listen, the crate is what we're after. Maybe it's in the baggage car already."

"Two of us find the baggage car," suggested Robert, "go in and bring the crate out."

"The porters could never allow us to do that."

"Can't we just tell someone in authority what's happening?" asked Robert. "We can go into the station and talk to them. You must know someone who works here, don't you, Jemmy?"

"Yes! Come on!"

Jemmy and Robert jumped out of the truck. Corax whined but Anya told him to stay.

"Wait!" cried Hattie. "Somebody has to distract Ouisel, or he might recognize one of us. Jemmy, you're the perfect one for that."

"I can try to get him talking."

"Look for a short fat guy with glasses. While you talk to him, Robert and I will try to find the crate."

"What about me?" cried Anya.

"That crate may be heavy, too heavy for you," Hattie decided.

"Heavy for anybody," said Robert.

"Right. Anya will have to drive the truck along the tracks to wherever we are. With any luck it will be straight down that way. Then we can load the crate into the truck and get out of here fast."

"Wait! Me? Drive the truck? I – I can't drive!"

"I'm going to show you how. Quick! Get in here. Okay, when

you see us waving at you, release the emergency brake. Look! Anya! Stop sniveling and pay attention!" Hattie showed her how the brake worked. "I'm going to leave this in first gear –"

"First gear?"

"– so you have to hold the clutch pedal down. Move over to this seat."

"I can't do this!"

"Push this pedal hard, all the way down to the floor. Now, after you let the brake off, slowly let that pedal up. Slowly! The truck's going to start to move. No, you can't sit. You're too short. Stand up. Do not release that clutch pedal."

"I can't hold it down! It's too hard!"

"You have to do your part, Anya! Listen to me! Whatever you do, remember: do not touch any other pedal. Only the clutch."

"The clutch."

"You know how to steer, right? Okay, so move the truck to wherever we are. Then push the clutch down again, pull the brake back on, and wait for us."

"I can't remember all that!"

"You'll have to. It's not that hard." Hattie turned to the other two and rolled her eyes. "I don't know about this," she said softly. "How much time before the train leaves, Jemmy?"

"Not sure. People are still boarding."

"Let's find Michael." Hattie, Jemmy, and Robert ran off.

"Wait!" pleaded Anya. "Don't leave me here, you guys!" Corax whined too, at seeing them go.

But, this was horrible! But she had to do her part. But it would be impossible! But they were counting on her. "But they all think I'm stupid," she complained to Corax. "I am stupid! Waaa!"

The dog snapped his head around in alarm – TENSION! His girl was wailing out loud.

Emergency brake, clutch. What are those other pedals? Why did she have to get stuck with the hardest job?

The other three ran toward the station, looking for Michael, but afraid of being spotted by Ouisel. The surprise was, when they found Michael Redbird, it wasn't Ouisel standing beside him. It was Ravilious. Little fat Ouisel had deserted Ravilious, not the other way around.

There was one other man with them. He and Ravilious both looked extremely jittery, and Michael wasn't looking any too calm, either.

Jemmy, Hattie, and Robert crouched behind a wagon loaded with luggage. "Look at that!" exclaimed Robert softly to Hattie. "I thought Ravilious was the double-crosser! It's the rotten little Frenchman who is trying to get away with the goods!"

"Which one of those guys am I supposed to talk to? That big greasy thing?" asked Jemmy. "He doesn't look like he'd give me the time of day."

"You're kidding, right?" asked Robert. "He's a man. You'll have no problem."

"But who's that guy wearing the suit?"

"That's the guy we saw driving the limosine, isn't it?" asked Hattie. "Remember? The day we arrived? That art dealer. Ravilious must have called him. We've got to get to the crate before they do. How can we get Mr. Redbird away from them?"

"I wish he'd look our way."

"If only he'd turn – "

"Here's what we'll do. I'll get them talking," directed Jemmy. "You two slip into the office and hopefully that will get Michael's attention. Okay, here I go."

"Take off your apron!" Hattie squealed.

"Oh yeah." Jemmy untied her apron, shook out her hair, and sauntered into the station. She made a point of bypassing Michael as if she didn't know him, hesitated, then turned to ask Ravilious a question.

As soon as Ravilious turned toward Jemmy, Hattie and

Robert darted into the station. Michael finally spotted them and pointed them into the office. Then he turned back to Ravilious and Lowe, the art dealer.

"Excuse me, gentlemen," Michael said pleasantly. "I'll just go see if they've located your crate."

He slipped into the office. "I thought you guys would never show up! Okay. So here's what's happening," Michael told them hurriedly. "I've convinced those two guys that the porters are looking for their crate. But actually, it's already in the baggage car. So I pulled another crate out of the store room, loaded it with junk, and nailed it shut. I just hope it looks like theirs. I want you to carry this fake one over to them and pretend it's theirs. Then get yourselves into the baggage car and off-load the real one."

"Anya's waiting in the truck. She'll pick us up. I hope."

"Excellent. We have exactly three minutes to pull this off before the train leaves. Put these jackets on so at least you look official. And hats." He handed them porters' clothes. "This jacket is too big for you, Robert, but it will hide your cast. It's good your hair is so short, Hattie. You can pass for a boy."

"Yeah, don't remind me," she huffed. "That was the original reason for this haircut."

Michael looked at them critically. He called to a man at a desk. "Bill, can we borrow your reading glasses? Robert, here. Wear these to hide your face. Pull your hats way down and keep your eyes on the ground."

"I can't even see the ground through these glasses," said Robert, swaying dizzily.

"Get going! Get going!"

Robert and Hattie each took a handle of the crate and stumbled across the office with short steps. Robert tried to keep his broken arm in a natural position, but the crate was heavy.

Mincing along, Hattie spoke softly and quickly. "Let me do the talking, Robert."

"Wh – ?"

"Just keep your mouth shut!" Hattie snapped, whispering.

"Bu – "

"Shut up, Robert. Remember, Ravilious has heard your voice, hasn't he?" They lugged the crate out of the office. "Right, Robert? You got it? Just keep quiet or I swear, I'll punch your lights out!"

"I –"

"Button it!"

Krimey! Whatever you wish, you little pussycat, thought Robert sourly. He hadn't called Hattie that name out loud, which proves some boys may have something between their ears besides snakes and snails, as the old saying asserts.

They were slow, the two of them, hardly able to lift the crate above the ground. Meanwhile, Ravilious was absently watching a red dog trotting down the platform. His mind was elsewhere, nervously watching for Ouisel, when – hold on a minute. A red dog? Where had he seen ...? Then he spotted two porters shuffling out of the office, struggling with a very heavy crate. The thought slipped away. He nudged George Lowe.

"George! Our crate! Here it is!" crowed Ravilious. He was almost giggling. "Thank goodness. Come on, let's get it out of here before Ouisel sees it." This was their moment of danger. This was the moment when Ouisel could happen to look out of a train window and see them with the crate. If he did, things could turn very ugly.

Ravilious snapped his fingers and gestured at the two porters. "Get a move on, you two!" He noticed the porter with the glasses. Again, his mind was twerping at him. Something odd? But no! There was no time! He bent to pick up his rucksack. Strange! That other porter had weird shoes, almost like a girl's .... Oh hell. The important thing was to get that crate out of here!

The porters set the crate at his feet. The porter with the glasses held his hand out.

"Give them a buck or two, George."

"Boys, take the crate to my limo," snapped Lowe, "and don't waste any time about it." He thrust a five-dollar bill into Robert's hand. "Go! We're in a hurry! Hey, grab the crate, will you? Let's go, let's go!"

"Sorry, sir."

"What? What? What's the problem?"

"Can't help you," Hattie muttered, pitching her voice low. "That's our train, about to leave."

"Hey! I'm not supposed to lift heavy stuff...!" "What about me? I'll have a heart attack if I ...!"

Hattie paid no attention. She hurried away to the baggage car, glaring at Robert as she went. He was fumbling one-handed with the eyeglasses. "Robert, move it!" she scolded, and pulled on his sleeve. "I thought I told you not to speak!"

Robert raised his eyebrows innocently and wadded the five dollar bill into his pocket. "Hey! Did you hear me say a single word?"

He smiled when he heard Hattie laugh.

They recognized Frank Rawlings, the porter they had met on their trip from Chicago. He leaned out of the baggage car, smiling and making a sweeping motion with his hand, subtly begging them to hurry. And just then, who should espy them from across the platform?

"What's Corax doing out here?" whispered Hattie.

"Quick, pretend you don't know him."

They tried to hurry over to the baggage car, but with Corax bouncing happily at their feet, ignoring him wasn't easy. Then the dog spotted Jemmy, standing by the door to the station. He bounded over, so glad to see her. Not knowing what to do, she took him by the collar, led him toward the train, and tried to lift him into the baggage car – an exercise in futility, no doubt about that.

When Corax realized what she was doing, where she wanted

him to go, he fought and squirmed as though he was trying to save himself from the jaws of death.

GET ON A TRAIN AGAIN? NEVER!

He was making a spectacle of them. Jemmy could not handle him and the clock was ticking. People were staring. Frank came to Jemmy's rescue. Dragging the squirming dog on board cost both of them a measure of dignity.

Porters were closing the doors on the passenger cars. The train was ready to leave. Hattie turned to see if Ravilious had yet realized that his crate was a fake. That was another mistake. He was looking straight at her, squinting. Oh no. Had he recognized her?

Frank offered her a hand and pulled her up into the baggage car. They still had to get the real crate of artifacts off the train, and fast, in case Ravilious realized he had the wrong crate.

Hattie stole another peek at Ravilious. He was walking their way. "Hey! Porter!" he was calling.

Frank had opened the door on the opposite side of the car. The crate full of artifacts was all ready to off-load. It was bound with metal straps and didn't really look like the other crate at all. If Ravilious got a look at this crate, he would know, for sure!

Hattie leaned out of the baggage car and beckoned frantically to Anya, who was parked back down the track a ways. Come on! Come on!

"Aaaa!" Anya wailed loudly. She would never get this truck moving! The emergency brake – so tight. She tugged and struggled. Her foot slipped off the clutch. The truck lurched alarmingly. Her head banged against the windshield so hard that it brought tears to her eyes. The truck was moving!

Quick! she admonished herself. Put your foot back on that pedal! The truck slowed. Her leg was shaking and she was getting nowhere!

The train blew a puff of steam. The air pumps began beating.

Hattie gestured madly. "Get moving! Come on, quick!" She groaned. The truck had hardly moved. "What is she doing?" Hattie heard Ravilious shouting for a porter again. "Help me!" she cried to Jemmy, dragging the crate close to the door.

Anya, without much finesse, let her foot off the clutch. The truck bounded into motion with a jerk and began to roll. Whoa! Too fast! "Aaaa!" She slammed the clutch pedal down to the floor. Another jolt! She saw Hattie gesturing angrily at her. Panic! I'm doing such a lousy job!

Without thinking twice, Robert jumped out of the baggage car, ran to the truck, and slid into the passenger seat.

"I can't —" Anya bleated.

"You're doing fine. Ease up. Quick, ease up on the clutch now. Now!"

She let her foot up.

"Good. Good. Turn the wheel a little ... Anya, hold straight! Hey! Don't hit the —! Straight! Aiy!" He hunched sideways in his seat.

They pulled up next to the open door.

"Stop, Anya! Stop! The clutch!" Robert yanked on the emergency brake and slid the stick into neutral. "Okay, take your foot off the pedal."

Frank was helping Hattie and Jemmy wrestle the crate to the ground. Still standing in the driver's seat, Anya took her trembling foot off the clutch, let out a huge breath, and rested the side of her head against the steering wheel. She looked over at Robert and blinked back tears.

Oh boy. That was the longest minute of her life!

"Good job!" Robert said. He leapt out.

Hattie came to the side of the truck and stood on the running board.

"That wasn't too bad," she lied. "Okay. Let me in."

Her legs like jelly, Anya almost fell out of the truck. Hattie scrambled in while Jemmy and Robert struggled to heave the crate into the back of the truck.

"This thing is heavy!" Jemmy groaned. And to Corax's everlasting relief, Anya lifted him from Frank's hands, just as the conductor blew the whistle.

"Get in! Gotta move the truck!"

There, up ahead! Hattie saw a place where she could hide the truck so Ravilious wouldn't see them, behind an old shack in a stand of cottonwood trees. She spun the wheels in the dirt and peeled away from the tracks.

The Santa Fe Chief began to move. Frank the porter leaned out the door and waved at their truck with slow arcs of his arm. They watched the train pick up speed and smooth away into the distance.

Hattie swerved sharply and pulled in behind the shack. She jumped out and peeked back at the station. Ravilious and Lowe were hoisting the bogus crate into Lowe's limo. No heart attack yet, thought Hattie. Too bad.

She saw Michael on the platform, looking up and down, searching for them. He caught her signal, got into his truck, and drove across the tracks to meet them.

"That's the right crate, I hope."

"Oh boy, I sure hope so," said Jemmy.

"Yeah, what if it's not?"

"How can we open it? Somebody put these metal straps around it."

"I've got some tin snips in the truck. We'll just take a quick look."

"Yeah, we'd better not hang around here too long," said Jemmy.

Michael worked at the straps with his shears and pulled the lid off.

"Wow." "Look at that." "Those – those creeps!" "Look at the

stuff they were hauling away." "They didn't even bother to wrap anything." "I hope nothing got broken."

Pitchers, chalcedony spear points, ancient vessels curiously shaped like frogs, heavily beaded necklaces, jars and bowls and jugs of all kinds for cooking and seed storage and for carrying water. And skulls, including a very small one.

The skulls made Robert think of the boy in the hut again, the child who had never been honored with a burial, who had only one beautiful blue object to accompany him into the Afterworld. He wished at that moment he could visit that boy one more time.

"I'll bet those criminals don't even see how beautiful this stuff is."

"They see money," said Michael.

He replaced the lid of the crate. "By the way, I noticed, Jemima Snow," teased Michael, "that you got the truck here in one piece after all. So you do know how to start it."

"Uh, no. Actually, Hattie started it."

"Hattie?"

"And drove it."

"Hattie did?"

Hattie shrugged. "The wire from the coil to the distributor cap was loose, that's all. I connected it and it started right up."

"Ah." Michael scratched his head. "That wire."

"I would check it, though, Mr. Redbird. It looked kind of chewed up. You might need to replace it."

"Okay." He widened his eyes. "I can't interest you in a mechanic's job, can I?"

"No," she laughed, "no thanks."

Michael smiled. "Well, folks. I have stuff to do. One of those grave robbers also stole a mare that belongs to Mrs. Frey and I have to find her. I'll meet you back at the ranch." He turned back. "Hey! Forgive me! I forgot to say thank you, everybody." He folded his hands together and seemed very touched. "Thank you all for saving this piece of our heritage. It means a lot. It really does." He waved. "I'll see you later." He drove his truck across the tracks and headed back to the station, leaving the kids and Jemmy standing beside the old truck.

"Well, you three hooligans," said Jemmy, "I think we make quite a team. Don't you agree?" Laughing, she circled them in her arms and pulled them toward her. "Seriously, you are the greatest!"

They were congratulating themselves. They were noisy. The dog was barking in excitement. They didn't hear the bang of a screen door.

"Hey, shouldn't we get out of here, in case Ravilious comes back? That guy scares the heck out of me," said Hattie.

"He scares you? He was going to shoot me!" answered Robert. "The French guy almost did shoot me!"

"Oh right. I'm sure, Robert," teased Hattie.

"That was after the lion —"

"Oh?"

"Yeah, the mountain lion —"

"The mountain lion. Uh huh. In your imagination, maybe. Get in, everybody. I'll drive. Oh wait." Hattie turned to Robert, her hand on her hip. "Before we go, Robert has a donation to make."

They looked at him, curious. He lowered his chin. They were all focused on Robert. They didn't notice someone coming to stand on the other side of the truck, watching them.

"Come on," Hattie insisted. "Give it up, Robert. Michael can use the money to repair the truck."

He pulled the wadded five-dollar bill from his pocket, flattened its wrinkles, and gave it to Jemmy.

"What's this?"

"Robert got those men to give him a tip."

"Robert!" cried Jemmy, patting his back. "How did you manage that?"

Robert shrugged. "I dunno." They all burst out laughing, even Robert. Even Anya. And Corax, delighted, pranced around and around the noisy bunch.

They didn't even hear the slide of the rifle bolt.

"Aawriight!" The hoarse drawl of a man startled them. "Whuzz goin' on here?"

They spun around. A man walked slowly around the back of their truck, as wary as if they were a nest of rattlesnakes.

They gawked at him, mouths hanging open. The first thing they noticed was the rifle he aimed at them because guns tend to get people's attention. Their eyes raised to his huge, very dusty cowboy hat. He had scraggly hair to his shoulders, a thick mustache, and a long dirty beard. But not nearly long enough.

Because, regarding his clothing, he wore not one stitch.

Boots. He did wear boots. Because he never took them off, never ever. Heavy old boots, unlaced, no socks.

"What you all doin' on my propitty?"

They gaped. They couldn't stop staring. Then, they couldn't look away fast enough.

"Sorry, sorry. We are leaving right now," Jemmy assured him. "Get in, everybody!"

Stunned, they jostled themselves into the truck – crickets under attack by a scorpion never moved faster. Hattie gunned the engine and the wheels tore up a storm of dust. They drove for a full minute before Jemmy started to giggle. Then they were all laughing til tears came to their eyes.

"It sure took a long time before that guy bothered to come outside to speak to us," Jemmy said.

"Maybe he was looking for his hat," Robert sniggered "Company comes, you can't greet people without your hat."

Anya sat forward suddenly and held up a hand. "Hey! Wait a minute. We never got to finish our lunch!"

"I'm starving again!" "Me too!" "So am I!"

"You know what? I am going to make you three the best meal you ever ate in your lives," vowed Jemmy.

And she did. And, as you might expect, to the end of their lifetimes, they would never remember a better one.


Meanwhile, Ravilious and Lowe, the art dealer, were speeding away from the train station, tearing at breakneck speed down the nearly deserted road to Santa Fe. They weren't hurrying for any special reason. George Lowe always drove like that.

"Ouisel is going to be out of his mind when he gets to Chicago!" crowed Ravilious in triumph. "Out of his mind! Oh, I really wish I could see his face when he finds out the crate has disappeared."

"So we've got the entire haul? He has nothing?"

"Not a thing. We got everything."

George Lowe laughed maniacally. "He's gonna pop a gusset!"

"You've got to sell this stuff fast though, George. He's gonna come after it. And he'll find you. You know he will."

"Don't worry. If the stuff is as nice as you say it is, I can get rid of it in a couple of weeks. Just in time for Christmas. With the money we make, you'll be able to afford to hide out in the Bahamas or somewhere for the rest of the winter."

"Ah! You don't know how glad I am that we pulled this off. That fat little creep was bugging the hell out of me. Imagine him trying to pull a trick like that, after all the work I did. I bought his train tickets, rented the tent, and the damn mule – hey! Slow down, George. There's a cop up ahead."

"What is this? A roadblock? Two cars! These guys are going to ruin some poor sucker's day."

"Sure looks that way."

"He's going to ding me good for speeding, though. Oh well. We can afford a ticket." George Lowe pulled up near the sheriff's car. He leaned over to Ravilious, smiling smugly. "It's the cost of doing business, right Snyder?" Very satisfied with himself, he lowered the window on the limo.

"Afternoon. How are you doing, Sheriff?"

Four more policemen came up, stationing themselves on both sides of the car.

"I was speeding. I know, I know. I'm afraid I got a bit carried away. These nice country roads, you know." George Lowe laughed. "You forget how fast you're going. Sorry about that. Who you guys looking for? Some criminal?"

Sheriff Alvarez was brusque. "Step out of the car, please." He opened Lowe's door and pointed at Ravilious. "Both of you. Sir? Yes, you too."

George Lowe knew how to jolly people up. "We have been very bad," he joked, stepping out and buttoning his jacket over his massive bulk. "Fortunately we didn't do any harm. We'll pay, though. We'll pay." He winked at the sheriff, dragged out his wallet, and pulled out a fifty dollar bill. He reached over and stuffed it swiftly into the sheriff's shirt pocket.

"Sir, I'll need you to open the trunk."

George Lowe stiffened. "The trunk?"

"Open it, please."

"My trunk?"

"Yes."

"Look! Sheriff, we were just joy-riding –"

"Sure."

" – acting like a couple of schoolboys, I'll admit."

"The trunk, sir."

"The trunk? Why – what do you – there's nothing –"

"Just open it."

Thinking furiously, George Lowe slowly walked to the back of the limousine. His eyes darted from side to side. He and Ravilious were surrounded by officers. Outnumbered.

Lowe opened the trunk. They all stared at the crate.

One of the officers produced a heavy screwdriver. Sheriff Alvarez passed it to Lowe, but kept his hand on the butt of his gun.

"Open it."

"What?"

"The crate. Pry it open."

Lowe paused. "Look. Sheriff. All right. Tell me what you need. Just tell me. A hundred bucks? More?" The sheriff stared. "Two hundred?"

"Open the crate."

Lowe was sweating by the time he got the crate pried open.

He lifted the lid.

His eyes bugged out of his head. He reached inside, then looked in fury at Ravilious.

"Just what are you trying to pull, Snyder?" he spat, purple-faced.

"What the –?"Ravilious was frantic with disbelief. Reaching into the crate, he pawed through thick volumes of old train timetables for every state in the union, an old spittoon, a vintage water pump handle, three almost-empty soda bottles, a broken Morse code transmitter, a pair of men's work boots caked with manure, one ripped up beaded moccasin, and underneath it all, a skull. It had large horns. He reached in and drew it out, aghast, apoplectic with rage.

Sheriff Alvarez nodded. "You realize it is against the law to remove artifacts from this territory?"

Ravilious shook the skull in his face. "This is nothing but a cow skull," he shouted.

"Skulls qualify as artifacts," said the sheriff. He pulled out the moccasin. "And this, as well. We'll send it off to the state experts. Let them analyze everything. Until we get the results, I am charging you with the theft of articles of heritage."

"You can't do that!" spluttered Lowe. "There's nothing here of any value!"

"If you have objections, I suggest you call your lawyer."

"My lawyer is in New York! It will take him three days to get here!"

"Well. Our jailhouse is clean and dry. Till he gets here, we'll give you a place to stay. For free. Handcuff them, boys. Hank, you take them in your car. I'll drive the limo back to town." Grinning, he rubbed his hands together, then pulled out Lowe's fifty dollar bill. "Oh, and boys? After we get these two locked up, I'll stand you to a dinner at Maggie's tonight."

Snyder Ravilious and George Lowe spent three nights in separate cells in the Santa Fe jail, waiting for Lowe's lawyer to arrive. They each had cellmates. You would think they'd feel happier and less lonely, having someone to help them pass the time. But it only doubled their punishment. Lowe's cellmate was overly friendly, so he hardly dared close his eyes all night. Ravilious's cellmate was unreasonably hostile and couldn't stand to hear anyone snore. He got up and gave Ravilious a good hard shake every time he fell asleep. The beds were wretched, the food more so. Both men were haggard with exhaustion by the time the lawyer arrived.

But if nothing else, at least they were temporarily safe from the wrath of Monsieur Ouisel. And that was something to be grateful for, as you might well imagine.

But truth be told, just what Honoré Ouisel's reaction was, when he got to Chicago, is unrecorded. He had watched his crate being loaded onto the train in Lamy. Now it was gone.

He had not insured any of the loot, naturally, because it was stolen goods. And he'd been in too much of a hurry to ask the stationmaster in Lamy for a receipt. "What crate?" the porters in Chicago had asked. There had been no crate.

Regardless of his reaction, when Ouisel returned home he would at least have the compensation of many happy memories of his trip to New Mexico. Midnight walks in dark canyons. Tenting in the November rain and snow with a congenial colleague whose body odor was not too objectionable, at least not on that day when he finally changed his socks. And oh yes, he had also had the companionship of a mule of surpassing charm. All safe-kept memories, as the poetess saith, tucked into his heart's treasury.


Late that Friday afternoon, when Jack and Hugh got back from the Painted Cave, they smelled Jemmy's dinner as soon as they crossed the river. They hurried up to their cabin, washed quickly, and headed back down to the lodge.

"We missed lunch," complained Hugh as they ambled along. "I deeply regret missing a single meal in this place."

"You're not talking about the food, are you?" asked Jack.

"What food?"

"You're talking about the person who cooks the food."

Hugh shook his head. "She's an amazing cook too, you've got to admit that."

"Is it fair to deduce, my friend, that you've fallen for something other than her cooking?"

Hugh groaned.

"Have you spoken to her at all?"

"I did. Sure I did. Yesterday when we were playing that game with the girls, I went in like you told me and asked her if she had an old can."

"You talked about tin cans?"

"I – I'm not sure what we talked about."

"Whatever it was, I'm sure you were very suave."

"Suave? Yeah. Well."

"If you want to talk to her, tonight is your last chance. We're leaving tomorrow."

Another groan.

"Too bad you can't find some work out here, Hugh, so you can stay longer."

"Stop it! You're killing me, man!"

Jack opened the door to the lodge and held it, grinning. "You're torturing yourself needlessly, you know." Hugh stopped in the doorway and looked at Jack earnestly. "Say something to her!" Jack leaned close and spread his hands. "Just speak! Open up and speak to the woman!"

Hugh was still digesting this advice when Jack urged him through the living room door.

"Here you are!" Jemmy exclaimed. "Just in time for appetizers. Would you like some bubbly? It's made right here in New Mexico."

"This is very elegant," Jack said. Hugh gingerly accepted a glass from her and muttered something incoherent. He shot a quick glance at Jack, then noticed Jemmy was smiling up at him.

"You're welcome," she said. He stopped, transfixed, his glass half-way to his lips. He was frozen in place even after Jemmy turned away to offer her platter of food to Anya and Hattie.

Jack sat down by the girls and finally, after Jemmy returned to the kitchen, Hugh was able to rouse himself and sit down too. He emptied his drink in one gulp.

"We had an amazing day," Jack told Anya and Hattie. "Hugh found – you tell them, Hugh."

"Me? Oh. Well I uh," he mumbled. He was suffering from a minor case of lock-tongue. "I, uh, I found a wonderful basket."

"Totally intact," inserted Jack.

"I turned a corner of a ruined wall, this crumbling old wall, and there it sat, hiding under a ledge. Just where someone left it, hundreds of years ago."

"How can that be?" asked Anya.

"It's the dry air here," Jack said.

"It was in perfect shape." Hugh was warming to his subject.

"It's been a great week. For me anyway. Just having the time to look around, record some of this gorgeous scenery. And only ourselves here, no crowds."

"And you, with your artist's eye, Hugh, you saw things I never would have noticed," Jack said.

"You took me to places I never would have found, Jack. We sure put the miles in this week."

"Yes we did. And what have you two been up to all day?" Jack asked the girls. "Just relaxing around here?"

"Oh no! We only got back a little while ago," said Anya. "I drove a truck, Dad!"

"You what?"

Jemmy came back and filled Hugh's empty glass, then sat down near him on the arm of the sofa.

"You won't believe what these kids did today, Dr. Netherby," she said.

"Please. I'm not sure I want to know. Did they give you trouble? What were you two girls up to?"

"Not just these two. All three of them."

Jack looked questioningly at Anya. "All three?" She nodded.

"Wait. Let me get Robert out here." Jemmy went to the kitchen door. "Robert! Come tell your uncle and Mr. Durant about your afternoon."

"I need him here," hollered Mrs. Snow.

"In a minute, Mama. He wants his moment of glory."

The four of them, Jemmy and Robert, Hattie and Anya, talked over and around each other, eager to tell how they saved a crate loaded with irreplaceable artifacts. Jack watched them with a small smile: Robert trying to monopolize the conversation; Hattie pushing him aside, not about to let him hog the limelight; Anya, mostly watching the others, smiling and nodding. Both girls laughing at something Robert said. Maybe, Jack considered, he had worried needlessly about ruining the whole trip by asking

Robert to come along. And look at the three of them this evening! Hattie's face glowing with health, Anya's eyes sparkling. Even Robert was so much more lively tonight.

When they were done, Jack said, "What do we do if Ravilious figures out what happened? He'll be here, pounding the front door down."

"I don't think so," said Jemmy. "Michael got the sheriff involved. I believe that guy and his partner might be spending tonight in the slammer. That was Michael's plan, anyway."

Mrs. Frey came in. "Jemmy dear, please don't sit on the arm of the furniture."

"Sorry, Mrs. Frey." Jemmy dropped to a seat on the sofa next to Hugh.

Hugh's universe rippled and gyrated. He tipped his empty glass to his lips, then looked at it in surprise, wondering who drank all his bubbly.

"So!" Mrs. Frey looked at them unhappily. "I hope you all have had a nice visit here. The weather hasn't been great for you, though we did need the rain."

"It has been wonderful," Hattie declared.

"I'm feeling very sad," Mrs. Frey went on. "This is your last night here and you are our very last guests. This house won't even be standing in a few more weeks. Why oh why does everything have to change? Why can't things just go on the way they always have?"

Hattie sighed and bent her head.

Yeah, said Robert to himself, his elbows on his knees.

"But," protested Anya, "I never would have found Corax if everything had stayed the same for me." The dog, hearing his name, looked up at her. She stroked his head fondly, remembering finding him as an abandoned puppy, and then remembering how her conflicts with Robert had forced her hand last summer. And with her remembering, the old bitterness snarled and knotted inside her. She was too embarrassed to look at her cousin. Even embarrassed to put something else into words: that the same unfortunate events that had caused girl and dog to come together had also brought her father back to her. Like a gift. But she looked up and saw Jack smiling at her, and knew that she didn't need to tell him so.

"I agree with you, Anya," said Jemmy. "Sometimes something good happens when you least expect it. That's what happened for me." She looked at Hugh, next to her. "What about you, Mr. Durant?"

"Hugh," he interrupted, and beamed at her. "Call me Hugh."

"You never say much. Tell us what you think. Don't you agree with me? Change is a good thing?"

"Well," he hedged, twirling his glass. He didn't want to change anything at the moment. Everything seemed grand to him tonight. Just – just everything. He beamed at his glass.

"Come on, Hugh," teased Anya. "Your life changed a while ago. You weren't always a photographer."

Hugh looked up and glared at her.

"Is that so, Hugh?" said Jemmy. "Tell us what made you change!"

"Eh," groaned Hugh. He shook his head.

"Know what?" Anya pretended to whisper. "When he had his other job, Hugh had a really pretty fiancée. Not only pretty. Rich too. But he dumped her. Right? Didn't you?"

Hugh stared at his glass and shrugged.

"You gave up a rich girl?" Jemmy nudged him.

"Okay. Yeah." He smiled. Two glasses of bubbly and he was practically a chatterbox. "I did do that. And if I hadn't left her, I never would have found this kid, that day when she came walking out of the woods all alone." He looked fondly at Anya, his glass twirling like mad in his fingers.

Anya was the only one who noticed that Robert, probably

panicked that his part in that story would come up, rose and quietly went back to the kitchen.

Jemmy reached over and poured Hugh a little more bubbly. "Go on, Hugh," she told him. "Tell us more."

"Well. I never would have met Jack. Never would have come here. I never would have ..." He stopped himself just in time. He stared at Jemmy's knees beside his on the sofa, and gulped some wine. "I never would have come to this wonderful place."

"I'm glad you've enjoyed yourself here, Hugh," said Mrs. Frey.

"Hey! You know what I think would be a great idea," said Jemmy, snapping her fingers and suddenly inspired. "You should stay on here, Hugh. Take photos of the artifacts we saved. And photos of this lodge before they tear it down. Then you could get pictures of the Conservation Corp while they work. Make a record of all their projects. Somebody would pay for that! Like the park authority or somebody. But most of all, I wish you'd preserve the way the canyon looks right now, before they mess it all up."

"What a great idea!" said Jack.

"You could take portraits of the workmen too, Hugh," suggested Anya. "Like you used to do last summer. The men would buy them to send home, wouldn't they?"

Jack said, "I bet you could get the park commission to pay you something. Hugh has just finished some work for the government. He'd be perfect for this."

"Oh, I would love that!" said Mrs. Frey. "Please say you'll stay and do that for us, Hugh!"

Flabbergasted, Hugh could hardly speak.

"I can't pay you," coaxed Evelyn Frey, "but I promise you won't go hungry."

Hugh stared at Mrs. Frey. "I – I ...." What had just happened? Was that legendary old Trickster just teasing him so he could laugh when Hugh's dream fell apart?

Hugh didn't have time to answer because at that moment,

Michael Redbird walked in.

Mrs. Frey greeted him and asked, "What is this we hear about someone stealing one of our mares?"

"That's true, and fortunately the horse found her own way back here," he said. "But you can't believe the commotion in that stable tonight. Some mule wandered into our paddock from who-knows-where and just made herself at home. She helped herself to the feed and cozied right up to one of the males. The other females are having a fit. She practically started a war out there. I tried to separate her but I can't get her to budge. I don't know who she belongs to. I wonder if Dick brought her in."

No, Dick had not brought a mule to the stable. She belonged, this mule of mystery, to Rossini's Pack Animal Rental Company, Inc.. "Mules, Ponis, Lammas, For Rent. Reasonible", claimed Gioachino Rossini's sign. His spelling was no better than his animal husbandry. Felicity – *SANTI BENEDETTI*, of course it was she – confirmed as much the moment she walked into Frey's stable. This place was nothing like Rossini's. A warm dry home, a handsome boy-mule – *CAVOLO*! She vowed never, never to go back to eating moldy hay at Rossini's dismal farm.

Shortly after Michael came in, Robert opened the doors to the dining room. "Dinner is served," he announced.

Isn't he the important one, Anya groused to herself, but at the very same instant, a new thought flashed into her mind: Robert hadn't tormented her once all week. Really. Not once. The thought stopped her in her tracks. That meant that she was meaner than he was, didn't it?

She was the last to file into the dining room. Her eyes met Robert's as she passed him. They both looked away, swerved apart, and took their seats.

So. Here they all were. Their last dinner at the Ranch of the The Ten Elders. They were less chatty tonight. Their holiday was ending and everyone seemed a little blue.

Indifferent even in these moments of heavy solemnity, Grandfather Clock scoffed at all their useless fretting over Change, their fretting over Endings and Beginnings, and their utter failure to appreciate *his* critically important yet mystical function, the measurement of Time. Not that he grasped the essence of it either, but the least they could do would be to applaud his efforts once in a while. However, he burped once and commenced his duties. His entire case vibrated faintly with the effort. First he tightened his springs with a twing of considerable duration. Then, with great and majestic pomp, he bonged the hour.

Dinner had finished. The kitchen was clean and quiet. Michael Redbird headed out to the stable, restless. He went from stall to stall, trying to settle the animals for the night, though he himself felt anything but settled. Accidentally, he sloshed water all over his pant legs. He ripped his jacket when it caught on a splintered board. He spilled feed. Even the apathetic mules were roused to stop chewing for one brief moment, to gawk at him with alarm in their eyes.

Michael was angry all over again at white men who think nothing of vandalizing graves belonging to his people. Especially those guys today. The sheriff had called to say those two snakes were bringing a high-falutin' lawyer from the east, to dispute the charges against them. They'd probably get off scot-free, unless the sheriff could get access to those new fingerprinting techniques. If he didn't, there was nothing that connected Ravilious or Lowe to the crate of artifacts. The men would surely claim they had never seen the stuff in their lives.

Michael swore aloud. He blamed himself. If I hadn't been so hasty, he thought, I could have figured out a better way to trap them.

Far away, he heard thunder mumbling above the mesa. Thunder, aha. For Michael, a hint. Here's what he needed to do.

His drum sat on a table in a corner.

A beautiful thing, that drum, almost sacred. A man from his tribe had taken the greatest possible care in making this instrument. He had painstakingly chosen just the right tree to provide wood. By hand, he had scraped the deerskin for the drumhead, not too thick, not too thin. Then he waited. He did nothing for a long time, waiting for a day when his mind was perfectly composed and at peace. Only then did he bring wood and animal skin together to finish this instrument. Tree and deer, plant and animal, the perfect synthesis, missing only one thing: the player.

When the day came that the drum was finished and Michael Redbird could hold this new instrument over his heart, he knew it was the drum he was meant to play. All he had to do was tap it to produce one of the deepest, clearest tones of any drum in the Rio Grande Valley.

Tonight, though peals of thunder were rolling closer, Michael picked up his drum and went outside. He smiled now. In the dark, he found a place to sit by the river. He tapped the drumhead softly with his fingers, just to warm it up. When he began to play, singing along softly, he started to feel better.

He played for the Old Ones. He played for Mother Earth. It pleased him to know that the sound of his drumming was healing to her. In response, the Earth healed him and, likewise, his playing could heal a listener, if he had one. Giving, receiving, passing the gift along – this is a concept basic to his people, and he became engrossed, caught up in the sound as it echoed through the canyon. Caught up in feelings, sensations. He, his drum, and the Earth, one instrument.

Just then, Anya stepped outside the lodge to take Corax for his evening walk. The dog was her excuse. In truth, she came outside because she was angry with herself, and maybe a little ashamed. She needed to blow off steam. She could not bring herself to make peace with her cousin, yet she couldn't forgive herself either, for being so stubborn. She had avoided Robert all week. She could have done better, but she hadn't.

The weather had turned cold again and she buttoned her coat collar. She heard distant rumbling. It must be storming up on the mesa, she thought. It was when the thunder paused that she heard the drum.

Someone drumming? Upriver a ways. The sound rose and faded on currents of wind. That rhythm she was hearing, it was like some strange antique language speaking to her heart.

After a few minutes, she heard a door open behind her. Her dad opened an umbrella as he came across the porch.

"Dad, listen."

Something from the ancient world, calling out. It put words into Anya's ear. "Come to us. Be quiet. Feel."

Little raindrops plinked into the Rio Frijoles and Michael echoed their rhythm. The rhythm of the rain blended with his drumbeat. He felt certain that something was being altered, somewhere, for the better.

This might be the last time for months that he'd be able to play his drum into the quiet of the night. Soon the canyon would be overrun with construction workers. He felt sad when he thought about the Old Ones who had once made a home in this canyon. Piece by piece, the white man will take their story and make it his own. Piece by piece, the old truths will be worn away. He had hoped the old world could save the new. Now, in this year 1933, this doomed decade, that hope hung by a thread.

Time was at fault. Michael knew that. Time, the oldest trickster of them all. Man thinks he invented it, but it follows no rules but its own.

At least, he thought, at least I had this night. Time cannot take that from me, as long as I have memory. He rose, covered his instrument with his jacket, and went inside.

Anya wished the drumming had not stopped. Her dad turned toward the porch and waited. She called to Corax and they went back into the lodge, just as the clouds opened and it began to pour.

TRICKSTER, BOUNDARY-CROSSER

Saturday

Time, that biting wind. Writing, erasing, rewriting. Keening through the canyons, scouring them bare, flowing ever onward. Who can measure Time's effects? Who can fathom its mystery?

For the last six hundred years, Frijoles Canyon had known hardly a footstep of man. But now, with the calendar about to turn to the last month of the year, two hundred men and their tools and their deafening machines will be moving in to begin "improving" the place, making it into something new. Gift shops, a road, a welcome center, lighted parking lots, vending machines, hasty tours led by bored guides.

Once again, the story of the canyon will be changed, rewritten. Frijoles Canyon, that ancient palimpsest, its old texts fading, crossing the boundary into the past.

Saturday morning is about to break and a soft breeze twirls down through the river canyon. By the time night has softened to pale dawn, the guests have long since departed and the canyon seems empty, its gods and the souls of the Old Ones notwithstanding.

At the Ranch of the Ten Elders this morning, three women sit silent at the small kitchen table, sipping tea and letting their minds roam over all that had happened in that house.

Evelyn Frey remembers moving in with their baby and young fruit trees and animals; Mr. Frey abandoning them, deciding that ranch life just wasn't for him; she and Dick shouldering all the burdens; keeping the canyon safe from trespassers of all varieties, two-footed and four-footed; building a wholesome life for themselves and a place of renewal for their guests; keeping things going even in these bitterly hard depression years; and bearing with a heavy heart the antagonism of the Puebloans. She loved so much about those people and yet they considered her a trespasser.

Jemima Snow and her mother, thinking back on how Blossom Snow had defied her peoples' tradition, and earned the resentment of many of them, by taking a job outside of the pueblo; eventually convincing her daughter, and finally even her son Michael Redbird that, to survive, they could work for a white woman and still come back to their pueblo values, still remember who they were.

All three women, thinking of the ranch as a haven where it, and they, had grown and changed from year to year, each taking on roles that none had foreseen.

Into their hearts' treasuries this morning, these ladies slip their memories. In a couple of days, they would be cooking for a large gang of construction workers and nothing would be the same.

Meanwhile, on that same morning, Dick Frey drives the departing guests across the plateau toward the train station at Lamy. Bumping down the dirt track, Jack Netherby savors the scent of still-damp sagebrush. He reminisces about his first trip here five years ago. At the time, he had been a broken man wracked by tragedy. Now he almost regrets that his new book will advertise this sacred and beautiful place to the world. He decides right then to make the book a celebration of stillness, of the ancient canyon as it was in the centuries between the Old World and modern times.

The three kids in the back seats are staring out the windows, not talking, looking at the landscape they see so differently this morning. Robert, Hattie, and Anya – today feeling as much reluctance to leave the ranch as he or she had felt about coming; each wishing they could have one more week, even one more day, here.

Only Hugh Durant stays behind, thinking about his future, how life turns on a dime. He looks forward to working here. Maybe he will publish a book of his own. Maybe he will never leave here. Maybe ..., well, Time will decide everything.

Oh, and of course not to be forgotten, is Corax, that spirited, indomitable dog. He has claimed his favorite place in the back seat of the car. Here he sits, with his nose snuffling eagerly at the slot where the window has been left open a crack. Corax – enthroned in the proverbial catbird seat, as the saying goes. A creature with but one flaw (for which he takes no blame): being zipped into a red fur suit of perpetual itchiness; red fur being but the slightest of drawbacks, he consoles himself, because otherwise he considers himself the most fortunate of beings.

Corax is not thinking of the past at all. He is not aware of a future.

He is just enjoying the moment on this, the very best day of his life.


As they speed across the mesa, who should be watching their car from the top of a pinon tree, but Raven. She watches them disappear around a bend. Then she rises into the clear morning air with a lazy flap of her inkblack wings.

Ah there he is! She spies him, her old enemy Coyote. That nefarious trickster! Look at him, trotting so jauntily across the plain.

*Aaugh*, she screams. Senor! I wondered where you were. You'd better brace yourself! I'm coming for you, you pathetic piece of filthy fur!

She does a deep dive, aiming straight for the back of his neck. He dodges just in time but she doesn't pull up fast enough, and her legs graze the nasty spines of a cholla cactus. In fiery pain, she screeches at him in her hideous voice. Her curse words echo far and wide across the mesa.

By the gods, she despises that skinny-legged mangy fiend, that matted pelt of flea-bitten carrion! Her most ardent desire is to see him dead and being picked apart by vultures. Until that day, she needs to make some drastic changes. The time has come. She makes a solemn vow. She will have nothing further to do with that beast. Relishing the thought of his rotting carcass, she wheels abruptly and heads into the west, never to be seen again. Well, hardly ever again. Or – probably not, anyway.

Ah, Raven. Will she forever drag her hatred around

like a corpse?

Is she really so evil as to wish death for her former friend?

Well, there's a belief among the natives here that Life,

brief and fragile as the breath of a fox on a winter's dawn,

is nothing more than a wind blowing through you,

and for some, as for Raven, it happens to be a dark wind.

Coyote is watching as she wings away across the plateau,

until she is nothing but a blot on the sky.

He knows she won't be able to resist coming back.

He, ever the Trickster, actually looks forward to her return,

because he enjoys stepping up to any game she offers.

He can disguise himself as an underling, a fool even,

and he can change the rules,

can cross whatever boundaries she sets for him.

What a laugh it will be,

when things don't turn out the way Raven expects!

But, you may ask, why do these two continue this antagonism?

Is our world that capricious,

the balance between opposites so delicate

that we so rarely reach equilibrium?

Are our mercurial bonds with each other

as fragile as ropes of sand?

It is true, that we never know what will happen

in this chimerical life.

We can't predict how things will turn out.

From his interplay with Raven, though,

Coyote has learned one thing,

something he feels he can rely on
with a fair measure of certainty,
one practically indisputable fact,
one nearly unassailable article of faith.
And, as it happens, there is a saying that sums it all up.
I offer it now for your consideration:
Some things never change.

END NOTE

I admit that I played with facts in this story, but only slightly, if you discount the bilingual mule. I was a little flexible with the map of the canyon, its trails and their length. Also, while Mr. and Mrs. Frey actually established the Ranch of the Ten Elders as a guest lodge in 1925, I suggest, for the sake of the story, they did so in the year 1916. I must also confess to romanticizing the appearance of the lodge. Sometimes the pen has a mind of its own and renders the author its helpless pawn.

For curbing the recklessness of said pen, I must thank two people, Dorian Kincaid and Henry Zielinski. Their contributions are invisible, but like all authors, I thank the Goodness for *simpatico* editors, and these two were invaluable.

An author must learn to allow her ink-people to disentangle themselves from the page, and she must watch, powerless, while they hoist themselves with their own petards. Help with their transformation is always very welcome. For background for this book, I turned to Janet Kessler's "Coyote Yipps" blog, a fascinating study of coyote relationships. Janet's research was very helpful in putting a face on the Trickster. Marc Garstein's dear hound, Red Dog, was and will always be the face of Corax. An image from Petra Fischer's beautiful art and photography site transformed Anya Netherby into a real girl. William Weliky convinced me that a locomotive could have a personality too, which is a wonder in itself, if you ask me. *Per aiuto con l'italiano, grazie a Barbara Ceglia, superba professoressa.* The person formerly known as Donnie Dilmore lent me photos of clockworks which gave untold depth to the character known herein as Grandfather, so now we all know what makes him tick. Many thanks to all of these folks for essential contributions.

If you enjoyed *Twist a Rope of Sand*, I would very much appreciate a review on a book site of your choice. You can view The World of the Book, its setting and characters as I imagine them, through a link found at www. kmdelmara. com. And finally, my previous book, *Vagabond Wind, the Adventures of Anya and Corax,* tells the story of What-Came-Before. It is an old-fashioned tale of cat-and-mouse but with the added twist of a dog hero, just to make things tricksier.